CUTTING OUT LOVE

KACI LANE

For the Clark family.

CUTTING OUT LOVE

CHAPTER ONE

Adrianne

Something about goats bleating in the background while I'm naked makes me feel extra vulnerable.

"Daisy, I can barely hear you." That's my nice way of communicating that her goats are getting out of hand.

"Sorry, Mullet is needing out."

I roll my eyes. For all Daisy's oddities, treating goats like literal kids has to be the worst.

I put the phone on speaker and step into my bikini bottom. A door shuts, and the bleating muffles. I pull my mop of brown hair over my shoulder, then tie my swimsuit top around my neck.

"There. Mullet's out. You sure you don't need me to come over?"

"No." I sigh. "I'm going to lay out and zone out for a bit."

"If you get bored later, we can get together, or do goat yoga."

I pinch the bridge of my nose. "Maybe to hanging out, definite no on the goat yoga."

"Fine, but goats are great therapy."

"I'm swearing off men for a while, not overcoming an addiction or dealing with daddy issues."

Daisy laughs. "Whatever you say, but goats can fill a great void."

I gather my hair on top of my head. What can I say that won't sound condescending? Responses turn in my head as I tie up my hair. Nah . . . I've got nothing.

"Adrianne, you still there?"

"Yep." I tighten my bun. "Just thinking."

"About last night?"

"No." *Yes.*

"It's okay if you are."

I plop down on my bed. "I feel stupid, that's all. Me of all people should've known better."

"No, he of all people should've known better. Imagine all the other women not smart enough to catch on to him."

I smile to myself. Daisy, quirky as she may be, always knows how to lift my spirits. "Thanks."

"I'm serious. In this modern era of technology, you've got to be pretty conniving to pull off dating three different women at once."

"Four." I wince at admitting that aloud.

"Four?"

"Yeah, apparently he covered enough sales territory to juggle four women at once."

"Well."

I lie back on the bed and stare at my ceiling fan like a toddler. "The worst part is now I have to get a new products rep."

Daisy laughs. "If that's your biggest worry, then you can hardly call this a heartbreak."

"Yeah, my heart's not so much broken *over* him as it is *by* him. It's like a culmination of many men taking tiny hammers to it over the years. No certain guy could break my heart, but this one just happened to have the final hammer to complete the crack."

"Don't beat yourself up. You're the prettiest person I know, you're smart, and sometimes funny."

"Sometimes." I balk, pretending to be offended. In reality, I'm tickled pink that Daisy called me smart twice in one conversation.

I don't get a lot of compliments on my brains. Most people tend to see me as surface-level only. The stylish hairdresser who can work magic with a curling wand. I'm sort of the unofficial fairy godmother for all eligible bachelorettes in Apple Cart County. But it's getting kind of old sitting on the sidelines for everyone else's happily ever after.

"We all know I'm the funny one."

"True." I laugh. Daisy is funny as in quick-witted, but also as in quirky. All around, she still gets more laughs than me, so I'll give her funny.

"Why don't you make a list of what you want in a guy?"

I blink at the fan. "I've done that before. Turns out what looks good on paper isn't always great in person. Like when an elderly woman comes in the salon with a magazine clipping of Taylor Swift. T-Swift's hair isn't going to translate well when worn at the retirement home."

Daisy laughs. "And you said you weren't funny."

I get up and retrieve the sunscreen from my bathroom. "Funny or not, I'm tired of funny business with men. Instead of making a list, I'm making a pact."

"A pact? With who?"

"Myself. No more men, at least until the summer ends."

"Why summer?"

"You know me. I thrive on goals, and summer offers plenty of shirtless temptations, from lawn boys to professionals chilling by the lake at Jack's lodge."

"If bare chests are your weakness, don't ever get into massage therapy."

"I didn't plan on it."

A large goop of sunscreen plops out when I squeeze the bottle. I rub gentle circles on my face with my fingertips until it's evened out. Then I rub the remaining lotion on my shoulders and neck.

A loud buzzing noise blasts outside my window. I stand and pull back the curtain. "Dais, did you hear that?"

"Hear what?"

"A loud buzzing sound."

"I heard something in the distance, but I'm not sure what. I've got goats and chickens scratching at my door."

"Oh well. As long as it's not a bear or something."

"There's no bears where we live."

My shoulders relax. Daisy was a real bookworm in high school and still reads a lot. That coupled with her obsession for unusual animals would qualify her to know about bears.

"You okay?"

"Yeah, thanks for letting me vent."

"Anytime. Feel free to call later. I've got appointments until five, then I'm done today."

"Thanks, Dais."

"Cheer up, buttercup."

I shake my head as she hangs up the phone. The buzzing returns for a few seconds, then stops.

You never know what's going on around here. We have all types of hunting seasons, so rednecks frequent the woods behind my house all year. I grab my headphones and start my favorite playlist as I exit through the back door.

Like most middle-class Southerners, I have the luxury of my own above-ground pool. After standing on my feet all week indoors, it's my go-to fix for relaxing my limbs and taking in some natural vitamin D.

It doesn't take long for me to settle onto my favorite float, belly down, and drift toward the middle of the water. Shania Twain belts out "Any Man of Mine," and I regret pushing away from my phone so soon. This is one track I'd prefer to skip today.

I mentally go over my grocery list and all the items I need to pick up for the salon. Of course, that leads my mind to products we're running short on, which leads to Marcus. Ugh, Marcus Farcus. Actually, Marcus Mosely, but Farcus is more fitting.

My brain takes on a table tennis match between productivity and the promiscuity of the man I last trusted to love me. Well, love is a strong word. I'll go with adore, or simply like. If only he hadn't liked a lot of other women as much as me—at the same time.

By the time the song ends, I'm worked up and ready to mix hair removal in his styling gel. As an evil little scheme cooks up in my head, something crashes beside me, sending me and half the pool water over the edge like a tidal wave.

My heart leaps in my throat as I rip out my earbuds, which are thankfully waterproof, and hold on to my Dollar General raft like it's a fragile ancient artifact. As I ride the wave to the ground, I notice the pool is split in half by a massive pine tree.

My heart races a million miles a minute as I scramble to my feet. It's a miracle I'm not dead!

"Are you all right?"

I lift my face to a scrawny guy with a soul patch and a mullet, wearing a sleeveless flannel shirt. It's like someone put

Joe Dirt and Morgan Wallen in a blender and this guy poured out.

I cross my arms over my bare stomach. Partly to hold in the nausea building from current events, and partly because I don't care for how Morgan Dirt is eyeing me.

"Whoa, mama."

"Hey." I'm about to chastise him for a sexist slur when I notice his eyes have now trailed to my roof. At least what remains of my roof.

All modesty takes a back seat when I rush toward the house. Pine limbs stick out of the top like Clark Griswold's Christmas tree.

"What have you done?!" I snatch my phone, which now has a cracked screen. Some lifecase.

Adrenaline rushes through me as I search for the sheriff department's number. I'll certainly need to put on clothes before Bradley shows up.

With my back turned to Morgan Dirt, I wait for Bradley to answer.

"Hello?"

When did his voice get so deep? And why does it sound like he's behind me rather than on the phone?

When I hear another ring, I turn to find another man standing by the scrappy soul-patch guy. My temperature rises, as this man looks like someone threw The Rock and Thor in a blender.

Except he's dressed like a Duluth Trading commercial and has facial hair. He looks vaguely familiar, but I'm certain I'd remember a guy like this.

Of course he'd show up when I'm in my new bikini, minutes after I've started my man fast.

Great sense of humor, God.

JoJo

I've had a lot of idiots work for me, and a lot of them have done a lot of stupid things. But this makes the first time one cut a tree the wrong direction and landed it on a woman's house.

I've also seen a lot of surprising things working in the woods. But I've never stumbled across a soaking-wet, hot girl in a red bikini. If Skeeder's stupidity wasn't going to cost me a fortune, I might say this was my lucky day.

She turns fully around, large gray-blue eyes fearful as a deer caught in headlights. I'm not a hugger, or even a toucher, but if she were wearing clothes, I might offer a comforting side hug. Instead, I try my best to apologize.

"Miss, I am so sorry. Do you need a ride to the doctor? My company will pay for all the damages." I hook a thumb back at Skeeder and shake my head. "And I'll be more than happy to fire this dumb butt if you want."

Firing Skeeder would be more of a favor to me and the whole work crew, but I thought it a noble gesture to offer her the decision.

"Oh no. Don't fire this man." She shoots a sympathetic smile his way. "He might have trouble finding a new job."

I chuckle.

"Oh, I didn't mean it like that." She winces at Skeeder. Then she presses a button on her phone and shakes her head.

"No offense taken, ma'am. You speak the truth." Skeeder bows like he just starred in a school play rather than crushed someone's house.

"Skeeder, why don't you go back and get some equipment for me to clean up this mess?"

He nods and starts toward our logging area. I think better of my instructions and call after him. "Better yet, send Homer."

"Right on, boss man." He continues into the woods.

I turn back to the woman and shrug.

She narrows her eyes. "Skeeder, Homer? Are those real names?"

"No. Skeeder can't say skidder correctly, which earned him that name. Homer likes to stay home until he needs money and decides to come and work."

She shakes her head. "Sounds like my employee."

"Oh, I'm JoJo. Short for Joseph." I extend my hand.

She gives it a firm shake. I'm used to firm handshakes, but they usually come with calluses rather than long painted nails. Her hands are small and smooth, and slightly shriveled from the water.

"Adrianne Reynolds."

I mouth her name. "You do hair, right?"

"Yeah. You must go to another salon because I haven't seen you in mine."

I lift my hard hat to reveal my freshly shaven head. She smiles and laughs. I'm not a smiler myself, but I find myself smiling at her.

It's rare to find a woman this attractive being so nice, especially when her property was just destroyed. Maybe she senses what I'm thinking, because she glances back at her house and drops her shoulders.

"Like I said, my crew will get this tree moved, and I'll pay for the damages."

"Oh no. I can't let you pay for it. I have insurance."

The loader hums nearby, and we both turn to Homer riding our way.

"I'm going to head inside to put on some clothes."

"I don't think that's such a good idea until we move the tree. Do you have a towel or something out here?"

She nods toward the cracked deck. A bright pink towel is crinkled under the bark.

"Oh." Without thinking, I unbutton my shirt and hand it to her. "I always end up in an undershirt by the end of a hot summer day anyway. Might as well prepare early."

"Thank you."

The corners of my mouth tick up a notch as she takes my shirt.

She rolls down the sleeves and puts it on. It falls almost to her knees, and the sleeves hit her knuckles. I watch her pinch the waist and examine the plaid.

"If I could get to my brown belt and cowgirl boots, I could turn this into a cute shirtdress outfit."

I laugh. "You sure are taking this whole destroyed property thing well."

She lifts then lowers one shoulder. "What choice do I have? I could cry, or go off on you, or slap that Skeeder guy. Regardless, my house still has a hole in it and my pool is still split in half."

I smile for the second time in the last half hour. More like the second time in the last half year. Similar to a pit bull, I show my teeth more out of frustration than friendliness.

Homer stops the loader, climbs out, and walks toward me. "Man, Skeeder did it this time. I'm surprised you didn't fire him."

"Well, it wasn't my decision." I raise a brow to Adrianne, who smirks. Then I turn back to Homer. "I'm going to grab this trunk with the claw. Keep her at a safe distance and watch for any flying branches."

"Ten-four, boss man."

I climb in the loader and wait until Adrianne is at a safe

distance. I hated to put her in the care of Homer, but it's best I be the one to remove the tree. We've already done enough damage. Besides, Homer might be lazy as sin, but he's a trustworthy guy.

I maneuver the claw and clamp down on the tree. The more I think about what happened, the madder I get. Skeeder had no business even cutting this close to her house without me around. He always wanders as far from the pack as he can to do what he wants. At least Homer has the decency to doze off in front of me.

The branches lift from her roof, taking some of the shingles with them. I lower the tree to the ground beside her house, which is now split halfway down the middle. Mud slings up from where the pool water soiled her yard.

I park the loader and return to Adrianne and Homer. "We need to get the rest of the crew out here with the chain saws and cut this monster up."

Homer nods and heads into the trees toward our logging site. I flare my nostrils at the mess we've made.

"I apologize again. We've ruined your home."

She shakes her head. "Don't feel bad. I know it was an accident. I'm just thankful not to be hurt." She sucks in a deep breath.

I watch her chest and shoulders fall as she exhales. Nothing within me wants a wife, or even a girlfriend. Still, I am a man, and a beautiful woman is wearing my shirt in the middle of the woods.

Let's just say that would make a great calendar photo.

"I appreciate you being so understanding." I adjust my hard hat and stare at the tree sinking into the mushy grass. "Do you have family you can stay with for now?"

For the first time, Adrianne's face falls. "None of my family lives in town anymore. But I do have a good friend nearby."

I nod. "I'll find a tarp to cover the roof for you. Jim Vann's calling for rain Monday."

She nods. "I appreciate everything so much."

"Don't thank me just yet. We still need to cut this big boy up and haul him off." I walk up to the house and grip the siding. What's not caved in already seems sturdy. "If you want, I can go in with you to make sure it's safe for you to gather some belongings."

The grin returns to her face. "Thanks."

She tiptoes past the mud and pine bows toward me.

I hold out a hand. "Watch your step."

She takes my hand and lifts her foot over a limb. "Whoa." Stepping between branches causes her to lose her balance.

With one arm, I catch her before she goes down. "Easy."

I scoop her up and hoist her over the branches and into the house. After I safely return her feet to the ground, our eyes lock. She doesn't say anything, but I get the sense she wants to thank me again.

Before more calendar images circle my mind, I clear my throat. "If you have some shoes close by, I can grab those for you. I wouldn't tromp around barefoot in here just yet."

"Oh yeah." She blinks, taking her focus off my face. "I keep flip-flops by the back door."

I step toward the back door, which seems unnecessary now thanks to the huge hole beside it. I find a pair of hunter-orange flip-flops. Before handing them to her, I wipe off a layer of bark and dust.

"Thanks." She slips them on and heads to the center of the house.

"Wait on me. Let me walk everywhere first." I stomp over branches to catch up to her. When I hear a bloodcurdling shrill, I'm afraid I'm too late.

"Adrianne, are you fine?" She looks fine—in more ways than one.

That is, until I notice the huge tears welling in her eyes.

"Did you step on something? Are you hurt?"

She shakes her head and points in front of us to an open room with half the ceiling and roof caved in on it. Her shoulders shake as she tries to talk.

At last, she mumbles, "My closet room is ruined."

I don't know what a closet room is, but it must be pretty important to break her after all this optimism.

Totally out of my character, I reach over and wrap my arm around her shoulders. She turns toward me and cries into my chest, soaking my undershirt with her tears and wet hair.

It's been years since I've held a woman in my arms, all due to my stubborn cavemanlike tendencies. My bachelor ways only worsened once I moved in with my elderly grandpa.

The last thing I thought I'd be doing when I went to work this morning was comforting a gorgeous woman wearing my shirt.

CHAPTER TWO

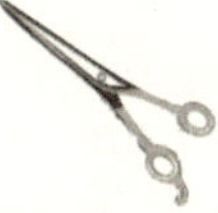

Adrianne

"Oomph." Daisy falls forward when she crosses the threshold to her bedroom.

"Are you okay?" I lift her by her arms.

"Yeah, all your poofy dresses cushioned my fall." She frowns at the pile of tulle and satin by her feet. "I knew you had a lot of clothes, but not *that* many clothes."

I laugh. "This is just a third of them. Most went to the salon. I'll get a good bit of these out of your way once I find some boxes."

Daisy arches a thin brow. "I should have some empty boxes in the candle room."

I nod. "Thanks. We can take these back to my car for now."

Daisy starts gathering skirts and hands some to me. Together we walk to my car, holding them high enough so the goats can't nibble at the material. I open the back door and fan my pile across the back seat. Then I take her pile and stack them on top.

Once I remove my hand, they expand to the roof of my car like a hot air balloon inflating. I fold a loose dress sleeve inside and slam the door.

"There."

Daisy stares at my window. The bright colors of my clothing swirling inside resembles a cotton candy machine.

Before she can comment on how many clothes I have in there—not counting all the ones in her house, at my salon, and already in the trunk—I turn and go inside. Daisy catches up to me.

Mullet follows us to the front door. I slide inside behind Daisy and shut the door behind me. He bleats a few times, but I try my best to ignore it.

She's had goats longer than we've been best friends, so I don't say much about it. But she reached another level with Mullet. He's more like a dog to her.

Although I've never cared much for animals in the house, I can understand people having a dog or cat. Maybe even a cute little bunny or one of those cool-looking lizards that changes colors. And fish. Those are fine.

But we as a society should draw the line at letting hoofed animals mill around on our hardwood floors. That's just responsible home maintenance.

I plop down on a chair and sigh. The idea of home maintenance has me a little on edge.

When the disaster first happened, I was in a state of shock and relief. A pine tree falling across your pool and house isn't something one plans for in everyday life. I'm lucky to be alive.

Between feeling incredibly lucky and blessed that it wasn't deadly, and spending half the day with loggers while wearing nothing but a bikini, this is the first chance I've had to really process anything.

I stare down at my orange flip-flops and bare legs. "Daisy, do you mind if I go ahead and take a shower?"

"Not at all. I'll show you where everything is. I have my last appointment soon. If you hear anyone, that's what it will be."

"Thanks." I gather my pile of toiletries and follow Daisy toward her bathroom. We pass Mullet in the hallway. "I thought I shut the door on you?"

Daisy laughs and waves a hand dismissively. "He must've used his doggy door in the kitchen."

I pinch my mouth shut and step into the bathroom. Daisy gets me a towel and shows me where anything else I may need is kept. She has plenty of goat's milk soap and goat's milk body butter on hand. That's one perk to having goats around all the time.

"If you need anything else, just text. I'll have my phone on vibrate in the massage room, but I can hear that."

"Okay, thanks."

Daisy exits the bathroom, and Mullet falls in line behind her down the hallway. I shut the door and make sure it locks. The last thing I need is a goat coming in on me.

I've got to hand it to Daisy—her house smells amazing to have so many animals. Must be all the candles and home-made soaps.

I turn on the hot water and suck in much-needed aromatherapy as the steam activates all the soaps and essential oils in the room. A warm shower is just what I needed. Between my luxury shampoo and her natural soap, I come out smelling like actual roses.

After slipping into some shorts and a top, I reach for my hair dryer. My mind often wanders when I dry my own hair. This time it leads to me debating where I'll sleep tonight.

The two spare bedrooms are currently occupied by a massage table and candle-making supplies for Daisy's businesses. I'd prefer not to sandwich between Mullet and Daisy in her double bed. I guess that leaves the hippie-like furniture in the living room that is anything but comfortable.

On the bright side, after the day I've had, I could sleep on the roof. Except maybe at my house, since I'd collapse into debris.

I sigh. JoJo said he'd bring some guys out tomorrow afternoon to clean up the remainder of the mess. Maybe then I can get the rest of my essentials out.

I fluff my hair with my fingers, then spritz a little holding spray on it. Then I start applying foundation to my face. I doubt we will leave the house tonight, but after spending all afternoon like a drowned rat, I need the confidence boost of a mini makeover.

I hang my damp swimsuit in the shower to dry the rest of the way and reach for JoJo's shirt. On impulse, I lift it to my nose and drag in the scent. Very sandalwood, with a hint of pine. It's a natural smell, and not overpowering. I never would've picked up on it among all the other scents had I not shoved it in my face.

Kind of like JoJo. He's pleasant, but nobody would know it by the way he carries himself.

Something about the scent calms me. I leave the bathroom with my wet towel in one hand and his shirt in the other. With the concoction of oils and soaps now behind me, I close my eyes and take one more long whiff of his shirt.

"Excuse me," a deep voice bellows in front of me.

My eyes pop open. "JoJo?"

I swallow audibly and drop his shirt from my face. When I go to retrieve it from the floor, he beats me to it. His calloused fingertips graze over my shaky hand as he fists the shirt.

I stand in slow motion like a kid called on by an intimidating teacher. "I was smelling your shirt to see if I needed to wash it before giving it back."

Idiot. Of course he'd want you to wash the shirt he worked in, followed by you soaking it with chlorine water and tanning oil.

He doesn't say a word, doesn't move a muscle. Except for his forearm. It flexes. Not that I was looking or anything, but it's hard not to notice when we're inches apart.

"Don't worry about it." He turns sideways and passes me.

I melt into the wall so he can pass without touching me in the tiny hallway. Then I watch him disappear into the front of the house and hear the front door shut.

What feels like an eternity later, Daisy exits the massage room, humming.

"Daisy? What the heck was JoJo doing here?"

She waves a hand towel and laughs. "Relax. He wasn't looking for you. He was here for his monthly appointment."

"Appointment?" I scrunch my nose. "For like a massage?"

She slings the towel over one shoulder and laughs more. "Well, yeah. You didn't think he took yoga or candle-making classes did you?"

I twist my lips. "No, I guess not. But I didn't take him for one to get a massage either."

"He has a standing appointment. A lot of men with strenuous jobs find that a regular sports massage helps them with aches and pains."

"Makes sense."

My mind drifts toward him lying on a massage table—shirtless. *I wonder if he has a hairy chest.*

"You okay?"

"Yeah." I shake my head, trying to dislodge its unruly thoughts. "Just, why didn't you say he was coming by when I told you about today?"

"I have masseuse-client confidentially. Besides, me pounding JoJo's back has nothing to do with your house."

I stare at the ceiling for a beat, then back at Daisy. "Technically, no. But since I spent half the day half-naked around him and his log crew, I'd think a little heads up he'd be coming by here might be nice."

Daisy grins. "He comes around this time one Saturday a month. So now you know."

Her eyes fall to the towel in my hand. She holds out the towel from her shoulder. "Can you take both of these to the laundry room? I need to start a load soon."

"Yes, ma'am." I take the towel and wait for her to cross the house toward her bedroom.

Before I go to the laundry, I inhale the towel she gave me. Too bad it's about ninety percent massage oil and only ten percent man scent.

Probably for the best, since I did invoke that whole man fast today.

JoJo

"Haul that to the burn pile, Homer."

"Ten-four, boss man."

Homer surprisingly agreed to come out here with me and sweep up the debris. I should've made Skeeder do it, but we don't need any more accidents. And I don't like paying him overtime. Homer, on the other hand, works as hard as a good employee would all the time when he knows he's getting overtime.

I hear gravel moving and turn to Adrianne's little red car flying up the driveway. At least, I think she's in there. The closer the car gets, the more I notice mounds of colors pressed against the glass in every direction.

She slams on the brakes at the end of the drive and opens her door. Adrianne gets out, and a pile of puff follows.

"What's that?" I walk over to her car.

She yawns. "More of my clothes."

I shake my head. "You have more besides what I helped you take to your shop?"

"Yes. I left some at Daisy's too."

Why anyone needs that many clothes is beyond me. "Why are they in your car?"

She balls up the wad of dresses and shoves them back in her car. "The closest storage unit is halfway to Tuscaloosa, and it seemed silly to rent a storage unit that far away for just clothes."

"It seems silly to rent a storage unit anywhere for just clothes."

She blinks.

Maybe that came out a little rude. "Sorry. What I meant to say was you can put them at my place if you need to."

"Oh no. You've already moved the tree, and you're tarping my house."

She points to Homer on the roof. He waves, then quickly regains his balance. I shake my head and silently pray he doesn't break anything—including himself.

"I couldn't ask you to store my clothes too."

"Well, you didn't ask. I offered."

Her mouth morphs into a grin, which is short-lived when she yawns widely. She covers it with her hand.

"Did you have trouble sleeping last night?"

"Yeah, but not because of this." She swirls a finger toward her house and stops it in front of me. Her cheeks redden, and she crosses her arms tightly. "I woke up on a wicker couch to a goat standing over my face."

"That might mess with my sleep too."

She shrugs. "And that was just at midnight. After that, I went in the massage room, where I knew there was a lock, and slept on the table."

"That's kind of comfy."

She narrows her eyes. "Maybe it is for a massage, but for someone who turns a lot in her sleep . . ." She yawns one more time. "Let's just say I eventually fell on the floor, then grabbed a yoga mat and stayed there."

I nod. "Maybe you can nap sometime today."

"I hope so. Daisy takes Mullet to the park on Sunday afternoons, so I plan on napping during that."

I catch myself smiling at her. Whether it's her cuteness or how well she rolls with the punches, I'm not sure. Maybe it's her entertaining goat stories. Regardless, I've never met anyone else who makes me smile like this.

We stand in silence for a moment. I take in her yoga pants, tank top, and hair twirled on top of her head. Then I turn toward the house before I'm tempted to eye the yoga pants any more.

"We swept up all the loose pine bark and straw. Once the tarp is secure, everything should be safe from the rain. Feel free to load those clothes and anything else of value in my truck. I can store it until you need it."

I turn back to her staring at me with her mouth parted.

"You don't have to leave your valuables with me. I didn't mean it like that. I know we don't know one another that well, just from passing in town and all."

"No, I was thinking how incredibly sweet that is of you to offer."

"Sweet?" I scratch my head. The only time I hear that word is when a waiter is bringing out sweet and sour chicken.

"Yeah. Everything you've done for me, are doing for me, it's really sweet."

Dang it. Either my neck and entire head are sweating, or I'm blushing. I swallow. Good thing I'm wearing a hard hat, because I'm certain my bald head is lit up like a bonfire.

"Thanks." I stare at my boots for a long pause.

When I raise my face, Adrianne is back at her car, digging out dresses. I go help her, then glance down at my hands. Calluses and dirty nails could do some damage to all that satin.

"Why don't I bring my truck over and make it easier for you?"

She peeks her head over the pile in her arms. "Thanks."

I drive my old dually around from the side of the house and park it beside her Honda. My personal truck is old, but it's clean and has plenty of space. Aside from a gun in the back glass and a few empty Skoal cans clanking under the seats, it's pretty bare.

I open the door to the back seat, and Adrianne drops the dresses inside. Then she meticulously smooths them out as if they hadn't just been on the ground and crumpled in her arms. I stand by, entertained, as she collects two more armloads from inside her car and two more from her trunk.

At last, she wipes her hands down her pants and sighs. "That's it."

I chuckle. "Are you sure?"

"Yeah, the rest are in my salon or at Daisy's."

"Okay." I turn toward the house. "It's safe to go inside and get more things as long as you stay away from the opening. I moved some things back in case the roof decides to cave in more after it rains."

I study her a second, then grab an extra hard hat out of my toolbox. "Just in case, you better wear this."

She pulls it over her small head, and with her hair piled

high, it almost fits. We walk side by side toward the house. I glance up at Homer as we pass under the opening.

"Don't worry. I'll go back and check his work before we leave today."

"At the risk of sounding like a broken record, thank you."

I raise my hand to dismiss her gratitude.

"No, really, don't say it's nothing. I'm filing an insurance claim as soon as the office opens tomorrow, and you've already cleared the mess and covered the hole. That will save me a lot of stress as I wait on the money to fix it."

"I told you my company can pay for it." We stop in the center and examine the opening. The sunlight barely seeps through the thick tarp overhead.

"No, please. You've done plenty." She puts her hands on my biceps and stares up at me.

I focus on her soft eyes and mentally snap an image of her wearing my hard hat. I'll add it to my imaginary outdoors calendar. Her wearing my shirt still makes the cover, but this will be a strong contender.

"All my family is moved away, and I've never had to deal with anything like this alone."

"You don't have to deal with this alone either."

Her cheeks redden again, and she smiles. My arms tighten under her hands. I hope she doesn't think I'm flexing on purpose. It's an involuntary movement. The same as every time she causes me to smile.

I open my mouth to say something, then close it. There's a weird current between us, drawing me closer. If I mess around too much, my mouth will gravitate toward hers.

We stand there like statues in a staring contest. Maybe she's searching for an appropriate response just like me. Her hands slide slowly as she pulls them away from my arms. My biceps twitch at the loss of her touch, and I take a step back just in time . . .

For Homer to fall.

Dust flies as the tarp sucks in around him. Adrianne's eyes bug as her face slides into shock. The pink in her cheeks is now ghostly white.

After the initial shock, she coughs at the dust and fans in front of her face. I kneel to check on Homer. When I pull back the tarp, he emerges like a baby deer testing out its legs for the first time.

"I'm all right. Sorry about that, boss man."

I widen my eyes and pat him on the helmet. "No worries, you get to help me redo the tarp for free."

CHAPTER THREE

Adrianne

Last night was a little better. I got a decent nap while Daisy walked Mullet. Then I took the wicker couch cushion off and spread it across the massage room floor for a better bed.

This morning was the issue. Mullet chewed the strap off one of my Jimmy Choos. Daisy made the unfortunate joke that smart little Mullet knew they were named "chew." That was pretty much the last straw.

I politely thanked her for opening her home, then spouted out that I found another place to stay. That led to frantic texting on the constant thread between my mom, my sister, and me.

Mama offered to rent me a room at Gamer's Paradise. I politely declined and explained that money was not an issue. However, I did like the idea and called Bianca to check on a room. When that didn't pan out, my sister called her sister-in-law in Apple Cart and arranged for me to stay there.

All this happened before seven.

Now I'm on my way to meet with the insurance agent before working at the salon all day, then going to stay with a single woman and her four kids. But as long as I can stay clear of trees and goats, it should beat my weekend.

I park behind my salon and push aside the bags in my front passenger seat. When I left Daisy's, I took all my belongings from her house as well. I look like the most high-maintenance homeless person ever.

The insurance office is also downtown, so I decide to walk. It's already warm, which is typical of summer mornings in Alabama.

Like my salon, most of downtown is old brick buildings. The largest building has several businesses inside, with one large reception area. Oddly enough, my insurance agent, a lawyer, and an accountant all share the same secretary.

I open the glass door and let it close behind me. The blinds hit against the glass when it shuts, causing me to jolt to attention. Lack of good sleep and no caffeine yet has set me on edge.

"Good morning," the lady at the front desk greets me.

"Morning, Rhoda." I try and hide my yawn with a smile.

Her haircut is adorable, but the color seems a little harsh for her small features. I narrow my eyes and imagine subtle highlights framing her face. That would brighten her eyes.

Of course, I don't tell her that. She's not my client. Besides, she looks great for someone in her fifties.

Last I heard, Rhoda goes to the other salon in our county. A lot of people a generation above me go there.

"Eric said he'd be ready whenever you get here."

I smile, this time without yawning. "Thanks."

I pass Rhoda's desk to a hallway with multiple offices. Eric's is on the very end. He had offered to come in over the weekend and help me when I called, but I told him first thing today was fine. It's not like the insurance agency as a whole would jump right on that anyway.

His door is open, so I enter and take a seat in one of the two chairs facing his desk.

"Good morning, Adrianne." Eric stands and shakes my hand, then smooths his tie as he sits.

"Hey, Eric. Thanks for meeting so early."

"No problem." He clicks his computer mouse. "I went ahead and input all the details you gave me over the phone yesterday to get us started."

My shoulders drop. I should've known he'd start on it early. Bless his heart. He's become a workaholic after his wife passed.

"I'll still need to go by and assess the roof and everything to make more notes."

I nod, then twist my mouth. There's a good chance more damage was done when Homer fell through the roof, but I don't mention that to Eric.

"Do you need any immediate assistance like a covering or cleanup?"

I shake my head. "JoJo tarped the roof and had his guys clean up the debris."

"Well, isn't that kind of him."

"I thought so." My chest tightens when I recall how much JoJo has helped me with this. If someone had to be responsible for a tree crashing into my house, I'm sure glad it's him.

"He's a good guy."

"Yes, he is."

"You need to keep any receipts that he spends on the tarp materials or that you spend on housing, et cetera, while we're waiting on the claim to go through."

"Okay."

"Do you have a place to stay? I know you mentioned your friend Daisy yesterday."

"Yes. And Bianca said a room will be open at the lodge eventually."

"Good, keep those receipts." Eric scrolls his computer and shakes his head. "It's a shame we don't have any decent hotels around here besides a hunting lodge."

I laugh. "Maybe Gamer's Paradise is the only tourist trap in Apple Cart County."

"Good point." Eric cracks his knuckles and stops scrolling. Then he turns his computer screen toward me. "Verify all this info for me."

I scan the screen, checking my contact information and the description of the incident and damage from my perspective. My eyes linger on the block titled "Marital Status."

Twenty-eight isn't considered an old maid in today's society. Unless I poll all the older ladies in the bridge club. And it's not like I live in my parents' basement playing *Minecraft* all day. I run a successful business and have plenty of friends—plus dates when I want them.

I'm totally fine with being single . . . for now.

"Everything okay?"

I raise my eyes to Eric's questioning stare. "Yeah, absolutely."

"Good." He turns the screen back to him. "I triple checked all your policy info this morning."

Bless his heart. Maybe I'm better off never having loved before. At least I know how to productively kill time without a significant other.

"Thanks for all your help, Eric. Especially for getting this in so quickly."

"Of course. Any way I can help you at all." He puts a fist to his mouth before continuing. "After all you did for Connie in her last months."

He tears up, and my own eyes dampen. "Don't mention it. She was a dear client, and what I did was miniscule."

He nods and chokes back his tears.

I stand. "Thanks again."

He nods once more, then turns to his computer, his eyes glistening with fresh tears.

I leave without saying anything more and shut his door behind me. If I'd stayed one more minute, we'd both be boo-hooing.

Connie was one of those people who made me vow to never take life for granted. She fought breast cancer for about a year, then passed just before her forty-first birthday. I did everything I could to help her keep stylish short cuts until she could no longer hang on to her hair.

I remember the day she came in wearing a cap. She'd lost chunks of her hair in the shower and wanted it all gone. Eric had taken off work and drove into Birmingham to buy her a wig, then brought it to me to style. I taught her how to style it and told her to come by anytime for help.

Three months later, she was gone.

I'm starting down the hall toward the main exit when I hear a familiar voice inside the lawyer's office.

"So you're telling me if I'm not married in the next year, you're selling your half of the business to someone else?"

I peek at the door and get a glimpse between the blinds. Sure enough, that was JoJo. He's sitting between two other men. One has silver-gray hair and his hand propped on the end of a cane.

"Talk some sense into my grandson. He needs some stability in his life before taking over the company."

The oldest is JoJo's grandpa. My interest is piqued. I step closer to try and get a better view through the slit in the blinds. Just the backs of three heads. But I can hear everything.

"Mr. Culp, with all due respect, I've never married myself," the female lawyer answers.

"Then why don't you marry him? Then I won't have to pay you cash. Kill two birds with one stone."

I hold in a laugh. This man is hilarious. I wish I could see Angela's face. She is like forty, and I've never seen her out with anyone, or even out, except for a jog.

She answers JoJo instead of the old man. "Regardless of what some of us think about business, your grandpa, as majority shareholder, can do what he wants."

I slink closer to the wall so I can hear more. I've got a few more minutes before I need to open shop, and this is getting interesting.

JoJo

"Don't you think I can concentrate on the business more if I'm *not* married?" I practically scream at Grandpa Joe.

My blood is boiling. Daddy sits between us, arms crossed like a disapproving father. Maybe he is. Grandpa and I are going at it like two cats in a paper sack. Grandpa must've chosen a small woman for a lawyer so she couldn't restrain us. Either that, or he really is trying to pawn me off.

"If you don't get married, then who's gonna get the business after you? You're killing my legacy by not having a kid."

"I don't need to be married to have a kid."

"Boy, I—" Grandpa steadies his cane and leans toward me.

Daddy stops him. "Grandpa, he's just joking."

I am, but I did make a valid point. Which leads to another good point . . .

"Grandpa, if you're willing to sell it to someone not in the family now, why not let me have it and sell it when I retire?"

Grandpa raises his hands and slaps his knees. "You think you're so smart."

"I'm smart enough to make decisions without having to go to you all the time. Daddy trusts me, why don't you?"

Daddy parts his mouth, but Grandpa interrupts before he can speak. "Any man not married at your age has to have something wrong with him."

I roll my eyes and push back my chair. "This is a waste of time. I'm going to service the trucks." I stand and open the door. When I slam it behind me, a brunette woman hurries past me. I'd recognize that walk anywhere.

"Adrianne?"

She stops and slowly turns. "JoJo, hi. Funny how we keep running into each other." She giggles nervously.

"Yeah. How was last night after I left?"

"Good."

I focus on her face. Behind all the makeup, I spot dark circles. She probably didn't sleep well last night either. I decide not to comment. For as little as I know about women, I've learned from having a mom and a sister that you never comment on their looks unless it's an obvious compliment. Saying she looks tired would not fall under that category.

"Are you headed to work?"

"Yes. Are you?"

"Yeah." I nod as we walk down the hall.

The more distance between Grandpa and me, the more my heartbeat steadies. Walking and talking with Adrianne could be contributing to my calming down as well.

When we get to the main entrance, a clap of thunder

rolls. The bottom falls out of the sky and a summer shower beats against the windows.

Adrianne's eyes widen. "I should've grabbed my umbrella. I didn't think it would rain this early."

"It wasn't supposed to." I stare out the window at the thunderhead clouds, then turn to her. "Come on, I can walk you to your car."

She laughs. "My car is down the block at my salon."

"Then I can drive you to your car."

She smiles and follows me outside.

"Wait here." I leave her under the overhang while I run through the rain.

I'm parked only a few yards away, but I'm soaked by the time I shut my door. I drive as close to the building as I can, then reach over and open her door. She climbs inside and slams the door, then inches closer to me to avoid the wet door. I'm just as wet, but don't dare mention it.

"Maybe I saved you from a few raindrops."

She brushes her hair from her face. "You did. Thanks."

I pull into the road and squint to see. The wipers run a mile a minute as the streets flood. Once it's clear enough to see the road, I head toward her salon.

"Park in the back near my car."

I pull beside her car and park close to the back entrance. A brightly colored suitcase takes up her front seat.

"You moving more stuff?"

"I am when the rain clears."

"Where will you put it?"

She wipes at her hair again. "Someplace in the salon."

I notice the back windows of her car filled with more things. "And you have room for all that?"

"I'll make room."

"If you need to put more in my basement . . ."

She waves her hands. "It's good. Most of this is stuff I use every day." I blink, and she shrugs. "What? You don't have essentials?"

"A toothbrush, toothpaste, and deodorant. I guess you can count soap, but that pretty much comes with the bathroom."

She laughs. "Comes with the bathroom?"

"Yeah, like if you go on a trip. They always have soap." I swipe my bald head. "And shampoo for those interested."

Adrianne gasps. "You should never use the shampoo in a hotel."

"Don't worry. I don't."

She smirks. "I mean in general. People shouldn't. It's watered down and can do damage to your hair."

"I think the damage has been done." I wipe my hand across my head once more, then smile.

She smiles widely in return. "Then don't use cheap beard products."

"What's beard products?"

Her face contorts. "You don't know about beard products?"

"Nope."

"They make combs and oils and shampoos—total kits. For beard maintenance."

"Beard maintenance?" Saying those two words together aloud is so unnatural.

"Yeah?" Adrianne answers like this is everyday knowledge. Maybe it is in her circles.

I shake my head. "I typically dust the crumbs out and call it a day."

She snarls her nose as if grossed out. My neck heats up, and I halfway regret what I said. Even if it is a hundred percent true.

"Seriously, if you need to leave anything else with me, I'll be glad to get it when it's not raining cats and dogs."

"Thanks, but this is everyday stuff."

"Can you not leave it at Daisy's?" This is none of my business, and I'm never one to ask personal questions—or even care what's going on. But something about Adrianne makes me want to take care of her.

"I'm transitioning."

I cock my head, trying to read into what she means by that.

"I'm staying with my sister's sister-in-law a few days, then getting a room at Gamer's Paradise."

"Okay. Too bad the inn is overrun with rats and winos."

Her eyes widen. "Yeah, I didn't even consider staying there."

"Good call."

A white Mercedes pulls up to the front of the salon. Adrianne cranes her neck to check out the car. "That's my first client. I've got to run. Thanks again, JoJo, for everything."

She reaches over and kisses me on the cheek, then opens her door and jumps out.

Before I can fully process what just happened, she slides into her salon and shuts the door. I sit and watch rain beat against my windshield for a few minutes. Then I decide it's best I head toward my place.

The longer I stay, the later I'll get to work on the log trucks. And the more I run the risk of coming off like a creeper.

Still, I can hardly believe the prettiest woman for a country mile just kissed me.

CHAPTER FOUR

Adrianne

I stand behind the chair and fluff out Angela's hair. The whole time I foiled her head, I couldn't help but think about the conversation I overheard this morning with JoJo's family.

Every time she mentioned work, I would make a vague comment, hoping she'd elaborate. Instead, she'd dive into talking about training for another marathon or the current book she's reading.

I'm more Zumba and magazines, so I find it hard to relate. I just nodded and hoped she'd mention JoJo eventually. But she didn't.

She must adhere to those privacy policies like Daisy with her massage clients. Maybe I should start making my clients sign some sort of waiver? If I had a nickel for every time I overheard someone say they heard something at my salon, I could retire yesterday.

"This looks so good, Angela."

She lifts her lips and studies her shoulder-length brown hair. "You always bring my vision to life."

I pull her hair up in the back. "I left just enough length for a full ponytail. That way you can put it up when you're running."

"Perfect." She grins.

"Hold still." I shade her eyes with my hand and spritz a layer of finishing spray. "All done."

I spin her chair to the side so she can exit safely away from the cords. She stands gracefully and digs in her wallet.

She's the only person I know around here who uses an American Express card. She's also the only person I know around here who flies frequently, so that makes sense.

Angela scribbles a generous tip on her receipt.

"Thank you so much." I smile as I stuff the receipt in the register drawer.

"You're welcome. Good luck with your house."

I sigh and nod. Angela presses her lips together and leaves the salon.

As soon as the door shuts, I unplug all my tools and sweep up her hair. My stomach rumbles as I dump the bird's nest of dead ends into a plastic bag. I always save hair clippings for Jack's lodge. Something about it helps control where the deer go.

My stomach growls louder, and I hold my hand across it. It's my fault for always scheduling clients across lunchtime, but I find it hard to tell people no when they need to come on their lunch break. Or to tell Angela no when she wants to come late after work.

I cinch the bag of hair shut, then lock up the salon. My legs stretch into warrior pose as I dodge a puddle between the door and my car. The rain didn't last long, but plenty of it fell in an hour's time. I climb in beside my suitcase and let my mind wander about what Morgan made for dinner.

She's a phenomenal cook and always has something homemade. It doesn't take long to get to her house from the salon, which makes my hunger pains more bearable. Worst case scenario about staying with her would be possibly gaining weight.

I park in her front yard and hear a blood-curdling scream, followed by yelling.

Okay, maybe the worst part would be her four kids. They're not bad kids. However, they gain power in numbers. Kind of like ants.

I proceed toward the house with caution, not unloading my bags just yet. Isabella, Morgan's oldest daughter, meets me at the door.

"Hi, Adrianne. Aunt Jessica said you may be staying here."

"Yeah, I'm afraid so."

"It's fine. Mama might not even notice you're here."

I laugh as if I meant the "afraid so" for them instead of me.

Isabella leads me through the foyer, where multiple tops are strewn across the floor. It's like déjà vu seeing clothes scattered everywhere. Except these are more suited for a young girl.

At the end of the breadcrumb trails stands Morgan, one hand on her hip and the other holding a sequin unicorn shirt.

"What do you mean this top is juvenile?"

Her youngest daughter rolls her eyes. "I told you, unicorns are for second-graders."

"You just finished third."

"Exactly." She rolls her eyes wider.

"Don't you roll those eyes at me, child. I'm not buying y'all nothing new until tax-free shopping weekend. Lord knows you kids will grow another four inches before then anyhow."

The girl cries louder. "But Mama! I have nothing to wear."

I take a step toward her. "Hey, Sophie?"

"It's Sophia."

"Sophia? You want me to take a look in your closet? I'm sure we can put together some cute outfits."

She rolls her eyes again. This time at me. "I don't need input from any more old women."

My jaw drops as she storms upstairs. I turn to Morgan, who calls up the stairs, "Child, you better give your heart to Jesus, because your butt is mine."

A door slams above us, and Morgan pinches the bridge of her nose. Then she lowers her hand and sighs. "I'm sorry, Adrianne. Come on."

She tugs my shirtsleeve and leads me to the kitchen. My mouth moistens with the anticipation of whatever dinner she's cooking. Instead, I find her youngest child wearing nothing but superhero underwear, pouring milk into a cereal bowl.

He keeps pouring until the milk overflows onto the countertop.

"Son of a biscuit. Andrew!" Morgan snatches a towel from the opposite counter and starts wiping the liquid.

It's already pouring onto the floor by the time she gets to it. I search for another towel and run into her oldest son, Ethan. He's holding a large dog by the collar.

The dog licks my shirt, leaving a sticky, wet tongue print below my boobs. I wince and decide to hang back.

"Take him outside." Morgan snaps her fingers and points toward the door.

"Wait, he's helping." Ethan pets the dog, who's now licking the milk from the floor. "Good boy."

"When did y'all get a dog?"

"We didn't. I'm dog-sitting while the long-term dog-sitter is away for the weekend."

"Oh."

Morgan wipes the rest of the counter while the dog licks the floor clean. Well, not clean, but clean of milk.

"I'm sorry, Adrianne. I'm a horrible hostess. Would you like anything to drink or eat?"

Between that statement and the cereal, I assume she didn't cook tonight. "Uh, some water."

I clear my throat to hide my growling stomach. It's like it knows we're in the presence of a master chef with ingredients nearby.

"I'll be glad to help you cook." Maybe she just hasn't gotten around to it yet. It's not like her hands aren't full with kids.

"Thanks for offering, but tonight is cereal night."

"Cereal night?"

"Yeah. I started it after getting my job at the Pig. On Mondays, they restock the shelves and send us home with expiring non-perishables. So they're still good, but some people who check the dates won't buy them. I load up on cereal for the kids."

Miraculously, my stomach stops growling.

Morgan opens the pantry door. "What you want?"

"I'm good. I actually just came by to tell you that I have another place to stay."

"Oh really?" Morgan pops a handful of Cap'n Crunch in her mouth.

"Yeah."

"Where?" she mumbles around a mouthful of cereal.

"Gamer's Paradise is getting me a room." Technically not a lie since I didn't mention *when* they're getting me a room.

"Cool." She cocks her head toward her two sons and the dog. "Can I come with you?"

I laugh nervously. "It's a single bed."

"Gotcha." She winks and pops more cereal into her mouth. "You're welcome to at least stay for dinner."

I shake my head. "No, I wouldn't want to impose any more than I have."

She wipes her hands down her leggings. "You're too kind." She engulfs me in a tight squeeze. "Thanks for stopping by."

I exhale when she finally loosens her grip.

She pats my back before fully releasing me. "We'll do a girls' night when your sister's in town and make my brother watch the kids."

"That sounds fun."

Morgan gives me a thumbs-up as I maneuver through the discarded tween clothing toward the door. Then I jump in my car and head back to the salon because what doesn't sound fun is trying to sleep in that circus.

JoJo

The worst part about being alone most of the day is I've had plenty of time with my thoughts.

I worked on the trucks in the shop with Daddy until lunchtime. He went home to eat and never came back. Perks of him being semi-retired. Which is another huge reason Grandpa Joe needs to wise up and sign his shares to me.

And I'm back to stewing over that again.

I park my truck farther downtown since Mary's Diner is like a beacon for the sea of busybodies in Apple Cart. Having skipped lunch myself, I need a good meal. One away from the house so Grandpa can't scold me more.

I've gotten a good fifty pounds on the man, but I'm still a little scared to turn my back to him when he's angry. He has some mad ninja skills with that cane. Note to self: Stop letting him watch *Cobra Kai*.

It's a little after eight, but most of downtown has already closed shop. Even Paul's lights are off. He's such an oddball that he's been known to open at random hours of the night for no particular reason.

My eyes gravitate toward the building across the road. Adrianne's salon. The lights are still on. Without thinking, I cross the deserted street to the sidewalk in front of her building.

Music echoes from inside, so she must not be closed. I pull the door handle and it opens.

Since I'm a dude and I shave my own head, I can't say that I've been in a hair salon before. As a little kid, Daddy would take me to the barber shop. I'd thumb through fishing magazines and read signs about the NRA while I waited behind a string of old men to get my ears lowered, as Grandpa called it.

I never understood why it would take Mama so long to get her hair done. The older my sister Dana got, the longer she stayed at the salon too. Thankfully, they never made me tag along.

There's a front area with some chairs, a couch, and a table. It resembles a doctor's office waiting area with fancier pieces. Nobody's in here, so I continue past the desk.

My neck itches at the oddness of being here, but I have a weird urge to check in on Adrianne. She's been displaced and has clothes stored all over the county. Despite her smiling and rolling along like everything's fine, it can't be.

A few feet toward the back, I spot Adrianne bent over the sink, humming to the radio. I approach quietly, not wanting to startle her.

I'm within a foot of her when she stops filling the sink and hikes her leg on it. Then she slides up her skirt and starts shaving her leg.

My neck is itchier than ever as I back up in an effort to sneak away. Except I back into a chair, and she turns her head. She squeals and throws a razor at me, then sprays me with the hose attached to the sink.

"Sorry!" I start running backward best I can. I don't want to turn around in case she throws more sharp objects. After managing to make it past all the salon chairs, the edge of the front counter hits me square in the back.

Seething, I bow over and hold my back. Before I can straighten, Adrianne is at my side. I blink. From being sprayed in the face and having the wind knocked out of me, my vision is a little blurred. I manage to refocus on her legs in front of me.

They're glossy with some kind of lotion. Long, lean, and tan. I close my eyes again. That's not what I need to focus on.

She loops an arm around my shoulders as I start to straighten. "Come on."

I allow her to lead me to the couch. She shoves a blanket out of the way, and we sit down.

"I'm so sorry. I didn't realize it was you. I was just . . ."

I face her. "Shaving your legs?"

Her face reddens and she nods.

My stomach buckles at the awkwardness of this moment. I may as well admit to why I'm here and hope it makes me sound like less of a creeper than more.

"I was in town and stopped by to see how you were

doing. The door was unlocked, so I thought you were still open."

She turns toward me slowly. "I'm good."

I nod and wipe a hand across my damp face. She stands and grabs a towel from the counter that spiked my spine a minute earlier.

"Here."

"Thanks." I wipe my face and neck, then set the towel beside me. "If you need me to get anything else of yours since I'm here, I'll be glad to take it back to my house." I notice an open suitcase in the corner of the room. "Unless, of course, you took it to your friend's house."

That's my nonchalant way of asking why she's shaving her legs over the sink. I know nothing about salon stuff and women's hygiene routines, but why would she shave over a tiny sink if she's staying in a house with a shower?

Adrianne sniffles, then reaches for the towel I used to dry my face. She drops her head in her hands and blows her nose loudly. When she raises her head, tears stream down her face.

"I'm not okay." Her voice squeaks so much I can barely make out the words.

She blots her eyes with the towel. I start to mention that she might want to make sure it's not the same side she used to blow her nose. But growing up with a sister taught me to never correct a woman crying.

Instead, I put my hand on her shoulder. When she doesn't flinch, I pat her gently. To my surprise, she falls toward me, burying her head against my chest. Her tears mix with my damp shirt as she continues to sniffle.

I slowly rub her shoulder, not knowing how to react. Before these last few days with Adrianne, the last time I comforted a woman was when we had a female employee who got her ponytail hung on some equipment. I obviously wasn't that great at it because she ended up with a bad haircut and a new job as a Waffle House waitress.

"I'm staying here."

I stop rubbing her shoulder and lean my head to hear clearer. "What was that?"

She lifts her head, putting her face dangerously close to mine. "I'm staying here."

My throat knots at her breath tickling my neck. I swallow and finally manage to ask, "Why?"

She leans back against the couch, but my arm is still around her shoulder. I start to move it, then she rests her head against my forearm.

"I went to Morgan's house and couldn't stay there. Her kids are like crazy, and she had a dog and no real food." She snarls her nose at a bag of pork rinds on the table in front of us. "Not that I have any sustainable food here, but at least there's not kids pitching fits." She sniffles again. "I'm the only one pitching a fit, I suppose."

I cradle her bare shoulder with my hand and try to ignore how smooth her skin feels against my rough hands. She doesn't flinch, but instead leans closer to me.

"I'll have a room at Gamer's Paradise soon, so I decided it best to stay here a few nights."

Maybe it's because my brain doesn't fully function when I've skipped lunch, but I say something that surprises even me.

"I live in a big house with plenty of space, and half of your clothes are already there. Why don't you pack up everything else and just stay at my place?"

She faces me and narrows her eyes. "Me? Stay with you?"

I shrug, realizing how ridiculous that sounds out loud— coming from her mouth. "Yeah. We'd both be working most of the time, you'd have easy access to all those clothes, and you've got a room coming soon. So why not?"

One side of her mouth kicks up as if she can't decide whether to smile.

I move my arm from around her shoulder and stand. "Tell you what. I'm going to Mary's for some supper. I'll stop back by here afterward. That'll give you time to think about it." I point toward her legs, all tan and shining in the florescent lighting. "And finish your legs or whatever else you had planned." I clear my throat, hoping that didn't sound as creepy to her as it did me. "Anyhow, if you want to stay at my place, you can follow me there when I stop back by."

I walk toward the door, then pause. I turn and hold up my palms. "No pressure or expectations on my part. Whatever you want to do. But I hate to imagine you sleeping on this short couch and taking sink showers."

This time both sides of her mouth turn up the slightest bit. "Thank you, JoJo."

I nod. "Anytime."

I leave the salon before I can do any more damage. Between a throbbing backbone and utter embarrassment, I've had all the awkwardness I can stand for one night.

That is, unless of course, she agrees to go home with me.

CHAPTER FIVE

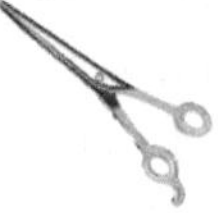

Adrianne

The door closes behind JoJo, and I stare at it. What in the world just happened?

Either I threw a razor at him and sprayed him with water, then broke down and cried on his shoulder, or I'm dreaming. Oh yeah, and he invited me to stay at his house, which I've never seen, even though I sent a third of my closet there earlier today.

Throw in a dead dog and some train tracks, and my life is a country song.

I start to tuck my bare feet beneath me to shield them from the cold concrete floor, but eye the shaving gel still on my legs.

Sighing, I lock the front door before returning to the sink. I don't want to chance any more intruders even more than I don't want to leave one and a half of my legs unshaved.

I'm sure I made a sight for sore eyes hunched over the sink in my sundress, shaving my shin. It's a miracle I didn't cut myself when I saw JoJo—or cut him when I threw the razor. At least I know I might stand a chance at warding off a real bad guy if one ever wanders in here.

As soon as my legs are shaved slick and towel-dried, I check my kitchenette area for more food than pork rinds. All I come up with is some wilted lettuce and a frozen dinner, both part of the remains I brought here from my home refrigerator.

Not wanting to ride the Weight Watchers train tonight, I slam my mini-fridge door. A small box of jewelry falls to the floor, spilling necklaces and bangles. I sigh and toss them back in the box. This time I put it on a higher shelf, safe from my temper tantrums.

I settle on the couch with my throw blanket and wiggle to get comfortable. This couch is as old as me. I bought it at an antique store for its chic appeal rather than its comfort. Now I'm paying the price for style as I try and relax. Kind of like the time I chose to work in cute new shoes over my usual orthopedic clogs.

If Morgan had cooked something, I would still be there. Her food is worth barking dogs, screaming kids, and spilled milk. Instead, I'm the one screaming and spilling water, followed by eating pork rinds.

I pop another piece in my mouth and frown. My mind drifts down the road to Mary's. I chug my water bottle and imagine JoJo downing a glass of Mary's sweet tea as he waits on something delicious.

He'll eat a nice, hot meal, then go home and sleep in an actual bed. I could go eat with him. What would that hurt?

Before I can talk—or think—myself out of it, I roll down the bag of pig skins and rummage through my suitcase. If I can't get decent rest, I can at least get a good meal. I change into jeans and a shirt. Even though my legs are now slick and smooth, I get cold when it's dark out. Plus, Mary is a huge fan of air conditioning—no pun intended.

I fold everything in my suitcase and zip it. My eyes land on the couch. How will I ever fall asleep on that thing? It's not even long enough for me to stretch out my legs.

My suitcase tempts me to take it. Do I dare? I have no clue about JoJo's living conditions except that he has enough room to store tons of women's clothing. Ugh, what if he has some sort of odd fetish for dresses? I shake that thought from my head, then leave for Mary's.

In the few minutes it takes me to get there, I'm almost certain I made the right decision. I park in front and go inside.

Despite everything in town closing by eight, there's still a decent crowd eating dinner. Mary never turns people away last minute, and sometimes stays open later after ball games. Tonight, there are a few couples and families, and JoJo in the corner. I cross the room, and Mary meets me in the center.

"Hey, sugar. You still working?"

"No, ma'am. I'm done for the night."

"Great, have a seat and I'll bring you an ice water."

Mary continues toward the kitchen, and I slide into the seat opposite JoJo. He lifts his head from picking at his short nails with a pocket knife. I get the urge to offer him a manicure, though I'm certain he'd decline. He may also go back on his room-and-board offer.

"I didn't expect you here."

I open my mouth to say that I'm only here for the food, but decide not to be so blunt. "Mary's sounded like a good idea."

He nods and picks at another nail. I bite my bottom lip and try not to focus on the damage he's causing his cuticles.

Mary brings out my water and a large plate of food for

JoJo. "Well, I didn't think about you sitting here, Miss Adrianne." She winks.

I've seen that wink before. It's Mary's way of telling me she knows something about me that I haven't yet figured out.

"Could I also get a Cobb salad?"

"Honey mustard?"

"Yes, ma'am." It's safe to say I order salads here regularly.

"You got it, sugar." Mary glances at JoJo, then back at me.

I sip my water slowly as she struts away with a smile so wide that I can almost see through the gap in her teeth. JoJo folds his knife and slips it under the table. Hopefully he put it in his pocket and isn't holding it as retribution for me wielding a razor at his head. In my defense, I'm certain his head isn't a stranger to razors.

However, he now has a steak knife, which he shoves into the center of his ribeye. I squirm and make a mental note not to get on his bad side.

I watch as he meticulously cuts a piece from the corner, then runs it along his mashed potatoes with his fork. He chews slowly, letting out a low moan. Should I give him and his meal some alone time?

Before I can excuse myself to the restroom or rethink my plans for the night, Mary brings out my salad.

"Thanks." I smile as she slides it in front of me.

I like everything Mary makes, but gravitate toward salads since I usually wait until I'm starved to eat anything and don't want to wait for something that takes longer to cook. A lot of people make hair appointments on their lunch break, which leaves me eating around two most days.

"You're welcome." Mary turns to JoJo. "Looks like you're enjoying your food."

He nods and grunts. She laughs and slaps him on the shoulder before checking on a nearby table.

I fork some salad and dip it into the dressing. JoJo has already devoured half his steak. As awkward as it is watching him wolf down more food than I eat in an entire day, I need to start a conversation about my arrangements.

"Thanks for inviting me to eat."

JoJo sets his fork down and stares at me. "I didn't invite you to eat. I invited you to spend the night with me."

I hear a gasp behind me, then turn to Mary standing at our table with a fresh glass of tea.

She slides it toward JoJo. "I'll just leave this here." She raises an eyebrow at me, then hurries off.

JoJo's expression is solemn, as if he doesn't notice or care that Mary read a little too much into that "spend the night" comment.

"True," I say, still shocked at his response. I chug my own drink and wish I'd ordered something caffeinated. I fork another bite of my salad.

JoJo continues eating the few pieces of meat left on his plate. He swallows, then clears his throat. "I didn't mean it like that. Of course I'm happy to have you eat. You're too skinny as it is."

My fork clinks on the table as my fingers relax. *What is that supposed to mean? Do I really want to stay with this guy?*

Just when I was beginning to see him as some sort of oddball superhero who pulled me out of dire straits too.

"That came out bad too. I'll just quit talking and eat."

He shoves half a dinner roll in his mouth, and his cheeks puff out like a squirrel.

I can't help but grin. At least he has the decency to catch himself when he says something possibly inappropriate. And would I rather him say that I'm not skinny?

"It's okay. And I've already decided to take you up on your offer."

JoJo's hand stops midway across his plate, where he was

sopping up the remainder of his potatoes with the last bite of his roll. He raises his eyes to meet mine. "It's settled, then. You can follow me home."

As if right on cue, Mary marches toward our table and slaps a bill in front of him. "I put her salad on your ticket. Least you can do is buy the girl a meal first."

I open my mouth to explain that it's not how it looks, but give up when she struts back toward the kitchen.

JoJo picks up the paper. "You can wait outside. I'll get this and leave a tip." He nods toward the counter. "And explain to Mary why you're staying at my house."

My shoulders relax. "Thank you."

I slide out of the booth and escape to my car in case the gossip train has already left the station. Maybe JoJo can straighten Mary out before it turns into a train wreck.

I nuzzle against the pillow, trying to soak in the last few minutes of rest before I have to officially wake up.

It took me a while to fall asleep last night, but not due to the accommodations. This bed, pillow, and entire basement suite are top-notch. Not to mention JoJo has my clothes stored conveniently nearby.

However, my mind couldn't overlook the fact that I followed an almost stranger home and agreed to camp out in his basement for an indefinite amount of time.

My body tenses as I sense someone's presence looming over me. It has to be sleepy brain fog kicking in, as I don't take JoJo for the creepy type, or even the nosy type. But I am in his house.

Curiosity beats sleepiness as I slowly open one eye. When

I make out a shadow of someone, I pop open both eyes. Then I scream—loudly.

The elderly man who was hovering over me staggers back a few feet. I bolt out of bed, then remember I'm wearing sleep shorts up to my booty and no bra. I hop back in bed and pull the covers to my neck.

The man blinks, then crosses his arms. "What are you doing in my house?"

I lift a brow. Either this is a super realistic dream in which JoJo has aged significantly, or JoJo is squatting on this old man's property. Better yet, a neighbor or former home-owner with memory loss has wandered into the basement. Regardless, I'm creeped out. I knew the luxury basement bedroom was too good to be true.

"What are you doing in the basement?" JoJo's voice booms behind the old man.

I sit up, careful to keep holding the covers up to my neck. JoJo moves from the stairwell to beside the man and crosses his arms. "You know better than to walk downstairs without help. Much less without your cane. What if you'd fallen?"

The old man scowls at JoJo. "It's my house, I'll do what I want."

"It's *our* house, and you'll do what the doctor told us you should do if you want to keep living."

The man pouts and stomps toward the corner of the room.

JoJo shakes his head and turns to me. "I apologize for his behavior."

My wheels start turning as I watch the back of the man's head. *This must be the grandpa.* I open my mouth to ask, but a loud thump calls our attention toward the stairwell. The old man is trying to walk upstairs and stumbling.

"Hold that thought." JoJo rushes toward the stairs and puts a hand on the man's back to steady him.

The old man curses under his breath, and by JoJo's reaction, I assume it was directed toward him. Together, they climb the stairs, with JoJo bracing the man's back and making him hold the handrail.

Once they disappear, I throw off the covers and cross the room. There's a perfectly good bra sitting inside my suitcase, and I intend to put it on before any more strange men pop out of nowhere.

I dig through and find a bra and some athletic pants that will cover my rear without sticking to it. While I'm at it, I find a less slouchy shirt as well.

I'm on my way to the basement bathroom when JoJo jogs down the steps and over to me. I shuffle the clothing in my arms in an attempt to cover my unprotected chest. I succeed in covering my chest, but drop my bra in the process.

JoJo's eyes gravitate toward the hot-pink bra on the floor. He stares at it like it's a rare animal in the wild. Not a far-fetched comparison, as it practically glows against the stained concrete and all the leather and wood furnishings.

I reach to pick it up, careful to hold the other clothing to my chest. He beats me to it and hooks his large pinky through a strap.

We both straighten, and he holds it up. I take it from his pinky and blink at him. It's hard to tell with the facial hair, but if the redness on his bald head is any indication, he's blushing.

"Thanks." My voice is breathy, and with the tingle in my cheeks, I'm certain my own face is red as a beet. "I'm just gonna go . . ." I nod toward the bathroom door. He steps back, giving me room to pass.

With all the worry about my chest, I'd forgotten about my shorts until I catch a glimpse of my thud in the full-length bathroom mirror. Thud is my made-up word for where the butt meets the thighs. Ideally, you want those to be two separate body parts. But every year I try on new swimsuits, I detect the beginning of a thud. I guess you can't fight gravity no matter how much Pilates you wield at it.

I quickly change and brush my teeth. I look in the mirror and finger comb my hair. I'm not a calm sleeper, and my hair often pays for it. It doesn't help that my silk pillowcase is back home, with ceiling flecks on top of it.

After a few minutes of turning to make sure everything on me is properly lifted and covered, I emerge from the bathroom. JoJo is planted in the same spot he was when I went in. *Has he been waiting on me this whole time?*

Not knowing what to do, I start making the bed. He comes within inches of me. Good thing I brushed my teeth. He helps me make the bed, then sits on the edge of it.

"Sit down."

I awkwardly lower myself. When I face him, the elephant in the room stampedes out of my mouth. "You told me you live alone."

"No, I said I have no pets."

"But you have an old man."

He lowers his head and chuckles before facing me again. "Grandpa Joe has been a widower for a while now. He's gone downhill in mobility the last couple of years, and we were either going to have to put him in a home or get some help. He hated everyone we hired to stay with him, so I offered to move in."

"Oh." My heart speeds up like it does when I see a hot man holding a baby. Something about taking care of his grandpa erases all the negative emotions that have hammered my mind since I woke up.

"I know. It's weird to live with an eighty-year-old dude."

He sighs. "But we've always been close, and I'm unattached to anyone, so it made sense for me to help."

"I think that's a very honorable and sweet thing to do."

He shrugs, and his T-shirt tightens around his broad shoulders. "I'm not a total saint. Technically, I'll inherit this house when he dies, since my sister is married and in another state."

"But you still don't have to live here now and take care of him."

"I know." He bites at his thumbnail and stares at the floor.

I place a hand on his shoulder. "If me staying here bothers him, I'll be happy to find someplace else until my room at the lodge is ready."

He shakes his head and grins at me. "No way. I can't sleep at night knowing we have this full basement while you're living in your salon or bouncing from house to house."

My heart melts a little. I can't think of a response worthy of that statement, so I give his shoulder a gentle squeeze before releasing my hand. I drop it to the bed, and a chill shoots up my arm as if it's mourning the loss of his connection.

We lock eyes for a moment, then turn to the stairs when the old man—rather Grandpa Joe—yells, "Get off that bed. Y'all ain't married yet!"

JoJo stands and stares at his grandpa. "I'm off the bed. Now go upstairs before you fall."

Grandpa peeks his head into the room and hits a wooden cane against the wall. "I brought my cane and only made it five steps down."

"Then go on up, I'm coming."

Grandpa draws his bushy eyebrows together and pouts, but turns and walks upstairs. JoJo stands at the stairwell and watches him, then starts up the first step.

"Wait," I say.

He turns toward me.

"What did he mean about we aren't married *yet*?"

JoJo's entire head reddens, and he palms the back of his neck. He walks back toward me and chuckles nervously. "We had a quick talk when I walked him up earlier. He assumed you were my girlfriend."

"And you told him I wasn't, right?"

He folds his arms and winces. "Yes and no."

I shake my head. "It's either yes or no. What did you say?"

"I told him you're my fiancée."

I almost fall on the floor. I don't care how comfy this bed is—it wasn't worth waking up to a fake fiancé!

CHAPTER SIX

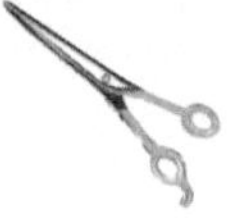

JoJo

"We're engaged!?" Adrianne's pretty face is the hue of a ripe tomato.

"No, we're not, but Grandpa thinks so."

She falls back on the bed and moans. After enough time for guilt to course through my veins like a blood transfusion, she asks, "Why would you tell him that?"

I clinch my jaw, afraid to admit the real reason. I need an alibi to get the company signed over to my ownership. The company that was promised to me long ago. Daddy owns forty-nine percent and Grandpa own fifty-one. It was assumed when Grandpa died, I'd get his part.

Yet due to Grandpa's condition, Daddy's been pushing him to go ahead and sign his share over to me. That way, whenever we need to make big business decisions, I don't have to crawl to Grandpa like a five-year-old asking permission to eat an extra piece of candy.

"It just kinda fell out of my mouth."

Adrianne narrows her eyes at me. "So you go around with 'she's my fiancée' on the tip of your tongue?"

I bite back a smile. Part of me enjoys her sarcasm, but it's overshadowed by how I'm a horrible person. I tried my best to take care of her house and take care of her. All my care unraveled with my tongue when I chickened out of telling an eighty-year-old man I'd get married if and when I pleased.

However, it did bring me a bit of relief when Grandpa smiled at the notion of me marrying Adrianne.

I sit by her feet on the edge of the bed, not caring if Grandpa comes down again. I'd rather be close enough to restrain her if she decides to chunk anything at my head as I try and explain my stupidity. Thank God, there's not a razor nearby.

"Look, Adrianne, Grandpa rides my tail all the time about getting married."

"Why?"

Because he somehow thinks I need a wife to run the business. "Because I'm thirty-four," I say.

She leans up on her elbows and cocks her head. "Huh, I took you for at least forty."

I frown, then she giggles. The flush has left her face, and I let down my guard a little. She wouldn't punch me while she's laughing. Would she?

I let my guard down even more and answer her. "Okay, I deserve that."

"I can relate. Anything over twenty-five is considered spinster in Apple Cart years. At least for a first marriage."

I laugh. "Can't argue with that."

She sits all the way up and challenges me with her stare. Crystal eyes shoot through me like ice picks. "Your age and singleness, I can empathize with. Your lying about marrying me, I can't."

"I'm sorry. I've just gone through a lot lately."

"I can relate to that too."

My stomach knots. "And it's all my fault."

Her features morph from condescending to sympathetic. "I didn't mean it like that. I simply meant I can relate."

I take a deep breath and exhale slowly. "Grandpa's mind isn't firing on all cylinders these days. There's a good chance he'll forget about the engagement thing by suppertime. If not, I promise to set him straight right after I come home from work."

She continues staring at me, then nods slowly. "I would appreciate that."

I stand. "Shouldn't be any harder than setting Mary straight last night. Trust me, I'm pretty good at putting out fires for not being a firefighter."

Her face pinkens, highlighting her cheekbones. Maybe she's picturing me in a firefighter uniform. I doubt it. She's probably picturing me having to explain our arrangement to Mary—or how I'll explain it to Grandpa.

How will I explain it to Grandpa? That's another problem for a later hour.

I reach for my wallet and pull out a business card. It's gritty with a film of dirt baked across the top, but still very legible. I hand it to Adrianne.

"My number is on here. Call or text if you need anything before tonight. Stay as long as you want and come as often as you need to. You have the key I gave you last night."

She reaches for the card, hesitating for a beat when our fingers touch. When I release my hand, she pulls it toward her and studies it. She flips it over, then back when there's nothing to see but more dirt.

"I gotta go to work. I'll be home around dark."

She raises her face to me and twists her lips. "What time is it?"

"Five thirtyish?"

Her eyes bug. "And you're going to work?"

I nod. "Yep. Ever heard the expression 'loggers' hours?'"

"Yeah."

"Now you know where it came from." I give her a slight grin, then ascend the stairs before I'm late.

The last thing I need is a ragtag team of men gloating that the boss showed up five minutes after them. Which has only happened once before when I hit a deer on the way to work. I made up for it by tossing the dead animal in my truck bed and letting them skin and cook it over an open fire for lunch.

Grandpa is in his favorite chair when I enter the living area. "Grandpa, I'm headed to the woods. There's some cinnamon rolls and bananas on the counter."

He blinks open one eye. "I'm not asleep, just resting my eyes."

"I never said you were asleep."

"Didn't have to say it."

I grit my teeth and grab a cinnamon roll from the kitchen counter, then a Mountain Dew and my lunch box from the refrigerator. "Don't go downstairs while I'm away."

"Sure, sure," he mutters before yawning widely.

Just resting his eyes? I roll my eyes at that and leave the house, locking the front door behind me.

The air swells as I step off the porch, promising another hot day by noon. A bird chirps in the distance, and my boots crunch against the gravel drive. Life doesn't get much better than this. Why on earth would I want to get married?

I follow the glow of the shop light toward my truck. If everyone would park the same each morning, I could maneuver there in the dark just fine. It's within Olympian spitting distance from the house.

Skeeder's truck pulls up a few seconds before I step onto

the concrete of the shop floor. Better him than the others. If Homer beat me to work, I'd never hear the end of it.

"Boss man." Skeeder gets out and adjusts his belt buckle.

I assume he's fixing his pants to stay up better since he's so skinny. But I turn my head in case he's preparing to drop them and pee against a tire. You never know with him.

"You have a hot date last night?" he asks.

"No. What makes you say that?" I scowl disapprovingly at his question.

He strokes his soul patch, then grins. Since he frequents Mary's Diner, I guess he saw us last night. I didn't see him, but I wasn't really looking at anything other than my food. And Adrianne.

It'd be lying to say having her sit across from me didn't beat my usual view of a historic photo of downtown Apple Cart hanging on the wall. Not that I have anything against history or buildings.

But given the option, I'd much rather gaze at a hot girl with light eyes and a smile that belongs in a dental commercial.

Skeeder points to the red Honda parked by the garage. The tag is personalized with CUTNDRY. I guess that gives away the owner.

"Looks like it went well too." He winks and pokes my arm with his bony elbow.

"No, you jackleg. She's staying here so she don't have to sleep under a tarp. All because you ruined her house!"

His grin straightens, and he slides away from me. Maybe the harshness of my tone will communicate how I'm still a little ticked about his blunder. Not only did he screw us up this time, but he ruined someone else's property.

I flare my nostrils and take a deep breath to regulate my breathing. When I speak again, it's in a calmer tone. "Can you fill the water coolers and ice down some Gatorades?"

"Yes, boss man." Skeeder nods and disappears into the shop to carry out his duties.

I run a hand down my face, then chug my Mountain Dew. I hope to God Adrianne has better folks working for her than this gang I've got.

Adrianne

"I'm here!" Misty sings as she struts through the front door.

I fight the urge to glance at the clock. What's the use? It was already well past the time I told her to arrive when I last checked. And I've foiled two heads since then.

"Could you look at my book and make the calls I have listed on that note?"

"Why of course, darlin'. It's my job."

I bite my tongue. When I reached out to the community college for an intern, Misty wasn't even on my radar. I'd expected some ambitious young woman who could help me with the books and towels and washing hair when I fell behind. Not a middle-aged diva who comes in when she wants and takes too many smoke breaks.

The joke will be on her when it comes time for me to give her work evaluation to the instructor.

If only Hannah hadn't talked me into taking Misty under my wing. All this mumbo jumbo about it being her last shot at making something of herself and how brave it was to go back to school at her age. You can teach a person a lot of things, but apparently work ethic isn't one of them.

After seeing Misty in action, Hannah now apologizes

profusely every time she's in my salon. I don't blame her. Hannah's good as gold and sympathized with Misty for having been divorced.

However, Hannah has only been divorced once, and not by her choosing. Misty . . . well, bless her heart and every heart she's broken along the way.

"Oh." Misty giggles into the phone.

I raise my eyes from my client's hair to check if she's on her cell. Nope, she's on the landline, but that doesn't mean it's not a personal call.

"I'll tell her." Misty pauses and giggles. "You too. Bye now."

She slams the phone on the base and rushes toward me, stomping through a pile of hair I'd just swept. I sigh at the hair tracing behind Misty's leather heels, which make the most impractical work shoes ever.

I return my attention to my client as Misty pauses to stare in the mirror and puff her hair. She's the only person alive I know who still uses Aqua Net hairspray. Everyone else using it has either realized there are far superior holding sprays or has died by now.

"Adrianne, that was JoJo Culp."

I gaze at Misty in the mirror.

"He called to say he would cook tonight." She wiggles her pencil-thin eyebrows. "Anything you care to share?"

I clear my throat and run my fingers through my client's hair to shake any loose clippings. "You're all set, Mrs. Augustine."

She smiles into the mirror and smooths out her hair.

"One second." I grab a bottle of finishing spray—not Aqua Net—and spritz her bob. "There you go. That should give you a nice, light hold."

"Thanks, Adrianne. Beautiful as always."

"You're welcome." I smile, then deflate my face when I

turn to Misty. "My assistant will be happy to schedule you another appointment."

Misty narrows her eyes. "What about JoJo?"

"Did he have a question?"

"Well, no."

"Then there's nothing more to discuss." I shoo Misty away with my hand. "Go help Mrs. Augustine."

Misty frowns, then follows the woman toward the front of the salon, taking a wad of hair with her on her heel. I shake my head and reach for the broom.

An involuntary smile crosses my face as I let Misty's message sink in for the first time. When I heard her say "JoJo," I immediately got defensive . . . as one should when needing to get ahead of any potential engagement rumors. Someone cooking dinner is a dream. None of my family lives close enough to cook for me regularly, I rarely have time to cook, and Morgan ruined my anticipation of a home-cooked meal yesterday. Needless to say, the bar isn't set high for JoJo's meal.

I make sure to sweep the hair in a dustpan and bag it up for the lodge before Misty can string it across the floor again. Then I head for the front to tell Mrs. Augustine goodbye . . . and to make sure Misty doesn't double book me.

I stand beside Misty and stare at the book. "Mrs. Augustine, had you rather come earlier?"

"If you can, dear."

"How about ten?"

"That's good."

I erase where Misty put her and move her up to ten. "Great, I've got you down. Misty will make you a reminder card."

I slide a card in front of Misty, who's now picking her nails. She sighs and grabs a pen, as if it might kill her to have to write another card.

I hand the card to Mrs. Augustine. "Have a good day."

"You too, ladies."

"Bye," Misty calls out as she examines her pinky nail.

As soon as the door shuts, she turns to me. "So, JoJo."

I raise a brow. "What?"

"What's going on with you kids? Spill the tea, girlfriend."

I try not to cringe at Misty using outdated middle-schooler slang. "There's nothing to say." I turn and lean back against the counter, rotating my shoulder to relax.

"Oh come on, word on the street is you two were looking mighty cozy at Mary's last night."

I roll my eyes. "Since when are men and women not allowed to be friends?"

"When they're both young and single."

I shake my head. "I'm not into every guy I share a meal with like some people." I pinch my lips together, realizing I just threw more shade at her than a covered porch on a cloudy day.

Misty elbows me and grins. "Maybe you should."

I exhale. Good, she didn't take offense. Or rather, she didn't get the hint I was referring to her.

"I'm just not interested in anything like that right now."

"Like what?" a male voice asks behind us.

It's familiar, but not in a good way. More like how you might recognize a family member's snore or an annoying kid's bodily smell. Thank you, Morgan, for that last analogy.

I clinch my jaw and sincerely hope this voice doesn't belong to whom I think it does. When I turn my head to Marcus, I throw up in my mouth a little.

"What are you doing here?" I manage to ask after swallowing the vomit. Then I reach for my water bottle on the counter.

"I'm here with the new line of conditioners." He lifts a large briefcase.

I choke on my water, and Misty beats my upper back like I'm a toddler. "Thanks," I cough out to make her stop. I glare at Marcus, and set my water down before it shakes out of my hand. My entire body tingles with rage. "I specifically requested they send someone new."

"They didn't notify me of a territory change. Perhaps management thought we make a good match."

He turns on the million-dollar smile that sucked me in months back. Oh, how I'd love to swipe a brush of my darkest toner across his pearly whites.

"Misty, can you fold the towels in the dryer?" I circle the counter and tug at Marcus's sleeve. "Come with me."

I lead him toward the back of the salon, my clogs echoing on the floor with every stomp. When I reach the kitchenette area, I drag him behind a rack of my clothes and let go of his sleeve.

"I put in a request online for a new rep. I never want to see—"

My rant is cut short by his lips on mine. I melt for a split second as memories of the good times flood my brain. Then my brain overpowers my heart and brings me back to my senses.

I put my hands on his chest and shove him against the wall as he's raising his arms around my waist. He straightens and gives me a dazed look. "What was that for?"

"Why did you kiss me? We're done."

"We don't have to be."

"Yes, we do. Done with work and done with whatever this is you're trying to create." I circle my finger between us.

He frowns. "If you give me one more dinner, just one more night to explain everything."

"No, Marcus! I am over you." My chest rises with confidence as this makes the first time I've had the guts to say that out loud. "I've moved on."

"This quickly?"

"Yes. I've found someone." I grab Marcus by the tie and drag him out from behind my rack of blouses. I continue pulling him toward the front of the building. "Who is kind, takes care of me, and even cooks me dinner."

"I knew it!" Misty yells, tossing an armload of fresh towels up in the air. Some of them land on a bowl of color, and the rest flutter to the floor, where I haven't yet swept.

That can wait. First, I need to throw out Marcus Mosely. I only let him loose once we reach the front door. Then I shove him out in the street, right in front of a doe-eyed Bianca.

She follows me back inside. "Who and what was that?"

"My ex, and showing him he's still my ex."

"You go, girl." She high-fives me, and I grow a few inches taller with girl power. "I'm here for the deer hair, and to let you know that I can have a room ready early next week. I'd hoped it would be sooner, but that's the only one that's not booked on and off for a while."

"Thanks." I twist my mouth and do the math in my head. "That should work." I smile at Bianca and go to collect the bag of hair.

One more week with JoJo. Easy-peasy. I bend to close the trash bag strings and notice gray hair on top. That reminds me of someone else I have to live with for a week.

Grandpa Joe.

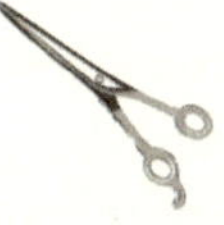

CHAPTER SEVEN

JoJo

Heels click on the hardwood flooring, and I turn to Adrianne walking toward the kitchen. Her long hair is pulled back and her eyes sag. She sets her purse on the counter and slumps her shoulders.

"Thanks again for cooking."

"No problem. I do it all the time. Everything will be ready in a minute." I glance at the microwave clock.

Good thing I didn't start supper as soon as I came inside. It would be cold by now.

"You always work this late?"

She shrugs. "Depends. A lot of my clients work full time, so they can only come evenings." She steps out of her shoes and scans the kitchen. "Where's Grandpa?"

I nod toward the opening that leads to the living room. "Sawing logs in his easy chair."

"Sawing logs? In the house?" Her nose scrunches.

I laugh. "It's an old expression for snoring."

"Oh." She laughs and palms the back of her neck. Her face contorts as she kneads the back of her neck and shoulders.

Out of instinct, I stand behind her and cover her slim shoulders with my hands. "Where does it hurt?"

She hesitates for a moment, and I almost regret touching her. The last thing I want is to make her feel even more uncomfortable being here. Lord knows, Grandpa Joe does enough of that. I'm about to step away when she lowers her hand and relaxes her shoulders.

"Below my neck, between my shoulder blades. There's a pinch there."

I press my thumbs between her shoulder blades and make slow circles up and down. She dips her head and relaxes her shoulders more.

"You're really tense. You should let Daisy massage you."

"I would, but I'm not one to mix business and friendship."

"You would be paying her, though."

"True, and I cut her hair."

"Then you should go." I press deeper around her spine, working into the knots around it.

I move my hands up and down until I hit what feels like a bra strap. The bright pink bra from the basement flashes through my mind. That makes me uncomfortable and I drop my hands to my sides.

"Uh, I need to finish cooking. There's an ice pack in the freezer if you need it."

I retreat to the stove and glance back at her before checking on the food. Her cheeks are flushed. Looks like I relieved enough tension to make her blush.

I pick up a spoon and stir the spaghetti noodles. When I

glance back, Adrianne is pulling an ice pack from the freezer. She turns and faces me. "Do you need any help?"

I shake my head. "Nope. Just need to toast some bread. It's not much, only spaghetti."

"I like spaghetti."

"Good." The corner of my mouth kicks up a notch. "I cook a lot, but I'm not used to making chick food."

She scoffs. "Chick food?"

"Sorry, that was chauvinistic of me. I meant like chicken salad and fruit trays and stuff."

She wraps the ice pack around her neck and relaxes against the counter opposite me. "This is dinner, not a wedding shower."

I shrug. "I don't know what women eat all the time. It's been a few years since I was home with Mama, and even then, she cooked stuff Daddy and me would eat."

Adrianne rolls her eyes. "We're human like you."

"I know." I swallow and focus on draining the noodles.

She's very much human, but not like me at all. She's feminine and dainty, with smooth skin and tiny shoulders. Not to mention long legs and a face worthy of framing.

I drain the noodles and start buttering slices of bread. Adrianne pushes off the counter and stands at the opening to the living area.

"Do we need to wake Grandpa up?"

"Lord, no. He gets cranky and will swear he wasn't asleep but just resting his eyes. He'll wake up eventually, and I'll save him a plate."

She turns back toward me and smiles. "Can I help by setting the table?"

"Sure." I direct her to the cabinets holding our plates and cups. "Get whatever you want to drink in the fridge. I'll wait and fix Grandpa some water when he wakes up."

"I'll have sweet tea," Grandpa's voice answers.

He's staggering toward the kitchen with his cane. He must've snuck up on us, which means he heard my comment about crankiness and resting his eyes. I'll pay for that later.

"It's too late for you to drink tea."

"Boy, I'll drink what I want. Who cares at my age? One glass of water might add fifteen minutes to my life. Not worth it."

Adrianne laughs and gives me a questioning look. I throw up a hand and shake my head.

"Sure, pour him some tea."

She fills three glasses with ice and pours tea into one, then hands it to Grandpa with a smile.

"Thank you." He shuffles toward the kitchen table.

The oven beeps, and I take out the bread. I fix spaghetti on the plates and set them on the counter for Adrianne to take to the table. I overhear Grandpa mutter something to her as I'm putting the bread on a plate to take to the table.

I take out some forks and frown at her shoes in front of the counter. They resemble covered-toe Birkenstocks, but with bright colors and heels. They're about the ugliest things I've seen, and that's saying a lot considering the people I work with every day.

She returns to the kitchen for the bread and forks. "Where's the napkins?"

"Uh . . ." I hand her a roll of paper towels beside the stove.

Grandpa and I don't do napkins. We lick food off our fingers and worry about our faces once we're finished eating. I don't tell her that, but I do rethink our cavemen ways of eating now that we're in the presence of a lady.

"Thanks." She takes the paper towels, and I follow her to the table.

Grandpa grins at us the way he grins at Miss Kitty on

Gunsmoke. Either he dreamed of Miss Kitty during his nap, or he's up to something.

"You kids make a mighty handsome couple."

Adrianne and I give each other side-eye as if silently asking the other how to respond. I'm convinced there isn't an easy response to this, especially since I have yet to explain to Grandpa how we're not engaged—or even together.

I'd promised Adrianne I'd set him straight after work. But the old geezer was out for the count when I walked in the door.

"Thanks," we say in unison.

Our voices are so in sync, it's almost frightening. Grandpa nods and stares down at the plate in front of him. Adrianne and I slowly take a seat on either side of him.

Every meal, he sits at the head of the table like he has since before I was born. Well, except for the rare occasion he's awake and I have dinner ready during *Wheel of Fortune.* Then he pesters me to bring a TV tray to his chair.

Adrianne picks up her fork and starts to spin it in her noodles. Grandpa reaches over and takes the fork from her. She stares at him, dumbfounded, until he clasps his hands together and bows his head.

I mouth *"we pray first"* from across the table.

She lifts her chin, then lowers her hands to her lap and closes her eyes. Grandpa clears his throat. He makes a sound similar to a hairball stuck in a vacuum.

I pat his upper back and whisper, "Get a drink. I'll pray."

He chugs some tea while staring me down. Then he wipes his mouth with the back of his hand—since we're not accustomed to having paper towels nearby—and huffs. "I'll pray. It's my house."

I lift my hands in protest as he begins to pray.

"Dear Heavenly Father, thank you for this food and for my grandson being a good enough cook."

I open one eye to Adrianne smirking, her eyes still closed.

Grandpa continues. "Please bless this food, and bless all our lives. We have so much to be thankful for, like the fact that I will live to see my grandson marry this beautiful, kind woman sitting at our table. Amen."

This time I open my eyes to Adrianne staring like a deer in headlights. She blinks at Grandpa, then gives me a different look. One that communicates I can go the opposite direction of where Grandpa directed his prayer.

I hope this spaghetti is good enough because it might be my last meal.

Adrianne

I force a smile as JoJo follows Grandpa to his room to make sure he gets in bed okay. Grandpa winks at me as he leaves the kitchen. Heat swirls through my stomach like I've drank a bottle of nail polish remover.

Either Grandpa really is losing his short-term memory, or JoJo forgot to set the record straight that we're not engaged. Of course, I need to set the record straight with a few people I ran into today that we're not together . . . but still, not the same.

I tug at a strand of hair hanging by my face and sigh. This is not good. My only sense of comfort is that since Grandpa no longer drives, there's a good chance he wasn't around anyone else today.

JoJo returns and starts picking up dishes. I stand and help, rolling around conversation starters in my mind.

There's not an easy way to ask someone why they didn't unlie to their grandpa about being engaged to you. It's not like Speech 101 at Apple Cart Community College touched on this situation.

I step back into my clogs and take the dishes to the sink. JoJo has already set his in there and is running water.

"Thanks." He rolls up his sleeves to rinse dishes and doesn't say another word.

After an awkward minute, I speak. "Did he already forget about you telling him we're not engaged?"

Maybe so. And if his memory is that bad, I doubt anyone in town will believe him.

JoJo puts down the plate he's holding and shuts off the water. He turns his head and stares at me. I cock my head, waiting for an answer.

"The thing is, I haven't gotten around to telling him yet."

I grind my teeth and narrow my eyes, trying my best to keep composed. When I do respond, my words are clipped and demanding. "You haven't told him yet?'

"Well, no. He was asleep when I got in from work."

"JoJo!" He flinches when I yell his name. "You had one job," I say quieter. "You have to tell him."

He picks up a towel beside him and fumbles it around in his hands. "You didn't exactly set the record straight either."

I shove my hands on his chest. It's solid as a rock wall, making me bounce back. He barely moves. No fair.

While it's nice to know my fake fiancé has a solid chest, I don't want him to be my fiancé—fake or for real.

"Adrianne, I'm sorry. Do you want me to go in there and tell him now?"

I bite my bottom lip and mull it over a second before shaking my head. "Nah, let him sleep. It's not like he's going to post this on Facebook before morning." My eyes bug. "Or would he? There's a lot of older people on there nowadays."

JoJo chuckles. "No, he won't. He falls out soon as his head hits the pillow. Plus, he can barely work a computer, much less a phone. Daddy got him one of those Jitterbug things for emergencies. Last time I saw him use it, he was cussing it out because it wouldn't call Quick Stop and order him a pizza."

I laugh, and JoJo joins me. Then I remember the purpose of this conversation and straighten my face.

"We still have to set him right."

JoJo turns and rests his hands on the edge of the sink. His shoulders slump. "I know. I'm sorry about ever saying anything. It just made it easier."

"For who?" *Certainly not me!*

He turns around and walks past me. Before he exits the kitchen, he motions for me to follow him. We walk past the living room, down a hallway, and into the last room. He flips on the light to a massive oak desk, and I see shelves full of logging photos and rolled-up papers, and a gun safe almost the size of the mirror in my closet room.

He goes to the safe and enters a code, then turns the large metal handle that resembles a ship's wheel. The door swings open to reveal more papers and an arsenal of antique guns. He pulls a paper from the top shelf and takes it to a leather couch in the corner of the room.

I sit beside him, and he slides the paper onto my lap. "What is this?" I ask as I lift it for a better view.

It's clearly an official document of some sort, but I've never been one for reading long scripts, especially in legalese.

"It's a document stating that Grandpa will sign over his half of the company to me when I get married."

I raise my eyes to him, and guilt washes over me when I see the desperation in his face. "I have a confession."

"You need to get married to inherit something too?"

I swat his arm, secretly thankful for a little comic relief to the tension of the moment. He half grins.

"No, weirdo. I may have overheard you and your grandpa and dad that day I was at the insurance place."

He stares at the ceiling as if recalling that day, then looks at me. "When I walked out of the lawyer's office and ran into you?"

I nod. "I shouldn't have eavesdropped, but y'all were loud."

He pinches the bridge of his nose. "Yeah, we're loud."

"Anyway, from my outsider's view—or sound, rather—I agree that you don't need to be married to run a business."

He drops his hand and sighs. "Thank you. Daddy and Mama agree with me, too, and I'm certain Angela would admit to it if Grandpa weren't paying her so well."

"I hate that you're in this predicament, but we can't let him believe we're engaged. That's not fair to either of us."

"I know. I just . . ." JoJo pauses and stares at the wall in front of us. "You ever say something to make things easier, only to find that you were better off keeping your mouth shut and dealing with the problem head-on?"

"Always." I smirk, and he turns to me.

My stomach pits at the memory of what I said to Marcus hours earlier. Although I didn't specifically say we are together to anyone else in the salon, I also didn't deny the rumor when Misty proudly proclaimed it. "I have another confession."

JoJo crosses his arms. "Oh."

I wince. "I kinda sorta let someone believe we're in a relationship." I wave my hands in front of my face when he grins. "Not engaged—just, you know, involved."

"Involved." He full-out grins now.

My stomach flips, and I squirm against the leather couch. "Long story short, my ex stopped by the salon and was messing with me. I said I'd found someone else to get him to leave me alone."

JoJo frowns. "Messing with you? Need me to ring his bell?"

My cheeks warm at the idea of someone jumping to my defense. I put a hand on his knee. "Slow your roll, Paul Bunyan, I can take care of myself."

"I know." His face softens. "But you're under my roof for now, so it's my job to protect you."

My limbs numb, and my hand tingles against his rough jeans. The last man who was that concerned with my well-being was the insurance agent trying to expedite a quote on my home repair. And I'm pretty sure his gallant efforts were a combination of my friendship with his late wife and him getting a commission for doing a good job.

JoJo has nothing to gain from being protective of me. Unless he's still not a hundred percent convinced I don't plan on suing them for wrecking my property with a pine tree.

"I appreciate the concern," I say once my mind recovers. For a moment, I daydreamed of JoJo rescuing me from a band of robbers like a rugged sheriff in a spaghetti western. Must be a side effect from eating spaghetti tonight.

"You're welcome." He uncrosses his arms and pats my hand.

That's when I realize it's still on his knee. I slide it back onto my lap beside the paper in my other hand. "I promise to correct my error at work tomorrow if you promise to tell Grandpa when he wakes up."

"That's one option."

I tighten my grip on the document. "Wait, you're not suggesting?"

He shakes his head. "Never mind. It wouldn't be fair to you. I have much more to gain from a fake relationship than you."

I stare at the paper in front of me. He's right. A thriving forestry business totally outweighs anything I stand to gain from proving my worth to Marcus or holding back friends from trying to set me up during my declared man fast. Then again . . .

"What are you proposing?"

JoJo grins. "That we don't deny any rumors." He shakes his head. "I mean, other than any that imply we're staying *together* together here at the house. I set Mary straight on that one."

"Good!"

He nods. "But if you need an excuse not to be with someone who annoys you or I need to quiet Grandpa a little longer, then we play along."

"What happens eventually?"

"You find someone you want to be with, and we break up."

I shake the document. "What about this? Do you plan on him dying slowly of sweet tea overdose and then claiming your right to the throne?"

He laughs. "I'm a little offended you'd suggest that."

"I'm not the one suggesting it." I narrow my eyes, but my grin gives away the amusement.

"I'm working with Angela too. She's scanning his stipulations with a fine-tooth comb and looking for loopholes. There's got to be a way Daddy and I can run Culp Family Forestry without me being married."

"Fair enough."

"So you want to carry on with this?"

"Being engaged?" My voice cracks on the last word.

"Only to Grandpa. To everyone else, we're just dating."

I blink. *Am I really considering this?*

JoJo stands and goes to the gun safe. He pulls something else from the top shelf and comes toward me. It's a tiny velvet box. He kneels in front of me and pops it open to reveal a huge solitaire diamond ring with a wide gold band.

I stare at it until the diamond clouds my view. I'm still focused on the ring when JoJo starts talking.

"Adrianne whatever your middle name is Reynolds, will you wear this ring around my grandpa and pretend to be my fiancée for a while but never marry me?"

The words "never marry" snap me out of my trance. Those words haunt my dreams from time to time, but in this scenario, they calm my nerves like a healing balm.

"Nicole." That's all I can manage to say.

"No? Okay, that's fine." JoJo shuts the ring box and starts to stand.

I pull him back down by his belt buckle. "Nicole!" I giggle. "I said, 'Nicole,' not 'no.'"

"Oh." He raises his brows.

"You need to know my middle name if we're going through with this." My hands tingle as I simultaneously release my grip on his belt buckle and the document.

The paper flutters to the floor. A metaphorical depiction that we no longer need to worry about its contents. At least, for now.

JoJo smiles and reopens the box. He carefully lifts the ring, the band disappearing between his thick fingers. With his other hand, he reaches for my left hand.

I spread my fingers and stiffen my knuckles to keep the shaking to a minimum. He slides the diamond up my ring finger. It's a perfect fit.

I hold up my hand and twist my palm. The diamond sparkles under the ceiling light.

"You and Grandma have the same size hands."

My heart speeds up as I imagine a younger version of his grandpa buying this ring. The fact that JoJo pulled this from a gun safe and kept it in a velvet box should've tipped me off it was an heirloom. But in my defense, people don't flash huge diamonds in my face every day—or any day, until now.

"Are you sure about this?" I suck in air, then exhale. "I mean, your grandma's ring?"

He nods. "It's only temporary, and you only need to wear it around here to sell the lie to Grandpa."

There's so much deceit in that one sentence. *Temporary, sell the lie . . . Grandpa.*

"Are we really doing the right thing?"

JoJo takes my hands in his, and they miraculously stop shaking. "Look at me."

I meet his gaze, our faces less than a foot apart. "You call the shots. I've got more to gain than you on this deal. If it ever gets to be too much, just say the word and we call it off. I can't promise how long it will take Angela to find a way around Grandpa's stipulations, but I can promise to treat you right and respect your wishes, even if we are just faking it."

I give his hands a squeeze and nod, unable to speak. He stares at me for another beat, then leans forward. Just when I think he may try and seal this deal with a kiss, he picks up the paper by my feet and stands.

He returns it to the safe and walks to the door. "Good night, Adrianne."

"Good night," I choke out as he disappears down the hallway.

I lean back against the cold leather of the couch and try and wrap my mind around what the heck just happened between us. The explanation he gave me tugs at my heartstrings. Whenever I am really engaged in the future, I want it to be to someone who respects me as much as JoJo.

CHAPTER EIGHT

Adrianne

"I can't believe you're staying with him," Daisy snarks in between bites of pizza.

"It's complicated," I offer.

"I'll say. You're fake engaged, but only in front of the grandpa, and you're fake dating, except in front of me."

"And you are sworn to secrecy. I shouldn't have told you, but I've got to vent to someone."

Daisy puts her fingers to her lips and imitates a locking motion, then tosses the imaginary key behind her back. "Sealed like Fort Knox."

"Better be."

She chugs a bottle of water, then slants her eyes my way. "But if we're gonna talk about it, I'm allowed to voice my opinion."

"I would expect nothing less."

"Good. You're insane."

I huff and pause from blotting grease off my pizza. "Tell me how you really feel."

Daisy laughs so hard she snorts. "You can always stay with me, you know."

Mullet saunters over and bleats. Daisy tears off a hunk of her pizza crust and holds it out. He snaps down on the end and bounces away with the crust. I shake my head and bite into my own slice.

"Thanks, but I have this basement apartment at JoJo's. It's very private." *That is, when an old man isn't milling around.*

I don't say that last part out loud. That would only encourage Daisy to extend her offer further, and waking up to Grandpa, scary as it may be, pales in comparison to having a goat in my face. Nosy as he is, at least Grandpa Joe smells like Old Spice instead of old spices from the candle-making room.

Daisy chews a large bite, then swallows. She nods at my hand. "Where's the ring?"

"At home."

"Oh, so it's home now?"

I sigh and roll my eyes. "I misspoke. At JoJo's."

She smirks. "Just messing with ya."

"I only wear it around there."

"For Grandpa?"

"Yeah."

Daisy shakes her head. "Can you at least tell me what it looks like?"

"It's a huge diamond. A solitaire." I set my pizza on my plate and stretch out my left hand in front of me. I curl my right index finger into my thumb, forming a circle the size of a small marble. "It's a pretty large round stone, wide yellow gold band."

I wiggle my left hand and imagine the ring. JoJo gave it to me last night, so I haven't seen Grandpa yet. I may or may not have used the basement exit to leave for work so I could avoid him. And I may or may not have slept with the ring on last night to get used to it.

Waking up with a rock on my hand was a pleasant surprise. But the moment I remembered this was all to fake out an eighty-year-old man, the excitement deflated like a balloon floating through a shooting range.

Mullet bleats again from across the room, interrupting my train of thought.

"All right, boy." Daisy stands and follows him to the open area near the kitchen.

He hops on a chair and sits at the table like a human. Daisy pulls a paper plate and begins shredding a slice of pepperoni and sausage into bite-sized chunks. She sets the plate in front of him as if they do this often.

That's all I needed to see to gain confidence that I made the right decision staying at JoJo's.

Daisy pets Mullet on the head, then pours some water in a bowl and sets it beside his plate. The tiny goat alternates eating and drinking like a toddler, except he's way less messy. It's safe to say this goat is housebroken. I'm actually impressed, but it still doesn't make sense to have a hoofed animal inside.

"Sorry about that." Daisy returns to the living area and picks up her own plate. "He takes his dinnertime seriously."

"I can see that." I watch Mullet chew the last piece of pizza on his plate, then lap water and hop down.

"So back to you. The deal is to wear the rock around Grandpa and fake date for Apple Cart?"

"Yes."

Daisy chews a bite of pizza and stares in front of her. This will be good. She's making her thinking face.

"What happens when Grandpa gets suspicious about y'all not setting a wedding date?"

I scratch the back of my head. Surely that won't be an issue. Eighty-year-old men don't think that deeply about wedding planning. Do they?

"This won't go on for long. JoJo has their family lawyer looking for a loophole to get us out of this mess."

"Right . . ." Daisy narrows her eyes at me.

"The plan is flawless, really. We keep Grandpa happy while JoJo finds a better solution. Meanwhile, I'm temptation free from going on any setup dates and guys aren't asking me out because everyone thinks I'm involved with JoJo."

Daisy cackles.

I roll my eyes. "I know it's not a normal plan, but it will work for us."

She shakes her head and coughs to stop laughing. "I'm not laughing at the plan, I'm laughing at you."

"Me?" My voice squeaks with shock.

"Yeah, you. You're the only person I know who would use a fake relationship to feed her man fast."

I lift then lower one shoulder. "Makes perfect sense to me. If I'm already in a relationship, I can't date anyone else."

"But you're missing the main flaw in your grand scheme."

"What's that?"

"JoJo is a man."

"Well, duh." *So duh.* More like a Greek god with a chest and arms of steel. I'd be lying if I said I haven't noticed.

"You'll have to show some affection or at least mild attraction to him while you're faking it."

Mild attraction? Check.

But I do see her point. I run my fingers through my hair and lean back against the uncomfortable hippie couch Daisy just had to buy on our last trip to the flea market in Mississippi.

"I get what you're saying, but it's not like I'll have to kiss him or anything. Just maybe hold hands or sit together."

"So you're going middle school?"

"Very funny, don't quit your day job."

Daisy smirks. "I'm not a fan of PDA, either, but this town of busybodies will see through any fake gestures of affection. A simple side hug or sharing a meal at Mary's isn't going to cut it. If you can't laugh and smile and the whole nine yards with him, then they'll see straight through it."

I swallow. She's right. "JoJo's an attractive man, so it shouldn't be a problem faking liking him."

Daisy sucks in a breath and widens her eyes.

"What?"

"Nothing. Just that you'd better be careful playing with fire."

I laugh nervously. "People have fake dated before. It's not like I need a degree in acting to pull this off. Even Tanner Nash made it believable."

"And how did that turn out?"

My body tenses. I coil into the couch and hug my knees.

"Adrianne?"

I turn to Daisy staring at me like a teacher does a student stalling on answering a question.

"Okay, okay. He and Hannah eloped."

"Exactly."

I bury my head on my knees and sigh. This deal may be even more complicated than I thought. Especially since the more time I spend with JoJo, the more I like him.

JoJo

"Where's the girl?" Grandpa yells in my face.

He doesn't mean to yell. He's just so dang loud. Years of operating heavy machinery without earplugs combined with old age means his hearing hasn't fared well.

I reach over and turn up his hearing aid. "She works late sometimes."

His hearing aid squeaks, and we both wince. He turns it down and tilts his head.

"Talk in my good ear, son."

I bite back a laugh. The only good ear he has is the corn on his plate. "She's working, and her name is Adrianne."

"Oh." He continues eating and mumbles, "Adrianne," around a mouthful of cornbread.

Bless him. I'm sure he's trying to commit her name to memory, but may forget it by tomorrow.

I scoop a forkful of peas and mull over my answer. I assume she's at work. She could be anywhere though, even with that ex-boyfriend of hers. And there would be nothing wrong with that. It's not like we're married, or even really engaged, or really together.

I shove the peas in my piehole. Grandpa continues eating, seemingly content with Adrianne being at work. I wish I were content with it.

Instead, I imagine her locking the door and flipping the sign to "Closed" when everyone has left the salon except an extremely handsome man.

In my mind, he is everything I'm not. Well spoken, outgoing, formally dressed, clean shaven, and with a full head of hair.

I take a big bite of cornbread and chew forcefully. *A full head of hair.* That's one thing a hairdresser would probably want in a man, and the one thing I can't offer her.

We spend the rest of supper making small talk about things that interest Grandpa. The weather, who all showed up for work today, the weather again, our upcoming outing to eat catfish, and the weather one more time. What is it with old people and the weather?

After we eat, Grandpa takes a shower while I clean the kitchen. If you can call it a shower. He has a seat and pulls down the showerhead, so it's more like a hybrid between a shower and a bath. But it keeps him from slipping and gets him clean.

Once he walks out in his pajama pants, undershirt, and slippers, I follow him to his room like always. It's our routine. He showers, combs his hair with the precision of a boy trying to impress his first crush, brushes his teeth, and shaves. Then he comes out for me to follow him to bed.

It's a habit that formed when I first moved in. He needed help getting onto his tall mattress. Now he can wiggle up on it and get down easily by himself. But he's gotten used to me walking in his room, telling him good night, and turning off the light so he doesn't have to stumble in the dark.

I suggested once we buy him a bedside lamp to solve the stumbling in the dark problem. He protested that he didn't want his end table cluttered. That was a lame excuse, considering the only thing on it is his favorite pocket knife and a small framed photo of Grandma when she was younger.

One night I caught him gazing at her photo extra long. That's when I realized how lonely he is. It's also when I quit suggesting we replace me with a lamp.

Grandpa flips on the light to his room. He stops a few feet from his bed and slips off his house shoes, toeing them against the wall. Everything in his room is in order. Combs of various sizes are lined up neatly on his chest of drawers, dirty clothes are piled in a corner basket, and even his underwear is folded.

I'm pretty organized for business's sake, but it took some time for me to get used to his over-the-top orderliness. The man still shines his shoes every Sunday before going to church.

Before moving in with him, I'd assumed shoe-shining went out with shoe-shine stands. Nope. Grandpa has a wooden box with polish, brushes, and a finishing rag. The lid even has a little stand for the shoe to sit on while he brushes it.

He pulls back the covers and climbs into bed. After he pulls them up to his neck, I stand by his head.

"You good?"

"Yes, son."

"Good night."

"Good night." He closes his eyes and sighs.

I turn the light off as I pass through the door. Any minute now, his sighs will turn into snores, and I can watch *Yellowstone* without him yelling in my ear about how much Beth needs Jesus.

I couldn't agree more, but it's hard to hear Rip over Grandpa's complaints.

No sooner than I settle into my own preferred recliner and reach for the remote, I hear wailing. I pause before clicking on the TV to make sure it's what I think rather than an animal outside.

Another moan echoes from the hallway, confirming my suspicion. I set the remote on the end table and hurry for Grandpa's room.

The first time I heard him cry out like this, it nearly scared me into a heart attack. I'd been living here about a month and thought he'd fallen.

Luckily, I was in the kitchen fixing a glass of water. Had I been in the basement, I wouldn't have heard him. After that night, I started sleeping in the master suite upstairs. The room he lived in when he was more spry—before the extra-tall bed and tile shower became too problematic. Now he's in the largest guest room, with carpeted flooring and a bath-room nearby that's easier to navigate.

I'm by his side in a matter of minutes, shaking his frail shoulders. "Grandpa Joe, wake up."

"Silvia. Gotta make it to Silvia."

My grandma's name trails on his lips. I shake him harder and pull him from his pillow. His eyes pop open as he mutters something else about making it home.

"Ah!" he screams in my face when he opens his eyes.

I wince, then hold him steady so he can recognize my voice in the dark. This is when a bedside lamp would really come in handy.

"It's JoJo. You were having a nightmare."

"A what?"

"A nightmare," I say louder. "Let me turn on your light."

Before I can stand, the light flips on. I turn to find Adri-anne standing in the doorway with tears streaming down her face. She backs into the hallway before Grandpa sees her.

"It's me, JoJo."

"JoJo." He puts his hands in the creases of my elbows. "I was in the war. I had to get back to my Silvia."

My stomach pits. I hate nights like these. His PTSD isn't frequent, but when it comes, it hits like a loose cannon.

I pick up Grandma's photo. "Here's Silvia."

He takes the photo from me and leans back into his pillow. "My Silvia," he whispers as he closes his eyes.

I sit a few more minutes, watching him hug the photo close to his chest. Once he's snoring, I ease myself off the edge of his bed and turn out the light.

Adrianne is in the hallway, tears still streaming down her face.

"Are you okay?"

She nods. "Let's let him sleep."

I follow her to the living room. She eases down on the couch, and I sit in my chair opposite it.

"Bad day at work?"

She shakes her head.

"Did your ex do something?" I ask in a more dominant tone that I hope conveys I'll axe his head if need be.

"No." She laughs and sniffles, wiping away a tear. "I'm sorry I walked in on you and Grandpa Joe."

"No, it's fine." My face flushes with a hint of embarrassment.

These are the parts of living here I didn't want her to experience. No woman has ever been around me this much to see the full scope of my life. I present myself as a tough boss man ninety-nine percent of the time. The one percent only shows up when Grandpa is panicked.

And lately when Adrianne needs something.

"For what it's worth, you comforting your grandpa was the sweetest thing I've ever seen. And I once judged a puppy pageant."

I open my mouth to ask if puppy means something other than a young canine in this instance, but decide to let it go.

"Grandpa Joe is really lucky to have you here to take care of him. Could you imagine what he'd go through if he were here alone?"

I shake my head. "Sadly, I can." I rock back in my recliner and turn to Adrianne. "Grandma said he used to have nightmares sometimes about the war. She'd wake him up like that, but he always woke up to her. It took me waking him up a few times before I thought to hand him her photo."

Adrianne swipes under her eyes. "How often does he have nightmares?"

I shrug. "Maybe a few times a year. Not too often, but I know it scares him."

Her forehead wrinkles, and she curves her mouth into a sad smile. "You're doing a good thing by staying with him."

"I guess. Sometimes I feel guilty, like I moved in more for myself to not have to buy a place until this house is mine."

She inches toward me and puts a hand on my knee. "Don't say that. You told me yourself you moved in to help him."

"I did." I sigh and try to ignore the calming effect her touch has on me. "He shouldn't have to be alone. I hate it Grandma can't be here with him still."

"He must really love her."

A grin crosses my face as I recall the two of them teasing one another on a daily basis. "Oh yeah, they were crazy for each other, as it should be. My parents have a good marriage, too, and my sister. That's why I don't like Grandpa shoving me toward the altar. I want to wait and meet someone worth dreaming about."

Adrianne brushes her hand lightly across my knee. Her blue eyes bore into me like a laser pointer to my soul. I hate vulnerability and have already said too much.

In an effort to keep my man card, I stand, letting her hand fall from my knee. "There's leftovers in the fridge if you're hungry. I'm going to sleep."

It takes every ounce of willpower for me to march across the living room toward my bedroom door without looking back at her. The more I'm around her, the more I'm convinced she's a woman worth dreaming about. And the fact that I'm thinking that way means I'm close to living out my worst nightmare.

Adrianne

The silver end of my curling wand catches the light when I pull it from the stand. *Silver. Silvia. Grandpa's nightmare.*

I blink to readjust my focus to the situation at hand. Glenda from the bank is in my chair, needing her hair finished before her lunch break ends.

I wrap a strand of her hair around the wand and try to push last night out of my head. Funny how about twenty minutes of material has dictated my entire morning.

When I got home from Daisy's, I heard some commotion down the hall. Not knowing if something was wrong, I followed the noise. That's when I heard JoJo consoling his grandpa.

I should've walked away. I wanted to walk away. That is, until he mentioned turning on a light. The practical side of me took the reins and flipped the switch within arm's length.

At least I backed away from the door before Grandpa

spotted me. I can't say the same for JoJo. However, I'm certain he would've concluded I turned on the lights either way.

I release Glenda's hair and pick up another strand. She's a good person to have in the chair right now, since she's fairly quiet and keeps to herself.

Anyone else would require me to talk. Although, that might make a nice distraction. Maybe Misty will come in from her vape break soon.

I finish Glenda's style and beam with pride as she examines herself in the mirror. She smooths her hair meticulously and smiles widely.

"You're a miracle worker, Adrianne."

"Oh." I bat a hand like it's nothing. "Come on, we'll schedule your next appointment."

Glenda stands, grabs her purse from the floor, and follows me to the front. Misty comes in, tucking a vape in the cleavage of her shirt. I call attention to the schedule book to keep Glenda from noticing her.

I really hope Misty doesn't ask for a full-time job when she graduates. I think I'll suggest she open her own salon. That would be the best advertisement for me.

While I'm scheduling Glenda, Bianca walks in.

"Hey," she calls as she passes.

"Hey, have a seat. I'll be there in a sec." I write out Glenda's card and tell her goodbye.

When I get to my chair, Bianca's nose is snarled and her brow furrowed. I follow her gaze to my extra chair, where a plain mannequin head is on a stool. Misty hums what sounds similar to a Miranda Lambert song as she adjusts a blonde wig on the bald stand.

Bianca and I stare until Misty acknowledges us. "Oh, Adrianne, mind if I use the curlers to perm my new Dolly Parton wig?"

"Not if you sweep the floor first."

"Oh yeah." Misty steadies the mannequin head on the stool and trots toward the broom.

I make eye contact with Bianca in the mirror and shake my head. She raises her paper-thin brows, and I make a mental note to suggest she grow them out. We have this discussion every few months, and she defends her over-plucking by saying she can't stand the in-between part when they get patchy.

I dig into her hair and finger comb to get a good view of her roots. "Same thing we did last time?"

She twists her mouth. "Maybe one shade lighter for summer."

"Okay, but you don't want to go too light if you'll be outside a good bit. It will brighten up once it's on."

"Whatever you think."

I nod. "I'll go maybe half a shade lighter."

"Sounds good."

I go mix Bianca's color, ignoring Misty's humming as I pass her.

As long as she's sweeping, I'll leave her alone. I move some towels from the washer to the dryer after I stir the color in a bowl. That should give Misty something to do in the next hour. Maybe by then, she will have her wig in rollers and not fuss about doing something useful.

I return to Bianca thumbing through a magazine.

"Sorry all my magazines are old. Most people play on their phones, so I canceled a lot of subscriptions."

"Fine by me. I come in here to get away from my phone."

"I'd think living so far out, y'all wouldn't have good service."

She looks up from flipping through *Health* magazine. "A few months back, we got satellite internet. It's not the best, but a big help with me working remote, and the guests like it too." She closes the magazine and smiles. "Speaking of, I almost forgot to tell you we have a long-term room opening Sunday night."

I pause from pulling foils. A few days ago, this would've been a heaven-sent message. So why am I not writing her a deposit check right away?

My stomach buckles. It's not because money is the issue. My business does well, and there's nothing to pay on the house until insurance comes through. I sigh.

"Something the matter?" Bianca stares at me in the mirror.

I shake my head and finish pulling foils onto my tray. They're stacked high as an eighties rocker hairdo. My blondes take a *lot* of foiling. I swallow as a montage plays in the back of my brain, highlighting the last few days.

Grandpa Joe and JoJo are the stars of this show. That would make it a comedy—or more like an episode of *Duck Dynasty*. Grandpa Joe is definitely Uncle Si. As crazy and odd as it's been, I enjoy staying in the basement and having their company.

"I appreciate it, Bianca, but JoJo offered me his basement, and I'm settled in there."

"Oh." She smirks, and I don't miss her tone.

"He wanted to make up for his employee wrecking my house."

"And he's in loooove," Misty's voice hisses behind my ear.

I flinch and brush my ear against my shoulder. She slides by us with a bin full of large perm rollers. Bianca's eyes meet mine in the mirror.

"We're not serious. He's helping—"

"Good afternoon!" A guy in a Carhartt T-shirt and jeans interrupts us.

He's holding a metal briefcase and smiling. I mentally

scan my schedule and don't recall any man haircuts until this evening. Then it hits me.

"Oh good, you're here. I've been waiting on you."

I smooth out the foils and lead him to the back of the salon. I open the bathroom door and point to the toilet.

"It flushes fine, but it's been making this hissing noise. I always have a high water bill from the sinks, so I can't gauge that to see if it's leaking."

He stares at me like I've lost my mind. "I'm your new product guy."

I tilt my head, taking in his stumpy stature and full beard. "Product guy?"

He flips open the briefcase to reveal a set of styling gels. My cheeks heat with embarrassment as I lift my eyes from the Redken to his face.

Redken is probably the color of my face right now. "Uh, I apologize." I lead him out of the bathroom. "Please, tell me more while I foil my client."

Bianca looks up from her magazine when we return, skepticism on her face. I'm not sure what she heard, but at this point, who cares.

The man sets the briefcase on one of my trays. "I'm Quincy, your new rep."

I extend a hand. "Nice to meet you, I'm Adrianne."

Quincy takes out a tiny pair of bifocals from his shirt pocket and adjusts them on the bridge of his nose. Bianca smirks at me from the mirror as I start piecing off her hair.

"Quincy, now that's an unusual name." Misty sashays over to us. The way she walks makes her leather pants squeal like dying ducks.

"Oh, thank you. I was named after the restaurant."

"The one with the yeast rolls that shut down?" Bianca asks.

Funny how everyone in the salon is so interested in this

stumpy little man with the Benjamin Franklin bifocals. I continue foiling Bianca's hair and pay them no mind.

"Yes, that's the one. My dad proposed to my mom at the one in Tuscaloosa. It was their favorite place to eat, so he hid a ring in the bread basket."

Bianca and I exchange a look.

Misty cups her hands under her chin. "Oh, how romantic! I love surprises."

Quincy smiles. "It actually worked out great because the ring was a little snug, so he had to butter her finger to slide it on."

I drop my comb, then take my time bending over to pick it up. It's hard to keep a straight face at a comment like that.

"So what do you have to show us, Quincy?" I bite the end of my tongue as soon as his name leaves my mouth to keep from laughing out loud.

"A new line of hair gels for all textures."

"Great, tell me more." I sound like I'm conducting a job interview or feigning interest in a guy on *The Bachelorette.* Which I may or may not have applied to once a few years back.

Quincy goes through each bottle in his briefcase, describing the benefits of each and their optimal use. I listen and ask questions when needed. Misty stays uncharacteristically quiet, staring at him from a few feet away. Maybe she's soaking in all the information since she's in hair school.

When he's finished, Misty drapes an arm around his shoulder and runs her long fake nails across his cheek. "Do we get a discount for buying the whole package?" She wiggles her eyebrows, dissolving any hopes of her silence indicating a hunger for knowledge.

She's obviously hungry—for something else.

"Misty, what did I say about touching the customers?"

"We touch heads in here all the time." She slides her arm away, tracing her fingertips through his hair along the way.

Quincy pushes his glasses up the bridge of his nose and swallows audibly.

Misty narrows her eyes at me. "Besides, I'd never think of stepping out on Woody."

That's a relief.

"But Quincy could cut us a deal, wouldn't you think?" She runs her hand over his head, massaging his scalp with her fingers.

He blinks at her, then takes a step back. "Tell you what, Adrianne. I'll let you keep this set for free and you can call me about an order."

I nod. "Sounds good."

Misty reaches for Quincy again, but he shoves the briefcase toward her. "You can have a discount if you please just never touch me again." He backs toward the door, leaving a card on the counter.

"Nice to meet you," I call as he hurries outside.

Misty slams the briefcase shut and smacks her lips at Bianca and me. "And that, ladies, is how it's done."

JoJo

I button my shirt and stuff my wallet into my back pocket. Since Grandpa gets in no hurry combing his hair, I took my time in the shower.

Today was extra hot and sticky, and I ended up with dirt and sawdust in places I'd rather not mention. Dog hair got added to the mix when Skeeder loaded a stray dog in the truck for the ride home.

I roll my shirtsleeves up to my elbows and leave my bedroom. The living room TV is blaring, which means Grandpa is ready.

Retro game-show music fills the air the closer I walk toward the living area. His gray head pops up from the back of his chair. I spot the top of Adrianne's head from the back of the couch.

I didn't expect her home yet. Not that she has to keep a routine, and not that this is her home. Still, I've grown used to her working until dark. I used to do the same before moving in here. Grandpa wants to eat supper by a certain time so he can get to sleep early and wake up before the sun.

That is not the schedule I plan to keep in retirement.

"Ready?" Grandpa doesn't acknowledge me, so I speak louder. "Are you ready?"

Still, nothing. I grab the remote from the end table and mute his show. He turns to me and scowls.

"Are you ready to go?"

"I reckon so, boy."

"Where are y'all going?" Adrianne looks up from filing her nails.

My chest tightens when I notice Grandma's ring on her finger. She's wearing it with sweats and her hair thrown on top of her head, like it's part of her regular attire. Her wearing it just seems natural, and that scares me.

"Catfish Camp."

She scrunches her brow. "Camp? Like a place to fish or a real camp?"

I chuckle. "It's a restaurant the next county over. Grandpa loves it, so we've made a habit of going once a month."

"Aww, that's so sweet."

I stare at my feet, feeling slightly demasculinized by her calling me sweet.

"You want to go with us?" Grandpa shouts.

I pop my head up and glare at him. "Adrianne doesn't want to go to a hole in the wall and eat catfish."

"What makes you say that?" She crosses her arms and pouts at me.

"I didn't mean you can't eat catfish with us, but it's kinda a dive, and we'd be the only people there under fifty."

She shrugs. "Then you shouldn't worry about someone else catching my eye."

Grandpa laughs and slaps the arm of his recliner. I narrow my eyes at him and shake my head.

"She may as well get used to going before y'all get married," he adds.

Adrianne and I exchange a look, then she smiles at Grandpa. "I'll go change."

"We'll be here waiting." He grabs the remote and turns the TV up louder than before, which I didn't know was possible.

"You could try turning your hearing aids up instead so the rest of us don't have to suffer."

"When I do that, I start hearing all kinds of things like I'm a dog."

I shake my head again and fall back into my own recliner. We stare at *The Price is Right* for a while. Grandpa guesses most of the right answers.

"How are you so good at this?"

"I lived through that era. I remember prices."

He can remember prices from the 1970s, but not the names of people he sees weekly at church. Dementia is complicated, but I'll never understand that.

Grandpa is about to guess the price on a new Corvette when Adrianne walks in wearing jeans and a bright orange shirt. Her hair is laid across one shoulder in a braid. And Grandma's ring is still on her hand.

"I'm ready."

"You look nice," I tell her.

She beams and crosses in front of us to the couch. She tosses her nail file in her purse and slings it over her shoulder.

"Okay, let's get in the truck."

"We usually take the car," Grandpa corrects.

"You're right." I turn to Adrianne. "We'll go in Grandpa's car. The pickup is harder for him to climb in with his cane."

"Okay." She follows us outside to the early 2000s model Cadillac.

For its time, this car was something. It's still in pristine condition, with cushiony seats and all the bells and whistles available two decades ago. I open the front door for Grandpa as always, but he goes to the back.

"What are you doing?"

"Let your bride sit by you."

I glance at Adrianne above the top of the car. She half smiles. I hadn't anticipated the two of us being in public *with* Grandpa. Luckily, we're going outside of the county. If the three of us showed up someplace like Mary's or Big Butts BBQ with her wearing Grandma's ring, we'd make the *Apple Cart Weekly* front page news.

She smirks, then dips inside the car. I get in and buckle, then start toward Catfish Camp.

It doesn't take long at all to get to the restaurant, since we live close to the county line and I take all back roads. Adrianne comments a few times that she's never been on some of these roads. That's probably a good thing, as I would hate to imagine her broke down in a place like Moonshine County.

We do a good bit of logging through here, and I've found more stills than I'd care to count. Needless to say, the place came by its name honestly.

A small metal building comes into view at the end of a dirt road. A light-up sign at the edge of the parking lot fizzles in and out, barely making the faded letters legible in "All You Can Eat Bufet." Yep, they left out one "f" in buffet. I assume it was a true misspell since there's no space in the word where a letter fell.

I park near the door in a handicap space. One of the perks to driving Grandpa's Caddy. As an added bonus, I don't have to worry about someone stealing the catalytic converter from under my truck while we eat. Most meth heads are too lazy to jack up a car.

A large catfish with a hook in its mouth stares down at us from the top of the building. Catfish Camp is spelled in mismatched tin letters underneath it.

Adrianne opens her door and stands back as Grandpa climbs out. "Here." She offers her hand and helps steady him on his cane.

She continues holding his arm until they make it across the few feet of gravel to the concrete pad.

"Thank you." He drops her hand and reaches for the door.

It's a screen door that I'm not sure even has a lock. I think Grandpa likes this place because the door opens easily and there are no steps to go inside. Well, that and their fish is as big as a plate.

We follow him inside, and I catch myself placing my hand on Adrianne's back. I'm not sure whether I did it to prod her forward or to sell the fake relationship. Either way, I drop my hand as soon as I notice it there.

She turns to me and lifts the corner of her mouth before facing forward and continuing toward the counter in front of the dining area. Does that look mean she's glad I put my hand there or glad I moved it?

"I see you have an extra guest tonight," Marsha greets us. She grabs an extra set of silverware from a bucket behind her.

"Yes, we need a table for three," I say matter-of-factly.

Marsha has been working here as long as I've known about the place, and she's our waitress every time. She smiles at Adrianne, then winks at me. Just great. Looks like I'll be getting the same matchmaking treatment I would at Mary's.

Marsha leads us to our usual booth. I hesitate for a moment while everyone else sits. Do I slide in beside Grandpa or Adrianne?

Grandpa likes to get up multiple times because he never puts enough on one plate, and I'm supposed to *be* with Adrianne. I bend down on her side of the booth, and she slides over for me.

I've never shared a booth seat here with anyone, and it's a bit crowded. Our thighs brush as I wiggle to get comfortable. The seats were probably made back in the mid-twentieth century, before most of America got fat or started doing CrossFit. Either way, it's a small seat for a grown woman with a few curves and me.

"Sweet tea for both of you?" Marsha asks.

I glance at Grandpa, then back at her. "Yeah, but no refills on his unless it's unsweet."

"Refill me with water. I'd rather drink dirt than unsweet."

"That can be arranged," I quip.

Grandpa scoffs.

Marsha laughs. "You two crack me up." She turns to Adrianne. "What about for you, hon?"

"Water is fine. For starters and all refills." Adrianne smiles, and Marsha smiles back.

"I'll go get those drinks. Y'all know the drill. It's Friday night, all you can eat." She nods and smiles, then hurries toward the kitchen.

Grandpa plants his cane on the ground and puts his

weight on it to stand. "Come on, boy, help me carry my plate."

I follow him to the buffet lines, where he gets one catfish filet and two pieces of toast. It looks like the meal Jesus multiplied for the five thousand. I hold his plate and take it to our booth before fixing mine.

No sooner than I get settled in and start eating, he'll be ready to return for some coleslaw or something else random. He uses the rule of getting a new clean plate each trip to pacify his distaste for food touching.

I pile my own plate full of catfish, shrimp, and hush puppies. I reach for the tongs to the onion rings, then hold back. Adrianne is sitting within a few inches of me. I can't chance onion breath when we're talking.

I drop the tongs and return to the table. Adrianne glances at my plate and twists her lips.

"What?"

She looks at Grandpa's. "He only has one piece of fish, and you have no vegetables."

"This is just our first trip." I notice she has both slaw and green beans on her plate.

She laughs. "Okay."

Grandpa meticulously folds his fish between the two pieces of toast, making a fish sandwich. Marsha returns with our drinks and some condiments. After we thank her and she hurries away, Grandpa clears his throat.

"Let's bless this, I'm hungry."

Adrianne's shoulders shake against my side, and I'm certain she's fighting off a laugh. Grandpa prays quickly, but doesn't leave out the part about how thankful he is Adrianne and I found one another.

My gut pinches with a tinge of guilt at our charade. As soon as he says "amen," I make sure to change the subject.

"Grandpa, I meant to tell you I have to change the oil in

several of the work trucks tomorrow. I won't be able to take you to get a haircut until later."

Adrianne wipes her mouth and looks at Grandpa, then me. "I can cut it for him."

Terror crosses Grandpa's face. "I've been using Lewis for forty years."

I swallow the shrimp in my mouth and shoot Adrianne a look that I hope is consoling. She nods as if she understands.

"Lewis at the Wisteria barber shop?"

"Yes. Downtown," I answer.

"I know him. I can take you tomorrow if you don't want to wait." She smiles at Grandpa, then looks to me as if asking permission.

"You don't have to take him. I can take him later in the day."

"I like going in the morning." Grandpa bites into his sandwich and frowns at me.

She bats her eyes as if pleading with me.

I sigh. "If it's not an inconvenience to Adrianne."

"I don't mind."

Grandpa swallows and grins ear to ear. "Great, it's a date."

Adrianne smirks. I hope she knows what she's getting herself into with him.

Adrianne

My phone alarm buzzes and I hit snooze one last time. Weekends are my days to sleep late. I'm always at my salon by eight and rarely get home until dark, so I catch up on sleep when I'm off.

I check the time and sigh, then slowly sit and stretch my arms toward the ceiling. According to Grandpa Joe, he's always Lewis's first customer on his appointment days. And Lewis obviously doesn't share my same business model since he opens at six a.m. on Saturdays.

My phone buzzes once more, reminding me that one way or another, the snooze time is over. I roll my eyes and end the alarm. Then I go to the bathroom and get ready.

JoJo promised to make sure Grandpa Joe had something to eat this morning so I could sleep as long as necessary. Of course, he then teased me about considering six super early. I can't help it that loggers land in the woods before the sun rises, like a gang of vampires. To me, he's the weird one.

I pull my hair into a ponytail and pick out some strands to frame my face. Even the simplest hairstyles need to look cute when I leave the house. My hair is free marketing that could make or break my reputation.

When my hairstyle passes the bar I set for stepping outside, I go upstairs to find Grandpa. I hear him before I see him, or rather hear the TV. It's on the Weather Channel.

Lacey O'Conner, who grew up in Wisteria, goes over the day's forecast in detail. I circle the couch and sit down. My chest puffs with pride at seeing one of our own Apple Cart County folks on TV for something other than a tornado. Okay, so she did mention a tornado warning in Oklahoma this weekend, but she didn't put the sound effects with it.

Grandpa squints and leans toward the TV. "I've seen that gal before."

"Lacey?"

"Yeah, the one with black hair."

"She grew up here. Her name used to be Lacey Sanderson."

"Sanderson," he whispers with a blink.

"Her parents are Joey and Robin."

"Who's her grandpa?"

"Ed Mayberry."

"Hmph." Grandpa snorts and points his cane at the TV. Then he stands, pushing in the legs of his recliner. "I don't care for Ed. Let's go."

I reach for the remote and turn off the TV before he decides to hit it with something. The look in his eyes communicates that he wouldn't care to watch her after learning of her connection to Ed.

I stand and offer Grandpa my hand. "Need help getting to the car?"

He stares at my hand, then at my face. "Where's Silvia's ring?"

My mouth goes dry. I spent half of last night with my hand under the table or in my pocket in an effort to hide it from our waitress and anyone else in the restaurant. Then I put it in the box when we came home. I assumed Grandpa wouldn't notice.

Until he did . . . as we're headed for downtown Wisteria, where everyone knows him, and a lot of them know me.

"I . . ." I swallow the lump to try and moisten my voice. "I don't wear a lot of jewelry when I dress casual."

"You got on earrings."

I reach up and touch the pearl studs in my ears. "Yeah, I guess I do." I squeak out a laugh. "Well, we better get going. I don't want you to be late."

He fans the hand not holding his cane toward me. "Ah, Lewis won't mind. Go get your ring. I'll wait in the car."

I puff up my cheeks. Should I protest? How would that even work? I'm not a controversial person, and he's an eighty-year-old man who's letting me live here for free.

Giving in, I trot downstairs to retrieve the ring. I slide it on my finger and try not to admire it as I head outside. It does fit me perfectly, and the elegant yet simple style is so something I would pick.

Maybe one day when I have a real engagement to a real boyfriend, I can remember this ring and find one like it.

I hurry to my car so Grandpa won't be late. He's nowhere to be found. Did he fall? Panicked, I twist around, gazing in every direction from the front yard.

A horn honks from the garage, and I jump. I jog toward the sound and find him inside his Cadillac. I open the driver's door and stick my head inside.

"Grandpa, we can go in my car. It's not hard to get in."

He motions for me to get in with him. "It's my trip, so we'll use my car and waste my gas."

"I—"

"Get in."

I do as I'm told and move the seat forward from where JoJo had it last night. Grandpa punches some buttons on the CD player and music fills the car.

Funny, we didn't listen to anything last night. Maybe JoJo doesn't like his music. Hymnals set to piano echo around us.

"Mind if I turn it down some?" I ask.

"Go ahead."

I turn it down a good bit. Grandpa leans back against the headrest, a content look on his face. I've heard the singer's voice somewhere before.

"Is that Elvis?"

"Yeah. This is his gospel album. Made back before he got crazy . . . and fat."

I snicker.

Grandpa smiles. "You know where the barber shop is?"

"Yes, sir."

He nods, then leans back again, soaking in the Elvis songs. I turn out of the driveway onto the main road. His eyes pop open, and he grabs my arm.

"What?"

"Slow down. This ain't a race."

I spin onto the main road and continue driving. Before we get another mile down the road, Grandpa grabs the steering wheel and turns toward the right.

"What are you doing?" I straighten the car, then pull over.

He points to a deer staggering into the woods. "You near about hit that stag. I ain't had a license in five years, and I drive better than you."

My lip trembles. *I will not cry.* "I know I'm a terrible driver. I'm so sorry." I hang my head and suck in a breath.

"It's all right." Grandpa pats my arm. "But I can't let you die just yet. Switch with me."

Before I can protest, he is in front of the car, pointing at me to get out. How he managed to move so quickly is beyond me. I get into the passenger seat and pray Grandpa's a better driver than me.

Turns out, he is. Even with slight arthritis and early dementia, he drives better than me.

We ride into town in silence, but it doesn't take long to get there. If anyone thinks Apple Cart is small, I point them toward Wisteria. They don't even have a Pig.

But they do have a barber shop. One of those old-school kinds with the spinning red-and-blue pole out front. The sign simply says "Barbershop," proving again that Lewis has a totally different business model than I do with Cut and Dry.

We park in front of the door, and Grandpa climbs out before I can get around to help him. He shuffles up the one step of concrete and opens the door. Obviously, he does this a lot. I follow him inside and let the glass door close behind us.

An older man dressed in slacks and an apron greets us. He's just three guys and a top hat away from being a barbershop quartet. If the getup is part of his marketing plan, bravo. Well played, Lewis, well played.

"Hey, Joe."

"Lewis." Grandpa Joe shakes Lewis's hand before taking a seat in the chair.

"Hi." I nod and smile.

"Hello, dear. Have a seat wherever you like."

I sit in one of the chairs against the wall and pick up a magazine. *AARP.* I decide that's not for me and go for the local paper instead. Unlike my place, the literature is current.

I assume most of Lewis's customers aren't scrolling their Jitterbugs.

"You didn't tell me you got a new driver," Lewis comments.

"Yeah, she's gonna marry my grandson."

I drop the paper, and it falls apart at my feet. My fingers shake as I gather the various sections as quickly as possible. Thankfully, our tiny paper is only three sections.

Lewis grins at me from the mirror. "You marrying JoJo?"

I giggle nervously. "That's the plan." *More like the scheme.* My insides twist like hair around a perm roller.

The bell on the door dings, and three more old men enter. I sigh and slump down in my chair, then cross my left arm over my stomach to hide the ring under my right elbow.

Lewis and Joe carry on a conversation about mundane things. At least, that's what I hear around the buzzing of the clippers and the other old men complaining about the price of corn.

I stare at the paper, reading all the upcoming events in the social calendar. Then there's wedding and engagement announcements on the opposite page. I imagine myself with my ring hand posed on JoJo's chest. I swallow. *How am I imagining this? Why am I imagining this?*

"Ready, Adrianne?"

I raise my head to Grandpa Joe standing a few feet in front of me. I fold the paper and stand. "Yes, sir."

Then I speed him toward the car best I can before anyone else spots the ring.

JoJo

I open the front door and wait for Grandpa to step inside. His dress shoes and the hardwood flooring don't always mix, so I stand behind him until I'm sure he's got his footing. I've tried to talk him into wearing boots to church, but he's old school and argues that boots can't be dressy.

I disagree. There's a huge difference in my high-dollar ostrich-skin boots and the steel-toed Georgia boots I lace up for work.

Whenever Grandpa gets a new pair of church shoes, I sneak them outside to scuff the bottoms against some gravel and concrete. It doesn't always help him not slip, but at least it gives me a false peace of mind.

We enter the living area to Adrianne scrolling through TV channels with a coffee mug in her hand.

She turns her head when we walk closer. "Good morning."

"Morning." Grandpa snorts. "It's already ten."

Adrianne laughs. "Then good mid-morning."

"Good mid-morning to you too." I plop down in my chair beside the couch.

Grandpa shuffles in front of his chair and lowers himself slowly. Instead of popping the recliner legs for a pre-lunch nap like he does most Sundays, he stares at Adrianne.

"We missed you at church this morning."

Oh, here we go.

Adrianne yawns. "So that's where y'all went."

"Yeah, it's where most people go on Sunday mornings."

"Grandpa," I scold through gritted teeth.

"What, boy? Don't you agree?"

I run a finger under my collar and pop the legs in my own recliner. Grandpa has no business lecturing Adrianne or bringing me into it. I lean back and stare at the TV as if I didn't hear him.

Grandpa ignores me and continues. "You really need to join us next week. Anyone who marries my grandson has to go to church."

I'm reminded of our little charade. It seems to slip my mind unless Grandpa mentions it or Adrianne wears Grandma's ring. I involuntarily glance at her hand. She isn't wearing it right now.

"We go to early service with the real music—hymnals. But there's another service going on in a bit with that new-fangled stuff where they use drums and plug in their guitars."

I make eye contact with Adrianne and try to communicate my apologies for Grandpa. When he starts to speak again, I interrupt. "Come on, Adrianne, let's go out for lunch."

She perks up and abandons her channel surfing in favor of handing Grandpa the remote. "What did you have in mind?"

I close my recliner and spring to my feet. "Anywhere that isn't here." I clear my throat and glare at the back of Grandpa's head.

Adrianne bites back a laugh.

"You can take her to second service first," Grandpa quips.

"Grandpa, that's enough. You need to leave Adrianne alone."

His face pales, and mine probably does as well. I've never stood up to Grandpa like that. I've argued my opinion plenty of times, but never point-blank told him to stop doing or saying something.

After an awkward pause, Grandpa turns from me to Adrianne. "I'm sorry, Adrianne."

She reaches over and pats his hand. "It's okay, Grandpa Joe." Then she stands and smiles at me.

"Change to go outside and I'll meet you back here in ten minutes."

"Can we make it twenty?"

"Sure." I sigh as she hurries toward the basement.

"Grandpa, are you hungry now?"

"No."

"Well, there's soup from last night you can warm up."

He doesn't say anything.

I talk louder. "I made you a bowl of soup to warm up. Just be careful getting it out of the microwave."

"Okay." He lands the TV on a game show and turns up the volume.

I go to my room and change out of my nice jeans and boots, then return to the kitchen. One perk to working in the woods most of my life is I've become an expert sandwich maker. I've had years to figure out the best combinations and ideal ratio between meats, cheeses, and condiments.

Bread is a game changer. I pull a baguette out of the bread box and start preparing a deli lunch that would put Subway to shame. I grab two small coolers from the walk-in pantry. One to hold the sandwiches, plus chips and fruit. To the other, I add some ice and drinks.

Loggers always have water bottles and coolers on hand. We can't afford to get stuck in the middle of nowhere with nothing to eat or drink all day.

I set the coolers by the door and hear footsteps on the floor. Adrianne walks into the room wearing shorts and a shirt, with these high-heeled sandals. I stare at her feet.

"You might want to change your shoes."

"Why?" She twists her leg and examines her feet.

The hairs on my neck stand up when her long leg flexes in those shorts. I force my gaze to her face instead. "We'll be outside for a picnic."

Her eyes widen. "A picnic?"

"Yeah, if that's okay?"

"Yeah, one minute." She holds up a finger and hurries back to the basement.

I lean against the wall and sigh. Maybe this won't take twenty more minutes. I watch Pat Sajak sell vowels for a few minutes, then turn to Adrianne's voice.

"Ready." She's now wearing jean shorts, a T-shirt, tennis shoes, and a ball cap.

"Good choice," I say, trying not to sound too surprised that she changed so quickly.

Grandpa cranes his neck toward us. "Where's your ring?"

Adrianne holds out her fingers, then glances at me. I half shrug.

She smiles at Grandpa. "Thanks for the reminder." Then she goes to the basement once more.

Grandpa winks at me and turns his attention back to the game show. I shake my head and gather the coolers. As soon as Adrianne comes back with the ring on her finger, we head outside.

I set the coolers in the back seat as she climbs in the truck. Adrianne runs her hand across the dash and studies the radio when I get in.

"I didn't notice when you drove me in the rain how the inside of your truck is the same red as the outside. It's probably the brightest red I've ever seen, including some of Daisy's hair colors."

"She does have some strange hair colors."

"You're not kidding. She once brought a tomato in the salon and wanted me to match her highlights to it."

I wrinkle my forehead. Daisy is a strange little woman, but I don't say so. She's a good friend to Adrianne and keeps my back in line.

"Where are we going?"

"There's a pretty spot where we're logging. There's a creek

and pasture nearby, perfect for a picnic. And I always keep bug spray and sunscreen in here, if that's a concern."

She smiles. "Looks like you've prepared for everything."

I cut my eyes toward her hand for a second. "Everything except Grandpa making you wear the ring. Sorry about that."

She holds her hand in front of her. "It's fine. I can always hide my hand if we run into someone."

I fight a smile as I watch her admire my grandma's ring. "There shouldn't be anyone out here unless we come across the landowner."

She smiles at me. "Good."

I stop fighting a smile and grin back. My neck heats up and a bit of excitement swirls in my stomach. I'm sure her response to us being alone is relief for not having to hide the ring. However, I'm glad it's just the two of us. No Grandpa or anyone else watching us.

We can just be ourselves. No faking it.

Adrianne

We pass my poor house with the tarp secure over the top and Daisy's house, where goats cover the porch. Either I'm losing it, or one is rocking itself in the porch swing. We continue past a few more houses down our country road, then turn toward a dirt road at the end.

"I've never seen this road before."

"That's because it's new. I made it last week to clear-cut this place."

"Oh." The trees are noticeably thinner in part of this area, and I assume more of it will be soon.

"How long are you working here?"

"A few more weeks." The road takes a slight turn, and JoJo points toward a row of pine trees. "That way backs up to your house."

I nod. "So that's where you were working the day the tree fell across my pool and roof."

"Yep. The day Skeeder disobeyed and screwed everything up."

I twist my mouth and turn to JoJo. "It hasn't been that bad. Aside from being temporarily homeless, of course."

He shakes his head. "You have a really positive spin on things."

I shrug. "Makes life more enjoyable."

"I suppose." He frowns at the windshield.

I hope he's recalling the blunder that messed up my house and not scowling because of me. I'd hate to think my staying with them is a burden. Then again, I get the sense he wouldn't have invited me had he not been one hundred percent fine with it. JoJo gives off vibes that he doesn't do anything he doesn't like.

The farther we drive down the dirt road, the more shaded the forest. There's almost a clear line of where they haven't cut yet. I watch the trees pass as we continue until the road ends. He parks the truck and gets out.

If he plans on eating on the tailgate, I don't understand why we needed to come out here. Hopefully he's not a secret axe murderer. Though that would explain why he only smiles at me.

I stay planted in my seat while he opens the back door and reaches for the coolers.

He sticks his head inside. "You coming?"

I turn, still buckled. "Where?"

"This is why you needed to change shoes." He gives me a slight grin.

The small part of me that believed him to have murderous motives calms down. I get out and meet him at the front of the truck. He has a cooler in each hand.

"Do you need me to carry one of those?"

"No, you need to be able to hold on to a tree if you lose your footing."

I raise a brow. "Where exactly are we going?"

"Through the woods, down a steep hill. There's a creek and pasture at the bottom."

He steps in front of me between two trees. "Stay close to me."

I fall in line behind him, watching my step as the hill starts to slant. Before long, my foot turns sideways, and I grab on to a tree trunk.

JoJo turns his head. "You okay?"

"Yeah." I steady myself and take a step down.

"Hold on to me if you need to."

I take a few more steps, then reach for a tree to my left. My hand lands on his back instead. He doesn't flinch, just keeps moving forward at a steady pace. I bury my fist in the back of his shirt for support.

He's every bit as solid as a tree, and his cotton shirt is much softer than bark. My ring catches the sunlight glimmering through the tree leaves overhead. I never imagined I'd be hanging on to him for dear life while wearing his grandmother's engagement ring, but stranger things have happened. Like a tree crashing my tanning time.

I follow JoJo down the massive hillside, bumping into him a time or two when I lose my balance. Once we make it to the bottom, I unball my fist, leaving a crinkled wad in the back of his shirt.

"I apologize for the death grip on your back."

He lifts the corners of his mouth. "I barely noticed."

I snicker. He's so dry, it's hard to know if he's being sarcastic.

"We're here." He nods past my head.

I turn to a wide-open field with avocado-colored grass. JoJo leads us toward it, and I hear water running when we're almost to the opening.

"There's a creek and some old rock caves next to the

field."

I raise my eyes to the sky, then pan the surrounding trees. "This place is breathtaking."

"The owner wants to thin out all the way to here and make it easier to access the field."

"What does he do with it?"

"It's a large green field in the wintertime. He wants to use it for hay, but it's too hard to get a truckload of bales back up as it sits."

"So he walks down here?"

"He rides a four-wheeler."

I nod. "I never knew this was so close to my house."

"There's all kinds of things people find in the woods you wouldn't believe. Some good, some bad."

"Bad?" My nerves tick as JoJo leads me to the edge of the field.

"Yeah. Mainly moonshine stills and stuff people are trying to hide."

"Oh."

"This is a good place to sit. I eat lunch here a lot. It's shady and not as hot near the creek." He dusts off a large flat rock in front of the creek area.

I sit on the rock while he unpacks the coolers. "Thanks for fixing me lunch."

"No problem. I needed a break from game shows."

I laugh. "My grandpa liked them too."

JoJo sits beside me, and his leg brushes mine. I try and ignore the rush it gives me. "What's he like?"

"He's no longer alive."

"I'm sorry." He stares at his boots.

After a moment, he raises his eyes to me. I wiggle on the rock, partly due to it burning my thighs and partly due to my conflicted feelings. JoJo leans closer, and I press my lips together, suddenly aware of their dryness.

Is he going to kiss me?

And . . . no. He reaches past me and pulls a sandwich from the cooler. The moment has passed, so I may as well carry on the conversation.

"No, it's fine. All my grandparents had passed by the time I was twenty. I never even met my dad's parents."

"I'm lucky to have Grandpa this long. I try and tell myself that every time he gets on my last nerve." JoJo takes a bite of his sandwich.

"You really are." I pop a grape in my mouth and admire the creek behind us, then turn to him. "For what it's worth, he's lucky to have you too."

"Thanks, maybe you should tell him that." He smirks.

"He appreciates you. Some old men aren't great at showing appreciation."

JoJo picks up an apple and stares at it. "I guess the apple doesn't fall far from the tree." He takes a huge bite and chews.

"You don't act as stubborn as him."

He huffs and finishes his apple in two more bites, then tosses the core into the trees. "Most people would disagree."

I study him for a moment. *Is he different around me? Is it because he feels responsible for wrecking my house?*

JoJo finishes his sandwich and balls up his trash inside one of the coolers. He lays his head back on the boulder and stares up at the treetops while I finish eating. Once I'm done, he sits up. "Want to see something cool?"

"Sure."

He stands and extends his hand. I put my hand in his and practically jump as he pulls me toward him.

"Whoa." I land at his chest and ease back sheepishly.

"Sorry, I'm used to lifting heavier things."

"I'll take that as a compliment."

He smiles, then releases my hand. My senses dull at the

loss of his touch. Would it be weird to grab his hand again? Probably.

I settle for walking close to him. I'm already his fake fiancée living in the basement. No need to make our situation any weirder.

We stroll along the bank of the creek for some time. I barely notice we've been walking at a slight slant until I look back and notice our coolers downhill from a distance.

"Look." JoJo nods to the left.

A small waterfall trickles through a wall of rocks. It's slow and steady and not quite large enough to make a lot of noise. Otherwise, I would've heard it by now, and I might have to pee.

"People pay landscapers big money to re-create stuff like this in their backyards. But it never lives up to the original."

"That's beautiful." I open my mouth in awe.

"Yeah, it is." JoJo's voice sounds close to my ear.

When I turn from the waterfall, I catch him staring at me. He jerks his head toward the waterfall, and his ears redden under his cap.

I smile and continue watching the water. A surge of excitement rushes through me, and I want to explore. I steady my footing against the rocks on the bank and start down the side.

"Careful, Adrianne. Those are slick." JoJo's voice carries behind me.

I get to the bottom safely but want a closer view of the stream. It would make a gorgeous backdrop for a selfie to remember this place. There are several big rocks above the water that I can use to maneuver toward the waterfall.

I'm making decent progress stepping from rock to rock when I come to a big gap. I'll need to jump to make it to the next rock. Not wanting to chance it, I pull out my phone and turn around. If I zoom a little, I can get the waterfall behind me from here. I just need to lean a little to my right . . .

"Ahhhh!" My foot slips against the rock and my leg comes out from under me.

I can't balance well enough and hold up my phone at the same time. I'm going down when something—or someone—scoops me up. My eyes land on a gray T-shirt stretched across a hard chest.

"JoJo?"

He steadies me on the rock. "Hand me your phone."

I do as I'm told. After the way he saved me from a wet butt and possibly a broken tailbone, I'd hand over anything I owned. Not that he'd want my house in its current state, or women's clothing, a compact car, and a hair salon, but still, I'd offer.

"I told you to be careful. Let me take this for you."

I clear my throat, feeling a little silly posing for a picture in front of him. But I get over it and smile as intended with my hand out, framing the waterfall behind me.

He stares at my screen. "Looks good." Then he hands me the phone.

I'm turning it to see the photo when he lifts me again, one arm under my knees and the other around my back. I relax into his arms as he effortlessly climbs the steep bank. Before I can even process what's happening between us—or maybe just to me—he sets me on solid ground.

"We best clean up our lunch and go."

I nod, unable to find a proper response. "Sure" doesn't seem to cut it. Then I follow him to where we left our stuff and back up the massive hill to the truck.

Along the way, I may have grabbed hold of him a time or two. Even though I didn't really need help walking up. Is that bad?

CHAPTER TWELVE

JoJo

Maybe I made a mistake taking Adrianne on a picnic.

My sole intention was to get out of the house and clear my head after Grandpa's interrogation. Instead, my head is more muddled than ever thanks to getting a little too close to Adrianne.

Catching her was necessary. I wasn't going to stand by and let her fall and hurt herself when I could do something about it. As for carrying her out of the creek and allowing her to lean on me up and down the path . . .

I can easily justify that as necessary too.

What I can't justify is why I liked it.

She's a very attractive woman, and I'm very much a man. It's probably as simple as that. The fact that she acts so comfortable around a gruff guy like me, all while wearing my grandma's ring, makes it odd.

Even odder, we're carrying out a charade to convince

Grandpa I gave her the ring with honest intentions on marrying her.

I sigh and pull my truck into the garage. Adrianne sits contently in the passenger seat as she has the entire trip. We've made small talk here and there, but she seems equally happy talking and in silence.

That may be why I enjoy her company. Most women either talk your ear off or ignore you and stare at their phones.

We park and get out. Laughter echoes from the back porch on the other side of the garage. It's Sunday afternoon, so I know exactly who it is. I glance at Adrianne, who raises a brow.

"Want to meet Grandpa's friends?"

A smile creeps across her face. "Are they half as entertaining as him?"

"Together, they're like the Three Stooges."

She laughs and swipes her hand for me to lead the way. When her hand falls in front of me, I almost ask her to take off the ring. I hesitate, then decide to let it go. Grandpa is less likely to mention anything if he sees her wearing the ring. Besides, the friend of his most likely to bring it up is blind as a bat.

We follow the laughter and voices to the back porch, where Grandpa and his two best friends sit around a table, playing cards. They're a sight for sore eyes, to say the least.

Grandpa with his bushy eyebrows and cane, still dressed for church. Merle is at minimum six foot six and skinny as a rail. He's retired from the coal mines and welds all kinds of lawn ornaments for his wife Connie. Then there's Ervin. He drove a truck for Grandpa until his bad eyesight forced him into retirement. Now he wears glasses thick as Coke bottles. He swings his gut over his jeans and wears suspenders rather than giving in and going up a size—or three—and he's never been married.

Merle notices us first, as he should sitting a head above everyone else. "Well, hey there, JoJo."

"Hi, Merle. How's Mrs. Connie?"

"Good. Digging in a flowerbed right now."

I nod. "How are you, Ervin?"

Ervin looks up from beating a pipe against his palm. He squints to try and focus on me. "All right. I've got crows in my cornfield again, but other than that, I can't complain."

"You got corn problems?" a high-pitched voice yells behind us.

We all turn to Wendall Jenkins—the final Stooge making up Grandpa's entourage.

"Get here when you can, Wendall," Grandpa quips.

"Hush it, Joe, I had to feed the herd." He adjusts his CO-OP cap and opens the screen door to the porch. He spits a lug of tobacco into the yard and pulls up a chair.

I barely hold off laughter when he sits beside Merle. Wendall is a tiny man, and his overalls practically hang on his frail shoulders.

"Deal me in, Joe." What he lacks in size, he makes up for in bossiness.

Grandpa shakes his head and deals out more cards. "Y'all have a nice lunch alone without me?"

I narrow my eyes at him. "Yes, we did."

A fly buzzes around the table, and Ervin puffs at it with his pipe. The fly swarms closer to the men, and Merle reaches out and flattens it on the table with his large hand.

"Y'all want in?" Grandpa glances at me, then Adrianne.

"What game is this?" she asks.

"Poker," Wendall answers matter-of-factly.

"I've never played."

"It's not hard," I tell her.

Some of the old men huff like she needs a PhD in Vegas card counting to play with them. Grandpa ignores them and deals us in anyway.

We take our time on the first few hands, showing Adrianne the ropes. I can tell Wendall is impatient teaching her, but that's what he gets for showing up late. The others don't seem to mind her playing with us. Especially Ervin, who squints at her extra hard. I don't blame him. I'm sure she looks good even out of focus.

I catch Grandpa smiling at Adrianne's ring when she pulls a card from her hand. Either his friends haven't noticed, or it doesn't matter to them. Probably both, considering we never formally introduced her and just joined the game.

An hour passes, then one more. By the time the sun lowers to that evening glow, Adrianne has won a few hands. Ervin even shakes her hand to congratulate her . . . or maybe he just wanted to touch a pretty young woman.

Once he lets go of her, we clean up the cards. The men gather their winnings, which are soft peppermints. Grandpa has a strict rule that they can't play for monetary gain on Sundays.

Other days, they've been known to play for anything from cash to crops. According to Daddy, Grandpa once lost a lot of land in a high-heated poker match before I was born. I haven't known of them playing for property, so that must be why.

Wendall spits the last of his tobacco out on the porch and pops a peppermint in his mouth. He sticks the remaining winnings in his front overalls pocket.

The guys chat about tomorrow's weather while I stack the cards in the box. Merle and Adrianne start a side conversation about flowers and gardens as we walk down the porch steps. Grandpa's friends always park in the back, so they're closer to the porch.

Ervin gets in the car with Merle, which is a relief since he can't see the broad side of a barn. Wendall hops in his own truck and spits once more. This time peppermint juice hits the ground. He cocks his head toward us and yells, "Go with us!"

I shake my head. That expression has never made sense to me. Nobody really means it when they say it, and Wendall is by himself, so clearly not an "us." When nobody takes him up on the fake invitation, he sits in his seat and cranks the truck.

We wave as they drive off, then start up the porch steps. Adrianne goes first, then Grandpa. On the third step, he pauses and holds his chest. He coughs, then stumbles.

"Grandpa." His eyes are closed, and he doesn't answer. "Grandpa!" When he still doesn't answer, I pick him up and hurry to the garage.

"Adrianne, crank the car!"

"Watch it!" I scream as Adrianne slides under a yellow light.

Apple Cart has one traffic light, and she almost wrecked under it.

"Sorry," she sighs before slowing down. "Maybe I should put my flashers on?"

"No, just drive safely." *If Grandpa does die, it better not be from a wreck.*

I never would've imagined her driving like a drunken NASCAR racer. I cup my hand behind Grandpa's head and pray he pulls through. My prayers must've worked, because we swing into the entrance to the hospital a few minutes later.

My stomach flips when she jerks Grandpa's car into park.

I gather him in my arms while Adrianne opens the back door. She helps me turn his legs so I can get out holding him.

Although he's frail from lack of physical work the last few years, he has the same large frame as Daddy and me. He may not be that heavy, but he's long.

We manage to get him out without bending his legs too much, then rush toward the door. I breathe in through my nostrils as I wait patiently for the swivel door to open toward us. We catch it at the opening and hurry inside.

The receptionist drops her jaw when I rush in with Grandpa. "Here." She jumps up and grabs a nearby wheelchair.

"Thanks." I place him in it gently as possible.

"You'll have to go to the emergency area."

I nod. "Thanks." I push him toward the emergency room.

Adrianne jogs to match my steps. "What do you think happened?"

I shrug and put a hand to his neck. "He's warm and has a pulse. I'm not sure."

She chokes back a tear and presses the button to the emergency room door. A few seconds later, it opens. We rush him to the desk behind the waiting area.

"JoJo, what happened?" Brooke's face falls when she recognizes us.

Grandpa may be ornery, but everyone in the county knows and respects him. A lot of people even like him.

"He fainted or passed out climbing the porch steps."

She nods and picks up a phone. "Dr. West, we have an emergency."

"We were all in the backyard. He was fine up until then. He went to church and—"

Dr. West rushes through the door and takes the wheelchair from me. He speeds Grandpa down a hallway.

Adrianne and I watch as the door swings behind them. Then we take a seat in the waiting area and stare at the floor.

"Do you think he skipped lunch?" I ask.

She shakes her head. "He said something about the soup when we were playing cards."

"Yeah, but we ate it last night too."

"No, he mentioned eating it for lunch. Something about it tasted too salty."

I sigh. "I put too much garlic salt. I hope that didn't mess him up." I prop my elbows on my knees and rest my face in my hands.

A gentle scratch moves across my shoulders. "It's not that, I'm sure. Don't think it's your fault."

Adrianne continues running her fingernails across my back. My body relaxes at her touch, while my mind races in a million directions.

I shouldn't have left him before he ate lunch. Why was I so short with him when we got home? Did Ervin's pipe smoke choke him out? Why didn't I tell Ervin not to smoke?

Adrianne's hand pauses on my collar and squeezes my shoulder. "Hey, look at me."

I turn my face to find her inches away. Her crystal eyes are misted with almost tears. "It's not your fault. He will be okay."

"He better be."

I lean my back against the chair and slump down. My eyes meet Brooke's for a second, and she gives me a sympathetic closed-mouth smile. Then she turns to her computer, and I stare at the wall.

Adrianne slides her arm from around my shoulder and rests it on my knee. I instantly wrap my hand around hers. Something about the small smoothness of her touch comforts me. I breathe in, then exhale, relaxing the slightest bit.

We sit in silence, side-by-side and hand-in-hand, staring ahead. A weird Adam Sandler movie plays on the TV in the corner. One of the florescent light bulbs fizzles in and out above the door, and Brooke's chair squeaks a time or two. Other than that, everything is calm and quiet.

My senses are heightened as I listen for any announcement—the door swinging, the doctor's voice, Brooke getting a call. Maybe that's why when Adrianne makes small circles in my palm with her thumb, every nerve ending in my body tenses.

I close my eyes and try to quit thinking. It partially works, as I'm not as worried. Instead, I'm thinking about Adrianne and me. Pretending this is real, that we're real. Except we're at home, on the couch, watching a movie of our choice.

"JoJo."

Her voice sounds strange.

"JoJo Culp?"

I pop my eyes open to an older nurse standing in the doorway.

"Right here." I spring to my feet, pulling Adrianne with me.

"You can see him now."

I speed toward the door, Adrianne still attached to my hand.

The nurse glances at her, then me, and frowns. "Family only, I'm afraid."

I want her there with me when I see Grandpa. No, I *need* her there with me. Without thinking of the consequences, I lift our intertwined hands so Grandma's ring shines in front of the nurse.

"She's my fiancée."

Papers slush behind us as Brooke drops an armful of files.

The nurse frowns again, then sighs. "All right." She half smiles at Adrianne. "Nice ring."

"Thanks." Adrianne blushes at me, then tightens her lips.

We follow the nurse behind the door, leaving Brooke to clean up her mess. Part of me regrets calling Adrianne my fiancée as I calculate all the damage control I'll need to do once Brooke and the nurse start gossiping. But for now, it was worth it to have Adrianne by my side when I see Grandpa.

The nurse leads us to a room down a long hallway. Grandpa is propped up in the bed, sipping on a juice cup through a straw.

"Hey, boy. Hey, Adrianne."

Dr. West glances over his shoulder from a laptop on the counter. "He's fine. Just a dizzy spell. I suspect he climbed the steps too fast."

I lead Adrianne to the bedside and rest my free hand on Grandpa's shoulder. "How are you feeling?"

"Much better, boy." He smiles at Adrianne and me. "I can't die just yet. I'm hanging on to see you two get married."

My chest tightens, and Adrianne squeezes my hand. The realization of this mess we've created must be settling on her now too.

Dr. West smirks at us. "Congratulations."

We mutter a "thanks" in unison. Then we share a look that communicates how deep we're in this mess. At least we're in it together—for better or worse.

CHAPTER THIRTEEN

Adrianne

I fan the mascara wand across Ashley's lashes one more time. Then I lean back and survey my work before removing the towel from under her chin.

"Okay, Ashley, you can raise up."

She pushes off her elbows and sits upright, blinking a time or two. I hold a mirror to her face. A smile blossoms across her cheeks as she admires her new lashes.

"Gorgeous, Adrianne!"

"Thanks." I hand her the mirror and step back for her to stand. "There's a new kind out that might not take as long to apply. I just need more practice with them."

She turns her head and bats her new lashes. "These are great." She glances at the clock on the wall and hands me the mirror. "Is it fine if I Venmo you once I get back to work?"

"Of course."

One of the downfalls in working in a small town is the spotty cell service. Customers with certain phone providers can't get their transactions to go through from the salon.

Another downfall is everyone commenting on your fake engagement, which has gone viral in the past few weeks following Grandpa's hospital scare. They usually say something along the lines of "that was fast" or "I'm glad you finally found someone." Both are loose translations of "bless her heart."

"Thanks, I've got to get back to work before Samuel has a fit." Ashley sucks in a breath, then smiles. It appears forced, like when a pageant contestant is trying to hold out a few more seconds after the judges call for more time to make their decision.

"How's that going?"

"Loan officer? I love it."

"Good. And with Samuel?" I lower my voice to not get the attention of Becki Douglas.

Her ears are always perked and ready to hear anything that might constitute as news for the *Apple Cart Weekly*. And she's currently ten feet away in my salon chair.

"He's great." Ashley's face lifts momentarily.

Too bad I see through her charade, and the fact that she commented on him personally and not *them* as a couple. I've never cared for the man, and many others around here share my opinion.

"That's good to hear." I put on my own fake pageant smile to not reveal my concern.

At first, Ashley comes off a little high on herself, but she's grown on me since switching to my salon. The more I get to know her, the more I realize she's just bougie. Trust-fund Samuel, by contrast, is just bratty.

"Congratulations on your engagement."

I laugh nervously and glance over my shoulder. I'm living on borrowed time before Becki catches wind of it.

"Thanks."

Ashley nods and grins a little wider before leaving the salon. I'd bet my bag of lettuce wilting in the fridge that her smile fell off the moment she turned her head. From one pageant veteran to another, I feel her.

I cross the room to Becki, hoping with every fiber of my being she didn't hear any of that. Part of me suspects she comes here for the juicy news around town. She always gets a basic blowout and trim, which she could get anywhere, even in Wisteria.

"Okay, Becki, I'm ready to dry you."

She raises her head and slides her phone under the smock. I swear, if she was taking notes.

"Ouch," Becki whines when I jerk a knot from her hair.

"Sorry." I truly didn't mean to pull her head, but if she was taking notes on my life, then I don't feel quite as bad about it.

Becki stares into the mirror as I carefully comb the rest of her hair and trim the ends. I've wanted to suggest she try highlights, but I'm not sure how to approach her. She's so calculated and serious that I do what she asks and nothing more.

I trim the usual amount to keep her hair at the length she prefers, then blow it dry. She's an attractive woman, but nothing stands out about her. Maybe she wants to blend in with the crowd to get more news.

When I set the hair dryer back in its holster, she smiles at her reflection. My chest warms at her satisfaction with my work. It's not one of my edgier or more complicated master-pieces, but a happy client is always a compliment.

Becki stands and walks toward the front counter. Misty

hums to herself as she files her nails. Becki waits patiently as Misty drums out a chorus with her newly evened nails.

"Misty, can you check her out?"

"Yes, boss."

"You don't . . ." I toss Becki's damp towel into the dirty towel bin. Metaphorically throwing in the towel on telling Misty not to call me boss.

She calls me many things, from boss to boo. I've tried nicely and firmly to remind her my only name is Adrianne. She doesn't listen, and at this point, I'm tired of wasting my breath.

Misty takes Becki's money and gives her a new appointment while I sweep hair from around my chair. As I'm dumping the hair into a bag for Jack, a delivery truck parks outside.

When the driver comes in, Misty perks up. "Well, hello."

If only she were that polite to our actual customers . . . maybe if more of them were men.

Misty continues to flirt with the delivery guy as I tend to the hair. Carolina comes in next and goes straight to me. Smart girl. She knows better than to mess with Misty.

"Hey, Adrianne."

"Hey, what's up?"

"Can you give me some dates that might work for my bridal portraits? I've got to confirm a date with the photographer."

"Sure." I slide behind Misty to check my appointment book.

The delivery driver is backing toward the door as Misty reaches for his bicep. He manages to escape about the time I find a few dates for Carolina.

"Everything going good with the planning?"

"Yeah." She laughs. "It's a little weird planning my own wedding after doing so many others."

"I bet."

"You'll see what I mean when your big day gets here." She winks.

My face flushes. "I'm sure."

I ball my left hand into a fist. Even though I'm not wearing the ring, my hand tingles as I read into that wink. *How far has news traveled? Did Becki hear anything I said, or was it all from the hospital?*

"Thanks, I've got to go look at a house we're reno-ing. I'll text you after I confirm a date."

"Sounds good."

Carolina pauses at the door and holds up the note where I wrote down the dates. "Congratulations, by the way."

"Thanks." I swallow and lean across the counter before I faint.

She opens the door to Woody. He's holding a bouquet of flowers and dressed fancy. Well, fancy like Apple Cart.

Misty claps her hands. "My love." She wraps her arms around him as if she hadn't just shamelessly flirted with the delivery guy.

I watch them embrace and kiss as if I'm not even here. When I sicken of their PDA, I turn my attention to the package. Woody and Misty gush over one another while I slice the packing tape with a pair of scissors.

"Bye, boss babe!"

I raise my eyes and smirk. "Bye, Misty."

They stroll out the front door, and I follow them to lock it and turn the sign to "Closed." Daisy is my last client tonight, and she knows to use the side door.

Once a month she comes in for me to color her hair, and we spill all the tea. I book her late so we can catch up without any interference from random citizens.

I'm halfway through unpacking products we ordered from Quincy when three soft knocks rap on the side door. I open it to Daisy wearing a shirt that reads, "I've Got Your Goat."

"Come in."

She sighs and plops down in my chair. "Pour me a strong color tonight, bartender."

I laugh. "Rough day?"

"I agreed to do a candle and soap fundraiser for Apple Cart Elementary School." She shakes her head. "Let's just say it was a huge success."

I laugh again. "That's got to be good for business."

"Yeah, but not for my hands." She lifts her tiny hands and moans. "Note to self: Don't massage on days that require extra goat milking."

I shake my head. "How do you want your hair?"

"Uh . . ." She runs a hand over her red ponytail. "A little darker."

"Okay." I pinch my lips.

For months, I've wanted her to soften the burgundy, but she always argues against it. Tonight, I choose to treat her like Becki and simply do as I'm told.

I mix her color and grab two bottles of water from the refrigerator. Daisy thanks me for the water, then goes into detail about what Mullet did today.

It wouldn't surprise me if Daisy has a house full of kids one day. Anyone who diapers a goat and feeds him at the table seems like the type itching to take care of a baby.

After some time, our conversation veers to her hearing engagement rumors in Piggly Wiggly.

"What are you going to do about it?" Daisy's eyes widen as she stares at me from the mirror.

I shrug. "Ride it out until the lawyer finds a loophole like we said."

"And if that doesn't work?"

"I guess I'll have to marry him."

Daisy chuckles. "Very funny."

"Come to the bowl." I lead her to the sink and lean her back.

The foils in her hair scratch the sides of the bowl. I pull the chair a little lower to accommodate her petite frame.

I undo the foils and ball them up before tossing them in the trash can by my feet. The light catches the tinfoil, making it sparkle, which reminds me of the diamond at home in my room. Except that's not my home or my room, it's JoJo's.

Strange how comfortable I've gotten living in JoJo's basement. Even stranger how wearing his grandma's ring makes me miss it when I don't have it on. I never wear rings to work, and lately I feel like I'm missing something without it.

I notice Daisy staring at me and turn on the water. She closes her eyes and relaxes once I start washing her hair. I apply her toner, then have her sit up.

Daisy opens her eyes to me pacing the floor in front of her.

"Adrianne, what's going on?"

"Nothing. Just thinking."

"About your fake fiancé?"

I scoff. "Whatever. You know me. I'm thinking about everything I have to do tomorrow."

"Like have dinner with your fake fiancé."

"Stop it, Daisy. It's all fake. Nothing to think about."

"Then why are you worried?"

"I'm not."

"You're pacing. You never pace. A freaking tree crashed your house and flooded your yard and you didn't panic."

"I was too focused on being blessed to be alive when that happened."

"Or focused on the Thor axe guy that came to your rescue."

"He is not a Thor axe guy."

"That's what you called him," she whispers.

"I heard that!"

Daisy crosses her arms. "What are you really thinking?"

I pull a rolling stool nearby and sit in front of her. "Hear me out. What if I did actually marry him?"

Daisy bolts forward, cupping her hands to my face. "You are on a self-induced man fast."

I pull her hands away. "Self-induced, so it's my call."

Daisy shakes her head. "You can't be serious. We don't even know the guy."

"*You* don't know him. I've gotten to know him pretty well."

"From a few weeks occupying his basement?"

"And meals and conversations."

"You can't be serious."

I shrug.

Daisy starts to say something else, but I shove her head back and start rinsing her toner. She grimaces as I massage her scalp and work the water wand over her hairline.

When I wrap a towel around her, she sits up and frowns. "At least promise me you'll let me and our friends get to know him better before you walk down the aisle."

I laugh. "Sure, more reason to have a courthouse wedding."

Daisy goes and sits in my salon chair and laughs. "Yeah, like you'd settle for a courthouse wedding."

"You never know." I smirk.

Before Daisy can come back with something else sarcastic, I grab the hair dryer. Neither of us can carry on a coherent conversation with wind blasting between us.

I go through the motions of blowing out her hair, all the while contemplating what a real relationship with JoJo might look like.

Once I turn off the hair dryer, my eyes meet Daisy's in the mirror.

She blinks. "It's . . . it's . . . When I said pour it on strong, I guess you did."

I wince. "I promise, I didn't do this on purpose." I finger comb her hair that is now a natural auburn color rather than the raving cranberry she prefers. "I must've rinsed your toner too quickly."

"Yeah, you were too antsy to shove my head in the sink and make me shut up."

I shake my head. "Daisy, I'm so sorry. I'll redo it for free."

She stands and pulls her hair up on the sides, examining it closer in the mirror. My nerves tense when she turns to me.

"I love it!"

"You do?"

"Yeah, don't you think it's pretty?"

I bend at the waist, laughing, then straighten when my stomach unknots. "I've been wanting to do something like this for months."

"Why didn't you just say something?"

I raise my hands, then let them fall. She has a point. Maybe I should say something to JoJo too.

JoJo

For the first time in my life, I'm at Double Drive for something other than a guys' night or clearing timber. I'm here on a group date.

Group date. I shake my head. That's something I haven't

done since high school, and even then, I was set up by a fellow football player.

But Adrianne suggested we go on an actual date for me to get to know her friends. Either she's super committed to selling this fake relationship, or it's some kind of trap.

Before I forget, I send Angela the same text I have every week for the last month.

Find anything yet?

Nope. Joe really did his homework on this one.

I sigh and run a hand down my face. Adrianne turns and hands me a golf ball. I slide my phone into the clip on my jeans and take it.

"I got the longest club they had." She hands me a golf club with a rubber handle duct taped at the end.

I turn it over in my hand and examine the tape. "Thanks."

She laughs. "You're welcome."

Jack walks over and extends a hand. "JoJo."

"Hey, Jack." I shake his hand.

"Funny seeing you here when it's not after-hours paintballing."

"Same," I agree.

"After-hours paintballing?" Adrianne raises a brow.

"Men stuff," Jack assures her.

She grins and joins her friends, who are picking out their own golf clubs.

"How's work?" Jack asks.

"Hot."

He laughs. "I hear that. I almost regret starting the fish ponds. It's a much hotter venture than hunting."

"More mosquitos, I imagine too."

"Yeah." Jack laughs.

Tanner walks up, laughing. "What's so funny?"

I stare at him until he quits smiling. He's a little too peppy for my liking. He clears his throat and stares at the golf course. "You ever played golf here, JoJo?"

"Nope." I've never played golf anywhere—mini golf and actual golf included.

Carolina and Jonah stroll beside us with their arms locked. It's rare to see one without the other now that they're running a business together and engaged.

I swallow. *Is that how all engaged people act? Should I act more affectionate toward Adrianne?*

As if right on cue, she comes over with the rest of the women. I wrap an arm around her shoulder and pull her closer to me. She doesn't fight it, but rather leans into me.

I resist the urge to enjoy her next to me. This is an act, and I have to keep my head in the game so I don't say something stupid. I've already outed our fake engagement at the hospital, then paid for that dearly over the past few weeks.

"We're ready to go?" Jack asks Bianca.

She slides her club under her arm and nods. "We're just waiting on Ashley."

Tanner groans, and Hannah elbows him.

"What?" he scoffs at his new wife.

"Be nice. She's been nice to us ever since I quit the bank."

I don't know anything about this group's drama, nor do I care to know. I stay in the woods with my own band of idiots, the way I like it. But I do know Hannah and Ashley once worked at the bank together. I guess that's what she means.

"It's not her. It's Samuel." Tanner rolls his eyes and drags out Samuel's name like a curse.

Hannah sighs, then touches the tip of Tanner's nose. "Be nice."

A small car pulls up and Ashley hops out. She bounces toward us, her blonde hair swaying behind her. She's wearing high, pointy heels, totally impractical for golfing. Not that this is real golfing.

"Sorry I'm late. Samuel made me work over tonight."

Tanner's face contorts like he's holding in a laugh, or maybe a fart. It's hard to tell the difference.

Hannah gives him side-eye, then smiles at Ashley. "That's fine."

"Is Samuel coming?" Carolina asks.

Ashley's face falls. "No, he's still at the bank. He had more paperwork to do."

Carolina nods. Everyone but Ashley looks relieved Samuel won't be joining us. Tanner looks downright giddy about it. Hannah grabs his wrist and pulls him toward the edge of the porch. They gather some scorecards and pencils while the rest of us start toward the green.

I drop my arm from around Adrianne's shoulder when we start down the porch steps. She glances at me and smiles. I walk beside her to the first hole.

Other than Daisy and Ashley, everyone is a couple. I dreaded coming here, but it's not hard to pretend I'm with Adrianne. Of course, everyone thinking we're engaged goes a long way to sell the lie for me.

I wrinkle my forehead as I scan the putting greens. There's quite the array of obstacles, from a fake bull with large horns to a pretend outhouse. At least, I hope it's pretend. No wonder Earl Ed makes us steer clear of this area during paintball.

We gather around the first hole while Tanner shuffles scorecards. "I'll keep score and go last."

"Well, that's nice of you," Daisy says.

Hannah and Carolina exchange a look. Carolina laughs. "Trust me, you want him to go last."

Tanner pops his younger sister on the shoulder, which gives Jonah a reason to kiss her cheek. As if he needed one. *Should I be kissing Adrianne on the cheek?*

I slide closer to her and wrap an arm around her waist. Best play it subtle. I shouldn't have to compete with Jonah, who's been in love with Carolina all his life. I just need to sell our love story.

Love story? Ugh. Someone take my man card, now.

Adrianne smiles up at me. "Have you played a lot of mini golf?"

I shake my head. "Never."

Her eyes widen. "Seriously?"

"Yeah. Never interested me. You?"

"Not much, mainly at the beach on vacation."

"We always went to the mountains. They had a golfing place or two, but my parents preferred dinner shows and wax museums."

She laughs. "Sounds creepy."

"It can be." I discover myself smiling back at her.

She stays locked in my arm until it's her time to golf. I watch her square her feet and bend slightly. Her long tan legs are a view I could get used to. And I can't help but stare at Grandma's ring on her hand.

When we arrived, that's the first thing the women commented on. I'm glad they approve of my ring choice, even if it was originally Grandpa's choice and I didn't really propose.

We golf through all the holes, with Adrianne by my side

the entire time. I find myself laughing and smiling more than I have in years—possibly all thirty-four of them.

We get to the last hole that has the outhouse.

"I've done this one before," Tanner announces. "You hit the ball in the hole in front of the outhouse door and it keeps it."

Jack steps up first to golf. Right as he hits the ball, the outhouse door swings open. I assume it might be a special effect, until Paul walks out. He has a deer-in-the-headlights expression on his face.

"Oh, I didn't know anyone else was around." He chuckles.

We stare back, and I'm sure I'm not the only one wondering if he actually used the outhouse. Jack frowns at Paul and retrieves his ball, which might've been a hole in one had the door not blocked it.

"Excuse me." Paul nods and steps over the edge of the green, then hurries off the course.

Once the weirdness wears down, we continue golfing until everyone's ball is in. Tanner tallies scorecards while we walk back to the front.

"What's next? Go-karts or food?" Jonah asks.

"I'd say it's better not to eat before go-karts," Jack offers.

The majority of us agree, so we pivot toward the cars.

We're greeted by Bradley tipping his tan cowboy hat from inside the track. When the current racers wheel in for the last time, he helps line up the kids and straighten the cars. After that group exits, we enter.

"Evening, folks."

Most everyone gives Bradley some form of greeting.

"You working here now?" Jonah asks.

"Just tonight. There's a ten-year-old party, and Earl Ed needed some help. I'm already patrolling a supposed meth lab nearby, so I offered."

We nod like the county sheriff helping with a kid's birthday party at a go-kart track while he's on the lookout for meth heads is nothing out of the ordinary. The strange part is that for Apple Cart County, it isn't.

"Ashley, how are you?" Bradley grins, singling her out.

Either he hasn't heard about her and Samuel, or he doesn't care. I never thought I'd think this, but in this case, I'm rooting for Bradley.

"Good," she answers shyly.

"Let me help you to a car." He offers his hand and helps her into a black car, leaving the rest of us to find our own. "You might want to lose the shoes, darlin'."

"Oh." Ashley takes off her shoes and settles into the car.

Bradley adjusts some of the cars and cranks others, while the rest of us settle in. Adrianne and I take one of the double cars next to Jonah and Carolina.

"Do you have enough room?" We're smooshed like a can of sardines thanks to my wide shoulders.

"It's good." Adrianne pats my knee after buckling her seat belt. "I feel safer this close to you."

I open my mouth to respond, but my face flames. What do I say to that? I can't tell her how it *really* makes me feel to hear that. Partly because I'm still sorting it out myself.

"Hey, Adrianne," Carolina calls over our car motors. "You never told me how JoJo proposed."

Now my entire body is on fire, and not in a good way this time. Adrianne gives me a sideways glance, then cranes her neck toward Carolina. My hands shake involuntarily, so I grip the steering wheel to try and steady them. *What is she going to say?*

"It was really sweet. He got down on one knee and told me all the reasons he wanted to marry me."

Whew. A load of logs lifts from my shoulders when Carolina smiles, satisfied with the lie. But it's not a lie. Adrianne just left out the fact that the reasons included ulterior motives about business and Grandpa.

"Go!" Bradley yells from the front of the line. Then he gives Ashley's car a shove, causing her to squeal.

"Hold on," I warn Adrianne.

She grips her right hand around the bar in front of her and braces her left hand on my knee. I glance at her hand with Grandma's ring shining on her finger before I speed off.

It's going to be a weird ride for a while, so I may as well enjoy it.

CHAPTER FOURTEEN

Adrianne

"Maybe turn it this way?" I shove the stuffed head sideways, and the teddy bear falls in through the front door, with me tumbling on top of it.

JoJo picks me up under the arms and laughs. "Are you okay?"

"Yeah, Brutus caught my fall."

JoJo laughs harder and bends to pick up the bear. It's a genuine belly laugh I've never heard from him, and it's contagious. I laugh along as he steadies me and picks up Brutus with one hand.

We ended the group date drinking milkshakes and playing arcade games. Everyone pooled their tickets together to "buy" us an engagement present. I picked the largest prize on the shelf—a huge brown teddy bear with an equally large nose.

Earl Ed was glad to see it go, as he complained about

having to dust it every week. Nobody had won enough tickets yet to get it, and he said he refused to take a loss on it.

We continue into the house, laughing and pushing the bear forward. JoJo hands me Brutus so he can shut the door and turn on the main light.

"What in tarnation?" Grandpa's voice booms from the kitchen.

JoJo and I walk into the main area, where we can see into the kitchen opening. Grandpa is at the sink, running water in a cup. A small light above the stove is on, illuminating his gray head.

"Hey, Grandpa. Why are you in the dark?" JoJo asks.

He hooks a thumb toward the stove. "I'm not. The kitchen nightlight is on."

JoJo nods, then smirks at me.

"What is that thing?" Grandpa nods at Brutus and cuts off the sink.

"A bear," JoJo answers.

"I know that, smart butt. Why is it here?"

"It was a gift from our friends," I say, hugging Brutus best I can. My arms barely fit around him.

Grandpa shakes his head. "Where have y'all been so late?"

Before I can spit out "Double Drive," JoJo shouts, "We eloped!"

I drop Brutus and nearly hit the floor myself. Even more shocking is Grandpa's reaction.

He sets down his cup of water and saunters over with his cane. Then he hugs both of us and laughs. When he pulls back, a smile stretches from one ear to the other.

"That's wonderful!"

JoJo blinks. "It is? Because I thought you wanted to see us get married."

Grandpa takes a gulp of his water, then waves a hand.

"Naw. I meant I wanted to see that you two are married before I die, that's all."

I look at JoJo, not sure where to go from here. One minute, we're coming home from an enjoyable—and seemingly real—date. The next, he's telling Grandpa we ran off and got married! I spent the entire night trying to find reasons not to fall for this man.

I think I've finally found his flaw—diarrhea of the mouth.

JoJo adjusts his cap on his head. "That's good to know."

Really? He can't come up with something better than that? Rather than stand here all night, conflicted about how to play this, I feign a yawn.

"Well, good night, guys. I'm headed to bed."

"Good night," they say in unison.

I arm up Brutus and start toward the basement.

"JoJo, ain't you going to at least kiss your bride good night?" Grandpa calls.

I freeze in my tracks. He's way too loud, and I'm still too close to act like I didn't hear him. If we don't kiss, he'll know something's up. Why wouldn't a freshly married couple want to kiss?

When I turn back to reply, JoJo is already behind me. His brown eyes focus on my face, as if he can see right through me. Maybe he can.

"We wouldn't want to disappoint Grandpa," he says.

"No." I slowly lower Brutus to the floor, removing the only physical barrier between us.

JoJo takes a step closer and drops his gaze to my lips. I moisten them and swallow in anticipation. As he lowers his face toward mine, I close my eyes.

My heart races and my body tingles when he gets close enough for his beard to tickle my cheek. Then he gives me the softest kiss on my lips. I breathe in once, and he pulls away.

I exhale and open my eyes to him still standing within a few inches of me. His face is red, and his lips curve into a slight smile.

"Good night, wife," he says loud enough for Grandpa to hear.

"Good night, husband," I whisper back.

My lips sting when the word "husband" leaves them. I've never called anyone that before. Even scarier than calling JoJo my husband is that it doesn't weird me out like I thought it would.

I lean down and grab Brutus, then turn and retreat to the basement. The entire walk toward the staircase, I fight glancing back at him. I'm certain my own face is flushed.

When I open the basement door, I decide the best course of action is to toss Brutus down the stairs. I do just that before stepping down myself. I'm about three steps down when Grandpa's voice echoes above me.

"Adrianne, I'm sending JoJo down to help you move your essentials."

Move my essentials? What in the world? Has Grandpa had a change of heart and decided to kick me out? Maybe JoJo caved and confessed our sham, making him mad. I twist my head to Grandpa standing at the top of the stairs.

He smiles down at me. "Don't worry, I'll have him move the bulk of your things in the morning. I know you're ready to get to bed."

"Move?" I clear my throat to talk around the lump forming in it. "Where?"

"To the master suite with your husband, of course. You think I'd expect you to spend your wedding night alone in the basement?"

That was my hope. "Uh . . ."

JoJo appears behind Grandpa and mouths *"sorry."* I grit my teeth at him. He shrugs and makes his way around Grandpa. "You can go to bed, Grandpa. I'll take care of things."

"You better." Grandpa laughs. "Now that I've gotten you married, my next mission is another great-grand."

I stumble down a few steps before grabbing on to the rail. JoJo jogs down and helps steady me. We make eye contact, and I realize he's just as scared as me. We've really gotten ourselves in a situation now.

His eighty-year-old grandpa is trying to pimp him out under his own roof.

JoJo sighs and looks up the stairs. "Good night, Grandpa."

"I'm not going to go to bed until I'm sure y'all are settled."

JoJo glances back at me. "Why don't you grab pajamas, or whatever you need for the night." He lowers his voice. "I'll sleep on the floor."

I nod, then turn toward the basement. My mind fogs as I kick Brutus out of the way and gather some pajamas and toiletries in my overnight bag. This is *not* the way I imagined my wedding night. Real or fake.

I take my time climbing the stairs with the bag. JoJo takes it from me when I meet him, then climbs the rest of the stairs with me. We turn off the light to the basement and stare at Grandpa.

He shoves JoJo forward and walks us toward the master bedroom. Never in my life have I witnessed a grandparent wanting their grandson to take a woman to his room. Is this the same man who scrutinized me for not going to Sunday morning church?

Perhaps he's afraid this is a shotgun wedding and wants to ease his mind?

I enter JoJo's bedroom in a daze of confusion. JoJo walks in behind me and shuts the door. At last, Grandpa is out of the picture. We both sigh audibly, then look at one another and laugh.

He swipes a hand down his face. "I'm sorry about all that."

I shake my head. "How would we know he'd react that way?"

JoJo crosses the room and sits on the edge of his bed. "I don't know why I keep saying stuff. I engaged us, now I've married us?"

"Just please don't make me a mom for a while."

JoJo gives me a guilty face.

"You didn't."

He laughs. I rush over and grab a pillow, then beat him over the head until his cap falls off. He laughs harder.

I smirk. "JoJo Culp made a joke. That must be a first."

"Maybe our child will get my sense of humor," he quips.

I hit him once more with the pillow. He grabs me and slings me across him to the other side of the bed. I laugh and lay my head back against the other pillow.

JoJo twists around, and we lock eyes. My chest tightens. He's got that same dreamy look in his eyes. *Is he going to kiss me for real this time?*

He stands, and my chest falls.

"I'm going to take a shower. Don't worry, I'll lock the door. You can change or whatever you need to do, and I'll check before I come out."

I nod. "Thank you."

"Go ahead and go to bed if you want." He tosses the pillow I pelted him with on the floor. "I'll grab a quilt from the closet and make a pallet."

I watch him gather some clothes from a drawer nearby,

then disappear into the connected bathroom. When the door shuts behind him, I glance around the room.

Crown molding, oak wood walls, a four-post king-sized bed that's even softer than my double bed downstairs. *If* this were my real wedding night, I wouldn't mind spending it in a place like this.

But it's not.

I'm not married, or engaged, or even dating the man currently undressing in the room beside me. I bite the inside of my mouth. What a mess. And to think it all started with a giddy old grandpa wanting to add another heir to his throne.

Had he just passed his business to his current heirs like normal people, we wouldn't be in this mess to begin with.

I sigh and hoist myself from the heavenly mattress to find my own pajamas. Luckily, I showered before our pretend date.

I grab makeup wipes and my brush from the top of my bag. It's hard to remember what I threw in for pajamas thanks to Grandpa's rushing me. I dig deeper and pull out a pair of shorts and a T-shirt. Good job on the shirt, which should go to my knees and cover most everything a man might want to see. Bad on the shorts. They will barely cover my butt, so the shirt will have to make up for it.

Still, a decent choice overall for having to pack up last minute like I'm fleeing the country.

I lift my shirt halfway over my head before jerking it back down. Before changing, I lock the bedroom door in case Grandpa decides to barge in and serenade us or deliver flowers. I wouldn't put it past him.

After that, I double-check that JoJo locked the bathroom door. Then I change into my booty shorts and T-shirt. I'll have to suffer through underwire chafing, since there's no way I'm going without a bra. Why didn't I think to toss in a sports bra?

Oh yeah, because I didn't have time to think.

I wipe off my makeup and comb my hair, then pull it back into a hair tie. As I'm looking for a trash can, JoJo knocks on the bathroom door.

"Is it okay to come out?"

"Yes." My voice is raspy. I swallow and try again. "Yes."

He walks out in a pair of gym shorts and a white undershirt. I bite back a laugh. His legs are pale as a piece of paper and his shins are slick.

He holds his arms out and turns. "It's fine. You can laugh at my legs. They never see sun."

"I can tell." A tiny laugh seeps out. I ease past him to the bathroom and shut the door behind me.

I throw away the makeup wipe and start to brush my teeth. I'm not sure if I grabbed my toothbrush.

I open the door and rush toward my bag. JoJo is a few feet away getting extra covers for himself from a closet while I dig through my bag.

He turns his head. "Need something?"

"You have an extra toothbrush?"

"Nope. But what's mine is yours."

I sigh. "It is tonight, I guess."

He shrugs. I toss whatever I rummaged out of the bag back in and go back to the bathroom. To my delight, we use the same brand of toothpaste, and he has floss. What a refreshing coincidence after feeling like I'm on an episode of *Married at First Sight*.

I brush and floss, then stare into the mirror. I wipe toothpaste from the corner of my mouth with the back of my hand. As I run my tongue across my freshly brushed teeth, I wonder what it would be like to kiss JoJo with mint breath. Like *really* kiss him.

My shoulders tense, and I cover my mouth with my hand. I shouldn't think that. Even if I'm sure he brushed his teeth with the same great-tasting toothpaste. Nope, not happening. I'm going to sleep . . . alone.

I ease open the door to JoJo fluffing a pillow on top of a folded blanket. His shirt is now off. I climb in the bed, but stay sitting for a better view. This won't help me forget wanting to kiss him, but I'm in too deep now.

He stands with his back toward me. On his shoulder blade is some kind of tattoo. I squint and lean forward to make out the design. Then I burst out laughing.

He turns and sighs. "I have no hair on my shins because my work boots rub them. I know, they look weird, especially since they're so pale."

I cover my mouth with both hands and try to stop laughing, but that makes it worse. Finally, I squeak out, "I'm not laughing at your legs."

He puts a hand on his hip and runs the other in front of him. "What? Because I have hair on my chest?"

I shake my head, still laughing. He has a nice chest. Very fit and manly. And I of all people appreciate a man with hair, even if he doesn't have any on his head.

"What?" he demands.

I cackle out. "Is that a bulldog on your shoulder?"

His face reddens, and he backs toward the wall, then flips off the lights. "Good night, Adrianne."

I slide under the covers and laugh to myself for a few more minutes before falling asleep. I may or may not have dreams about a bulldog pulling logs.

JoJo

My back is killing me. It's not until I roll over and open my eyes to the rug that I remember volunteering to sleep on the floor. Why didn't I bring an air mattress in here?

Oh yeah, because as far as Grandpa's concerned, last night was my wedding night.

I roll onto my stomach and raise onto my hands, stretching my back before I stand. Adrianne is nowhere to be seen, and the bed is made. Either she's already up and dressed, or she ran away. If my stark-white hairless legs and chest hair didn't do it, I guess the bulldog skidding logs pushed her over the edge.

The stupidest mistake of my youth. Okay, maybe not the stupidest ever, but definitely the one with the longest-lasting consequences. Nothing says don't settle a triple dog dare when you're half-drunk like getting a dog tattooed on your upper back. A dog skidding logs with a chain tied to his shoulders, to be exact.

Since I'm not much of a beach or pool person, nobody outside of my family has seen it in years. Until last night.

Thanks to not seeing it myself without a mirror, I sometimes forget I have it. And I naturally took off my shirt, rather than feel like I'm sleeping in a sweaty straitjacket. Had the tattoo crossed my mind, I'd have turned the lights off before baring my back to Adrianne.

I stretch my arms and yawn before heading to the bathroom. At least I can go without a shirt around her now. The damage is done.

I open the bathroom door to a wet woman in a towel, screaming. My ears bleed, and I jump back, scrambling to make it out the door.

Adrianne screams again, then slams the door at me. Too bad I'm still in the bathroom with her.

I grab her shoulder and shush her. Those crystal eyes dart around like a crazed cat. With one hand, she holds the knot on the towel under her arms. With the other, she pulls out tiny earbuds.

"Did you not hear me coming?"

She holds up the earbuds and takes deep breaths. Her chest rises and falls as she breathes. I focus on the shower door to keep from focusing on her pink skin.

"Waterproof earbuds."

I take a step back. "Sorry, but you can't scream. We could scare Grandpa."

She nods. "You just surprised me, that's all."

"I didn't know you were in here. I thought you were already ready since the bed was made."

"No." She sets the earbuds on the counter and folds both arms across her chest over the towel. "I guess I should've showered in my room, but I had all my hair products and body wash up here."

I cock my head. "You remembered all that but not a toothbrush?"

She pouts. "I'm a hairdresser, not a dentist."

I shrug. "Fair enough." I take a step toward the toilet. "If I can have a minute to drain my faucet, I'll get out of your hair and let you get ready."

"Drain your faucet?" She scrunches her nose.

"Pee." I sigh. "I didn't want to say pee in front of you."

She giggles. "We're standing here half-naked, sharing a room, and you can't say 'pee' in front of me?"

I palm the back of my neck. "I guess married people say 'pee.'"

She shrugs. "Like I would know."

"Same." I grin, and she grins back. Her cheeks redden even more.

She shifts awkwardly. "Oh yeah." She backs out of the bathroom and closes the door behind her.

Once the door is fully closed, I do my business and brush

my teeth. Then I open the door to let her know the bathroom is hers.

I change into church clothes and go to the kitchen. Adrianne made us some banana bread Friday. I cut a few slices for Grandpa and me to eat and start a pot of coffee.

Grandpa eases past the kitchen and sits in his recliner about the time the coffee is ready. Despite his hearing, vision, and mind going a little, his sense of smell is sharp as ever. Coffee calls him in from a mile away. I should hire him out for Folgers commercials.

The weather report comes on loud and clear, which means he's found the remote. I pour two cups of coffee and carry them to the living room.

"Thank you, boy."

"I've got banana bread too." I go back for the bread slices, then join him.

Grandpa bows his head before taking a huge bite of his bread. "That's some good eating." He swallows. "You lucked out marrying a girl who can bake."

I press my lips together. My new plan is to stay as quiet as possible. Every time I talk, the plot gets thicker. Much more talking, and I'll need the excavator to dig us out of this mess.

We eat in silence and watch the weather. Even though I try and monitor his sugar intake, I debate giving Grandpa another slice of banana bread to keep him from talking.

But I can't drive him into a diabetic coma to cover up my lies. If that's not an episode of *20/20* waiting to happen . . .

I stand and take our plates and my coffee mug to the kitchen. As I refill my mug, heels clack across the wood floor. I turn to red shoes and follow them up to tan legs and a red sundress.

Adrianne smiles. "Good morning, again." Her smile fades quickly, and she points at me.

I stare down just in time to pour coffee over the rim of my mug. I set the pot down and tear off some paper towels. While I wipe the counter, Adrianne comes over and wets a towel.

"This needs cold water so it won't stain." She dabs at my stomach.

I look down and notice a coffee splash on my shirt. "I better go change."

She nods. "I'll have Grandpa ready when you get back."

"Ready?" I assume she means church. "Wait, where are you going?"

"To church with y'all." She smiles.

"You are?"

She shrugs. "I might as well. After all, we are *married* now." She makes air quotes at the word "married."

I raise my eyebrows. "Good point. I'll be right back."

I hurry toward the bedroom, half dreading what kind of stir her showing up with us at early service might cause.

Adrianne yells from behind me, "Lay out that dirty shirt so I can take it to the cleaners tomorrow."

I shake my head. I've never taken anything to the cleaners, but if my *wife* insists . . .

In no time, I'm back in the living room, fresh shirt on. Grandpa is standing beside Adrianne, his cane in one hand and his Bible in the other. She clicks off the TV and sets the remote on the coffee table.

Nobody says a word while we file in his car and head to church. Aside from Grandpa's comments about the weather and how nice Adrianne looks this morning, we're all pretty quiet. I'm too afraid to say something else stupid, and Adrianne looks a little tired. Maybe she slept okay last night. I hope my being nearby didn't bother her.

I'll make a plan for her to sleep elsewhere without Grandpa knowing if need be.

Grandpa perks up when we pull into the parking lot. He gets antsy if we don't get the same spot every time. We have to park two spaces over, but he doesn't say anything.

Instead, he comments how he's glad Adrianne joined us. I help him toward the ramp, and we climb the slight slope to the door.

Everyone at church smiles and greets Adrianne like she's a celebrity. She gets tons of compliments on her looks, as she should. Some people already know her from the salon or milling around the county, and others introduce themselves.

She's wearing Grandma's ring, which is common nowadays. However, we somehow manage to sidestep saying we're married, or even engaged. She uses words like "I'm with JoJo" to not put any definite labels on us. I've come to appreciate her cleverness in these situations.

We find a seat near the middle of the sanctuary. I scan the crowd, which is mainly older people. Most people my age go to the second service, where they play contemporary music. I'd bet Adrianne would like that better, as would I, but Grandpa needs someone to drive him. As long as he's with me, I can manage singing hymnals.

Brother Billy greets everyone and makes a few announcements before we sing a song. Then we all turn to "I'll Fly Away," one of Grandpa's favorites.

I hold a book out in front of Adrianne and me. Grandpa leans against the row of seats in front of us and claps. He has every word committed to heart.

Adrianne smiles at him, then me. I smile back. For all his aggravation, it's good to see him happy and full of life.

The last chorus ends and the piano player hits one more key.

Brother Billy stands again. "Please sit." We all take a seat.

"Before we continue our worship this morning, are there any prayer requests or praises we need to lift up to the Lord?"

Grandpa grabs his cane and eases himself back to standing. I prepare to exit out the side in case he needs to go to the bathroom.

Nope. He stands and raises his hand. Brother Billy smiles and points.

"Brother Joe Culp."

Grandpa reaches over and pats my shoulder. "I have a praise. My grandson JoJo and his lovely girlfriend are now one in Christ, joined together in marriage."

Holy . . . things I shouldn't think in church.

I freeze. Applause rings out all around the church, and I can't move. Can't speak, can't blink, can't even turn to see how Adrianne's handling this.

All I can do is think that in order to unravel this mess, we will now have to get a divorce for our fake marriage.

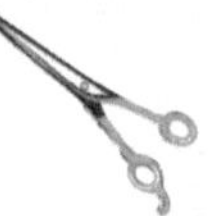

Adrianne

"Good morning!" Misty floats in with dark sunglasses over her eyes.

With her high heels, sequin top, and sunglasses, I'd think she'd come from a club. Except she's married, middle-aged, and it's nine a.m. Then again, it is Misty.

"Morning," I greet her, then return my attention to my client.

Olivia turns her head toward Misty, then tilts it the direction I had it. She makes a concerned face in the mirror before dropping her eyes.

I try not to laugh. She's the dean of the college that sent Misty to help me. Today she's seeing firsthand what I'm dealing with.

I continue trimming Olivia's hair while Misty settles in for the day. By that I mean plops down at the front counter and slurps an Icee from Quick Stop.

"Misty, can you confirm tomorrow's appointments, please?"

She removes her glasses for the first time, revealing eyelashes almost the length of my pinky finger. I choke, trying not to laugh, and reach for my water bottle.

"Sure thing, boss babe."

That moniker is all it takes for me to lose my sense of humor. I cut my eyes at Misty.

"Adrianne," Misty corrects, batting her eyelashes.

I nod my approval and finish Olivia's style. She turns her head to the side and smiles in the mirror. I fluff her hair once more, then remove the smock.

"You're good to go, Olivia."

She stands and retrieves her purse from beside the chair. "Thanks as always."

"You're welcome. Misty can set you up with another appointment." I smirk.

Olivia smiles back at me. "My apologies."

"Not necessary," I say before glancing at Misty.

She's actually on the salon phone, which I hope means she's making client calls. Olivia and I walk toward her.

"Dr. Carter." Misty grins at her, batting her eyelashes.

"Misty, good to see you. How do you like working here?"

"Oh, Adrianne's a peach," she answers.

"Hello?" a voice calls through the receiver on the phone.

"Oh." Misty fumbles the phone, then holds it to her ear.

"I've got it, Misty." I smile and take the phone so she can help Olivia.

"Hello?" Ms. Dot yells from the other side of the phone. I hold it a few inches from my head. She continues to speak loudly and clearly about her appointment tomorrow. I talk with her a few minutes to confirm that she'll be here on time.

I'm almost off the phone when the front door opens and

a goat walks in. This goat has a collar, which can only mean one thing . . .

"Daisy."

She waves to us as the goat saunters over. It sniffs Olivia's purse.

Olivia holds it closer to her side. "Oh, it must smell my gum." She laughs and makes a comment about needing to get back to the office ASAP.

Between Misty and the goat, I'm certain she's ready to get back to work.

Olivia says her goodbyes and hurries to the door. I frown at the goat. The only one I know by name is Mullet. There's so darn many. I'll have to scold its mama instead.

"Daisy, get that goat out of here!"

"It wandered in. I told her to wait in the car."

I pinch the bridge of my nose, then give her a stern look. "Why did you have it in the car?"

"I'm on my way to the vet, and I needed to ask you something."

"Okay?"

The goat raises its tail and starts to squat. I grab it by the collar and pull it toward the back door. A puddle streams around my feet before I can open the door. I groan, open the door, and shove the goat outside.

Daisy rushes to me. "You can't leave her alone. She's just a baby."

"You left it in the car."

She twists her mouth as if that never occurred to her. "But that was in the car."

I shake my head, then turn toward the front. "Misty, can you babysit a goat for a minute?"

"I'd love to!" She jumps up and laughs giddily.

I shrug at Daisy. "There you go."

"Do you think she can watch her?" Daisy whispers.

"She has like five or six kids."

Daisy hugs the goat close until Misty arrives. "Guard her with your life," she instructs through gritted teeth.

Misty salutes her and takes the goat by the collar. They shuffle across the gravel lot, Misty bent over, wobbling in her heels.

"My car is out front with the windows down," Daisy calls out. She cranes her neck to make sure they find it, then comes fully inside.

I shut the door behind us and cross my arms. "Now that that's settled."

Daisy scrunches her nose. "What was on Misty's eyes?"

"I haven't asked, but my guess is she tried to give herself fake eyelashes."

"How many times?"

I laugh. "Good question." I sit in a dryer chair and pat the one next to it. "Now, what's your question?"

Daisy sits beside me. "This is going to sound like total gossip, which is why I had to ask you in person."

I circle my hand to spur her to get to the point.

"Anyway." She sucks in a breath, and her eyes widen. "I went by Piggly Wiggly, and Morgan told me that Brooke told her that she did an X-ray on someone this morning who said she heard from her cleaning lady who heard from her grandma who heard from her sister who goes to Wisteria Worship Center first service that you got married to JoJo."

I half listened through the Apple Cart County roll call, but when I heard Wisteria Worship Center, my ears perked. Sure enough, the rumor is out. Big time.

"Wow."

"Wow?" Daisy leans over and stares at me.

"Yeah, we were there like maybe twenty-six hours ago, tops. And that many people are talking about it already?"

Daisy balks. "Are you wanting people to go around saying you're married?"

I run my right hand over my left knuckles, which are free of rings for now. "No, but that is the newest rumor."

Daisy sits back and sighs. "So it is a rumor?"

"Well, yeah, for now."

She snaps her head toward me. "What does that mean?"

I lift then lower one shoulder. "I don't know. Just the more I'm with JoJo, the more I wonder what it might be like to really be with him."

"That's understandable. But marry him? We barely know him. He's this elusive, grumpy older guy who lives the next town over."

I cross my arms, suddenly offended that my best friend would dis my fake husband. "What about Friday night?"

"Y'all seemed good together, but he's very unsociable."

"So you don't like him?"

"I never said that. He's just kind of grumpy and quiet."

"He's actually not when you get to know him. He even has a good sense of humor."

Daisy half smiles. "You really like him, don't you?"

I stare at my lap and let that question sink in. When I'm not working or checking on the house, I've spent all my time and energy faking it with JoJo. I've suspected true feelings cropping up, but always beat those back down. Why?

Why should I have to hide how I anticipated—and enjoyed—our forced kiss to appease Grandpa? Or ignore how JoJo only seems to joke with me? Or pretend I'm not physically attracted to him?

I lift my head and half smile. "Yeah, I do like him."

Daisy laughs. "I can't believe you're falling for your fake husband."

"Me neither."

She smiles. "But I'm happy for you, and I'm relieved to know you didn't elope without telling me."

"Never."

She smiles wider. "So why the marriage rumor now?"

"JoJo joked with Grandpa that we eloped, and he took us seriously."

Daisy covers her mouth and cackles.

"Apparently, JoJo doesn't joke much."

"I'll say! You're in a pickle now."

I grip her knee. "Look at me, Daisy." Once I have her full attention, I say, "Nobody can know about this. Divorce is a big deal around here—fake or not. You've got to keep it between us that it's fake."

Daisy blinks. "How long are you going to play this out?"

I sigh and drop my hand. "Until we find some sort of loophole with their family lawyer. It will be easier to say it's all fake then and break apart."

"Is that what you want?" Daisy's almond eyes bore through me.

I swallow, forced to honestly ask myself that question for the first time.

After a long pause, I say, "I'm not sure what I want."

"Do you want him?"

My ears burn like they're letting out steam from my racing mind. *Do I want him?* I swallow again as a montage of all our interactions play in my mind like a highlight reel. If this were a movie, it would be set to some cheesy love song. If it were a Facebook album, there would be heart-smiley emojis in the title. I think I have my answer.

"I do."

Daisy's heart-shaped lips curve at the corners. "Does he know that?"

I laugh and pick at a seam on my shirt nervously. "I'm not even sure I knew that until five minutes ago."

"Now that you know, what are you going to do about it?"

I stare at my friend, mulling over all the possibilities. Do I tell him how I feel? Do I ask how he feels? And if he feels the same, where do we go from here? Do we start real dating while we're fake married? That's strange.

Daisy is staring at me for a response when Misty bursts through the front door. Her top is missing some sequins and hanging from one shoulder. Her hair is tousled, and some eyelashes appear to be missing.

Although the latter is probably for the best, she's a hot mess.

"Daisy." Her voice is breathy and frazzled to match her appearance. "You've got to get this goat."

Daisy hops up and hurries toward the door. She pauses halfway and turns to me. "We'll continue this conversation later."

I lift my chin, not ready to nod in agreement to that. The only person I need to have this conversation with is JoJo, and I need to sort some things out before that.

JoJo

"N-twenty-seven. N-twenty-seven," Brother Billy calls into the microphone.

I double check Grandpa's card and mine, while Adrianne checks hers. Grandpa's usual ride to Thursday night church bingo is home with a cold. Instead of rushing to find someone to drive out to get him, I decided to drive him. He insisted Adrianne ride along. Little did I know he'd also insist on us staying.

We could be eating at Waffle House right now while we wait on Grandpa to finish. But because Adrianne can't seem to tell him "no," we're in the church gym eating old women potluck food and marking bingo cards.

"I-sixty-five."

I put a dot on my square, then check Grandpa's. Adrianne isn't marking hers either.

"Looks like I'm the only one with an interstate square."

Adrianne laughs, and I smile at her. Finally, someone gets my dry sense of humor.

Some of the older ladies come around with plates of brownies and cookies, offering them to everyone. I take a brownie, and so does Adrianne. I get Grandpa a cookie, since he's had a lot of delicacies tonight.

He slinks his arm around me and snatches a brownie. When I open my mouth to protest, he snaps, "Boy, when you're my age, you've earned the right to eat what you want. If not eating that brownie adds fifteen minutes to my life, who cares?"

He's spent at least fifteen minutes this month giving me that same excuse. I reach for his cookie to put it back.

He slaps my hand. "Did you not hear what I just said?" He smiles at the lady holding one of the plates. "Thanks, Genene. I'll keep both."

She nods and smiles, then puts her free hand on my shoulder. I shudder a bit, as I don't really know her or care for her touching me.

"Congratulations! Where did you two get married?"

"The courthouse," Adrianne offers before I can think.

Genene's face drops. "You didn't have a wedding?"

Adrianne shakes her head. "I help with so many weddings, I'm over it all."

"Awwww." Genene finally releases her grip on me.

She sets the plate of brownies in front of Grandpa and wraps her arms around Adrianne. I slide the plate toward me as Grandpa eases his hand toward another brownie. He pouts and bites into his cookie.

Adrianne's eyes bug as Genene gives her a squeeze before releasing her. "You should have a wedding. You're so beautiful!"

"Thanks?" Adrianne glares at me in a silent cry for help.

I bet she's regretting coming to bingo night about now. I tried to convince her Waffle House was a step up from this.

"We can plan your wedding if that's all it is," Genene offers.

A lump gulps down Adrianne's thin throat. "No, really. I'm very busy with my house and business."

"Really, it's no trouble. Y'all could get married here at the church."

Adrianne's eyes are like a cartoon cat's staring into a fish tank—wide and nervous as she plots her next move. I've got to save her. "We're already married, Genene."

"Yes, but that doesn't mean you can't have a wedding after the fact. People do stuff out of order all the time nowadays. Like have babies before they marry." Genene rolls her eyes disapprovingly.

I bury my head in my hands and attempt to tune her out as she spouts out ways she can decorate the church. Every other sentence, she clarifies that Adrianne won't have to lift a finger to help.

"Genene, we're fine, really. I wouldn't want to have a wedding as if we're not already married." Adrianne says that way more politely than I could have.

She makes eye contact with me, as if realizing she literally lied this time. We're *not* already married. We've had like one very chaste kiss to call Grandpa's bluff, and I don't even know her birthday.

Should I know her birthday by now?

Ugh. I glare at Genene, giving her a look that communicates she can shove her plate of brownies where the sun doesn't shine. She starts to say something that better end in an apology.

But before any words leave her mouth, Grandpa yells, "Bingo!" He holds the edge of the table and stands, waving his card.

Applause breaks out, and someone nearby asks Genene for a brownie. She frowns, realizing her interrogation is over, and picks up the plate. Brother Billy comes by to check Grandpa's card.

He didn't bingo. He marked one wrong square.

The crowd sighs, and Brother Billy tells him, "Better luck next time."

"That's fine," Grandpa announces loud enough for the room to hear. "I best be getting home to take my pills. Thanks for a great night."

Everyone claps as Grandpa shakes Brother Billy's hand and shuffles behind people toward the end of the table. I grab Adrianne's hand, and we follow.

Nobody says a word until we're in Grandpa's car. Adrianne climbs in the back and leans her head against the seat. I glance in the rearview mirror and give her a relieved look. She smiles.

I crank the car and leave the parking lot. When we're turning into the road, Grandpa speaks up.

"I'll let y'all know when I think of a way you can thank me."

I wrinkle my forehead. "Thank you. For what?"

"For lying in church."

My face heats up at the word "lie." For a moment, I

think he's on to us.

"I knew I didn't bingo." Grandpa grins.

I let out a breath and laugh. "Then why did you say you did?"

"To get that crazy woman to leave you kids alone. There's nothing wrong with having a courthouse wedding. Your grandma and I had one, and it was a lot less stress than when your daddy married your mama."

"Really?" Adrianne leans up, interested in his tale.

"Yeah. I got married in dungarees and boots."

She glances in the mirror with a questioning look.

"Blue jeans," I translate.

She nods. "What did Grandma wear?"

Grandpa's face lights up as he recalls in detail the Sunday dress my grandma wore when she married him. For the life of me, I can't comprehend how he can remember every feature on a homemade dress from sixty years ago but has trouble remembering what he ate the day before. Maybe the memory of marrying Grandma is so powerful that even dementia can't touch it.

That's true love.

He continues to tell us about their wedding day all the way home. By the time I pull into the garage, Adrianne is grinning like a possum. I smile at how much she enjoys Grandpa's stories.

I always worry he's boring people with his lengthy tales. The older I get, the more I appreciate stories from my family's past, but I realize it doesn't mean as much to people not in my family.

Adrianne's face is glowing as she helps Grandpa out of the car. If she's faking interest in his stories, then she's a great actress.

She's done an award-winning job of faking interest in me so far. However, I'm beginning to wish she weren't faking it.

CHAPTER SIXTEEN

Adrianne

After an eventful night at bingo, we're in the living room watching *Lonesome Dove* with Grandpa. It's got to be one of the most depressing shows I've watched, but Grandpa's comments help keep me in high spirits.

According to JoJo, Grandpa watches this miniseries at least once a year and knows it by heart. That would make sense, as he normally doesn't like people talking while the TV is on unless it's the weather. Then he's all about open discussion for opinions on rain, crops, and if the weather report lines up with what his *Farmer's Almanac* predicts.

Grandpa dozes off in his recliner sometime before the credits roll.

"Come on, Grandpa." JoJo wakes him up gently.

"What?" Grandpa glances around, then smiles at me before turning to JoJo.

"You fell asleep. Let's get you to bed."

He blinks before closing the legs of his recliner and following JoJo down the hallway.

I tell them good night and head to the master bedroom to change. All of my things are now out of the basement, except for the overflow of clothes.

It took a few days, but JoJo and I have fallen into a routine of sharing the bathroom. We've learned when the other tends to take showers and always knock, not unlike college roommates. I suppose our situation is similar to that.

Except for the part where he's sleeping on the floor, and I'm wearing his grandma's diamond.

I kick off my sandals and gather my pajamas to change. At least now I have access to pajama pants and my own toothbrush.

Not knowing when JoJo will come to bed, I lock the bathroom door behind me. I change into my pajamas and go through my nightly skincare ritual. Then I comb my hair and pull it out of my face.

JoJo isn't there when I finish, so I pull out a new set of eyelashes I've been wanting to try for Ashley. I spread the kit on the bathroom counter and work with the glue and tweezers to try and add the small pieces to the base.

They look pretty good once I finish. I set them on the counter for the glue to cure and put up the remaining lashes. I'll test the other one tomorrow for more practice.

I clean up my workspace, then zip the eyelash kit. That's enough learning for one night. I open the bathroom door to JoJo walking in the bedroom.

"Is Grandpa asleep?"

"Yeah." He goes to the chest of drawers and pulls out some clothes.

Is it weird that I've gotten used to seeing his dirty clothes in the corner of the bathroom? Probably not as weird as me washing his and Grandpa's clothes. They thought I volunteered to help with their laundry out of the kindness of my heart. In reality, I didn't want them seeing my underwear.

It took me a few weeks to stop washing my undies at the salon. The day Quincy came by and noticed lacy bras hanging in the back room was the day I decided Grandpa and JoJo would be less of an embarrassment. From then on, I've washed all my clothes at the house.

JoJo nods toward the bathroom. "You need in there before I change?"

I pull back the covers on the bed and shake my head. "No, I'm done. Thanks."

He nods and goes in the bathroom. I settle under the covers and prop a pillow behind my back. I'm scrolling Pinterest for cool new braids I can use on my younger clients when loud bangs come from the bathroom.

I turn toward the noise, hoping it will stop. It doesn't.

What is going on? Should I check on JoJo? I mean, I want to respect his privacy, but if he's hurt . . .

"Die!" His voice echoes from behind the door.

That's it, I'm going in. I toss my phone on the bed and hit the floor running. Of course, the door is locked. I knock loudly.

"JoJo, are you okay?"

The door swings open in my face. He's shirtless and sweaty, clutching a towel in one hand. He pushes me farther into the bedroom.

"Stay in there where it's safe."

"What is going on?"

He catches a breath, then exhales. "There's some kind of odd spider on the counter. I'm trying to kill it, but it's legs pop back up every time I beat it."

I narrow my eyes and crane my neck to see around him. "I don't see a spider."

He frames his large body in the doorway. "Don't move. It might be on the loose."

I shake my head and stay put. This is a little ridiculous, and probably not the best time to announce that I killed a huge spider in the basement last week.

JoJo turns his head toward the counter. "It's still there." He reaches and grabs a can of hair spray. "Can I use this?"

I shrug. "It's like six dollars a spray, but by all means, this spider sounds deadly."

"Not funny," he says through gritted teeth as he squirts about three days' worth of styling spray toward the spider I never saw.

JoJo grunts, then sprays once more. "Die already!"

"You sound like me bleaching a brunette," I joke.

He turns and sighs. "I was trying to protect you, but if you think you can kill it, be my guest."

He steps aside and fans out his arm for me to enter. I hum the dinner scene song in *Beauty in the Beast* and curtsy before passing him. I take the can from his hand, preparing to beat the spider with the bottom of it.

When I'm in full view of the counter, I bow over and burst out laughing.

"What is so funny?" JoJo steps behind me. "It's still there."

I finally regain my strength to stand from laughing so hard. Then I reach and grab the eyelashes with my fingers. "You mean this?"

He jumps back.

I laugh harder. "Oh, JoJo. You've been trying to kill fake eyelashes."

He wrinkles his forehead. "Eyelashes? Why are they so long and curly, like tarantula legs?"

I giggle one more time. "They're some Ashley wanted.

I'm experimenting with them." I hold them up to my own eye. "What do you think?"

He scrunches his nose. "You look like you work at a gas station."

I laugh again, and this time he joins me. We laugh so hard that I drop the lashes on his bare foot. He hops and kicks them across the tile floor. That makes us laugh harder.

We end up sitting on the floor, both curled over, laughing our heads off. After several minutes, I can barely breathe. I slump against the wall and hold my side. JoJo slides beside me and relaxes his shoulders.

"I can't believe I thought that was a spider."

"Me neither. What a weird night it's been."

He shakes his head. "Sorry about Genene. I hate that kind of crap. It's people like her meddling that make people not want to go to church."

"It's fine. Trust me, I've lived in Apple Cart my whole life, and I own a salon. Small-town meddling is commonplace to me."

JoJo turns to me and frowns. "I know. But just because we're all used to it doesn't make it right. For what it's worth, she likely said all that to make herself feel important. I seriously doubt she would plan us a wedding."

I laugh. "I hope so. The last thing we need is a fake wedding to top it all off."

"But we could get a real cake." He raises his eyebrows.

"We don't have to have a wedding to have cake."

"Can you bake me a cake, then?"

I pinch his arm.

"Ouch." He rubs his bicep. "What was that for?"

I grin. "I'm not your Betty Crocker."

"But you made me banana bread."

"I didn't want the bananas to rot."

"Uh-huh."

I give him a death stare until his face forms a smile. We lock eyes for a minute, and I study his face. I'd give almost anything to read his thoughts right now. His eyes lower to my mouth, then raise back to mine. He leans closer and cups his hand around my face.

My cheek ignites when his fingertips rub across it, then land at the back of my head. He gently moves my head toward his and presses his lips to mine.

Then he kisses me.

Not the quick, awkward kiss we shared to derail Grandpa's suspicions. This is the kiss to end all kisses. The kiss that makes me boycott my man fast like a desperate dieter taking a bite of cookie dough ice cream.

His mouth is cookie dough, and I haven't eaten in a long time.

I kiss him back with no worry as to what this might do to our complicated situation. It can't get any more complicated than it already is, so I may as well enjoy myself, right?

As I'm deciding this is even better than real cookie dough ice cream, or cookie dough, or ice cream—heck, all three— he pulls back. Then he kisses me gently on the forehead and stands.

"Good night."

He grabs his shirt and shorts, then closes the door behind him.

I suck in much needed air and exhale as I melt into a puddle on the bathroom floor. The cool tile stings against my heated skin. I stretch out and breathe slowly as I wait an appropriate amount of time for him to change into his shorts. Then I peel myself from the floor and crack open the door.

Sure enough, he's already wrapped in his bed of covers in the corner of the room. I tiptoe toward him. I really want to ask what made him kiss me like that. Is that weird? Maybe that's why I'm still single?

His back is to me. I step closer, then tense when he snores loudly. I guess I'm not getting any answers tonight.

I hang my head and tiptoe back to the bed. It's probably for the best. Now if only I can manage to fall asleep after that kiss.

JoJo

"Homer, watch that branch." I sigh and shake my head.

Homer ignores me and continues sawing a log, not noticing the attached branch above his head until it falls on his hard hat. He shuts off the saw and steps back.

"Stupid branch."

"I told you to watch out," I yell.

He snarls at the branch now on the ground beside him. I walk toward him and cross my arms. Skeeder laughs.

"Don't you laugh. You do stupid things all the time." After scolding Skeeder, I turn to Homer. "And you should know to be more careful. I don't have time to babysit y'all."

"What crawled up your butt and died?"

I turn around to see who said that. "Excuse me?"

The group of guys behind me clams up and stares at the ground. Nobody fesses up.

"Boss, you are kinda in a mood today," Homer comments.

I prop my hands on my hips and flare my nostrils. "I

don't mean to be." I soften my voice an octave for the next statement. "Just be careful, that's all."

I'm starting toward my machine to load more logs when I hear whispers. I turn toward the group, and everyone stops talking but Skeeder.

"I told y'all it's 'cause he didn't get no honeymoon."

"What's that, Skeeder?"

He turns to me, and his face goes pale. "Nothing, boss."

"Well, it's not lunchtime yet, so get back to work." Apparently, playing nice doesn't work with this bunch.

Skeeder nods. I turn and walk a few more steps, then stop. I twist my head and call loud enough to get everyone's attention. "From now on, whatever you think or hear about me and my wife, keep it to yourself. And by yourself, I mean just you, not your little gossip group. My personal life is none of your business and should have nothing to do with us working in these woods. Is that clear?"

Nods and yeses come from everyone. I nod, then look directly at Skeeder. "We clear?"

"Yes, boss man."

"Good." I climb in the cab of my machine and resume my work.

Who would've thought a group of roughneck men would be as bad as a bunch of middle-aged church women? Change their appearance and clean up their language, and it would be hard to tell the difference.

I swear, is there anyone in this community who doesn't have an opinion on my love life?

I sigh and turn music on my headphones. I need something other than silence to fill my mind while I work. Otherwise, Adrianne will fill it. As she does again when a familiar song comes on.

Great.

The guys are right. I am extra ill today. Even worse, they're not entirely wrong in my reason for acting like this.

We didn't have a honeymoon, but that's because we didn't have a wedding, which means we don't have a marriage. Every night, I roll up blankets and stretch across the hard floor in my own bedroom. Meanwhile, the most wonderful woman I've ever met is a few feet away in my bed.

Talk about torture.

Many nights, I've held back from crossing the room and lying beside her. Not to do anything other than hug her and kiss her good night. But I don't want to come off as a pervert or lead her to believe I'm after something else.

I finally gave in a little and kissed her in the bathroom like I've wanted to for so long. Well, not that I've dreamed of kissing her in the bathroom, but at this point, I'll take what I can get.

I pull levers to lift the log in the claw and spin it to fit inside the rack attached to the eighteen-wheeler. Then I glance back to make sure my crew is still being safe while they get their job done sawing limbs and getting the logs to the pile.

They're good . . . for now. That means I can go back to daydreaming about Adrianne, for better or worse.

A few days have passed since I kissed her. That's all I've wanted to do every night since, but I've held back. I'm a naturally intimidating person, and the last thing I want to do is pressure her into a relationship with me.

I've already convinced the woman to be my fake fiancée, then threw her under the bus by declaring us married. Any future decisions should be entirely up to her.

Besides, what would happen if I find out she doesn't want to kiss me again?

It's not like I'm going to kick her out before her house is ready. The woman has been through enough. And we can't go back to her living in the basement with Grandpa sniffing around. I've already got Angela working overtime trying to find us a way out of this mess.

The least I can do is not trap Adrianne in an unwanted relationship. Even if a real relationship with her is the only thing I want right now.

Well, that and for Grandpa to wise up to how ridiculous his document is.

I load another log and clear my throat. *Trapped?*

Adrianne is such a kind, cheerful person. She'd never admit to feeling trapped with us. What if I gave her a break for a while?

Shoot, I could use a break myself. Between work and Grandpa's controlling nature over my life, I just need to get away for a while.

Maybe some time away would do us both good to really clear our heads. That's it. We need to get out of Apple Cart County for a while and figure out what we really want.

JoJo

Adrianne's car pulls up a little before dark. She'd gone to Daisy's house for the afternoon.

I'd been in the shop all day with Daddy until he left about an hour ago with Grandpa. They went to visit some cousin who lives a few towns over. One of those family members who I see periodically and act like I know so Mama won't get offended.

What is it with Southern women assuming we remember everyone we're kin to? They say stuff like, "You know her, she was there when you were born." Sure, that really rings a bell thirty-four years later.

With Grandpa out for a while, it's the perfect opportunity to surprise Adrianne.

I grab a rag and wipe the grease from my hands as she climbs out of her car. She notices me when I make it to the opening of the garage. A smile stretches across her face, and she walks toward me. We meet halfway between the house and the shop.

"How was goat yoga?"

She rolls her eyes. "I didn't participate."

I frown. "I thought that's what y'all were doing."

"Hannah, Ashley, and Daisy did it. I did normal yoga, no goats."

"What's the difference?"

She giggles. "One is with goats and one isn't."

"Well, yeah, but did you go in a room without goats?"

"Yes. I refuse to have animals standing on top of me while I'm bowed over with my butt in the air."

I widen my eyes. "I don't blame you."

She laughs. "Have you been working all afternoon?"

I nod toward the shop. "Pretty much. Daddy was here earlier, then left to take Grandpa somewhere."

"How long are they gone?"

"They should be back at a decent hour."

"Want me to cook us something to eat?"

I smile. "That would be nice."

Adrianne twists her lips. Every time she does that, I want to untwist them—using my own lips. But I don't.

This next week will prove if she really wants to be with me or not. I need to play it cool until then.

"When will you be done working?"

"Whenever you need me to be."

She smiles. "Give me an hour, and we can eat."

"Good deal." I smile and head back to the shop to finish my tasks.

I need to make sure the trucks are the way I want them before I leave tomorrow. Daddy gets to unretire from running the crews this week, which I'm sure some of the guys will like. Most who worked for him are long gone, but everyone enjoys it when he comes out with us.

For the last several years, he's mainly handled the truck schedules and assisted Mama with keeping the books for us. That helps him tend to Grandpa during the day for doctor's visits and such, plus gives him a bit of a physical break.

Logging is hard work. Luckily, I've learned from Grandpa's and Daddy's aches and pains to take precautions. That's why I wear ear protection and get monthly massages. I may be destined to become an ornery old man like Grandpa, but I don't want to be half-deaf and stooped over when I get there.

I work a little longer until I'm satisfied with leaving the trucks. I'd hate to leave a potential burden on Daddy. With him taking my place, Mama will need to help with Grandpa during the day. Then one of them will need to spend the night at the house with him.

And now I'm realizing why I never go anywhere.

Not that I'm complaining. Oddly, I thrive on responsibility and work.

That's why I planned to go to Texas this week and check out a sawmill owned by a buddy I met at an equipment sale. For several years, I've wanted to start our own sawmill. Both for convenience and for more revenue. It would cut our costs, plus add more money for us and jobs for the area.

I turn off my radio and lights, then shut the shop door. The sun starts to set low in the trees as I walk to the house. Delicious smells hit me when I open the front door. My stomach growls as I pass the kitchen.

I continue to my room and take a quick shower. I'm sure Adrianne doesn't want to smell or see my grease while we eat.

Once I'm wearing a clean change of clothes, I walk toward the kitchen in my sock feet. Adrianne stands in front of the oven with mitts on her hands.

"Perfect timing."

My nose agrees it's perfect timing when she pulls a pan of

lasagna from the oven. She sets it beside a pan of garlic bread and pulls some plates from the cabinet.

"I made enough in case Grandpa gets back hungry."

"That's sweet of you." I don't have the heart to tell her there's no way I'm letting him eat something like that this late. He'd be up all night.

"If he's already eaten, we can have leftovers for his lunch."

I fix a plate and grab two glasses while Adrianne fixes her plate. "What do you want to drink?"

"Water is good."

I pour our cups and take them to the table, then return for my plate. She already has it in her hand, so I get us forks. We walk to the table and she sits across from me as always. She smiles as she slides my plate in front of me.

"This looks great, thanks." I stare down at the squares of gooey cheesiness on my plate. My stomach growls, and she laughs.

"You're welcome. I can't believe I haven't cooked this for y'all before."

"Yeah, we've been living off my makeshift meals too long."

"Your food is good too."

"It gets us by, and Grandpa doesn't complain . . . much."

We laugh, and I'd bet she's recalling the time he complained about my bacon. I forgot to rotate it in the oven. One end was chewy and the other was crunchy. Grandpa told me to pick one way and stick to it.

"Maybe we can cook together tomorrow," she offers.

"About tomorrow. I kinda have a surprise."

"Oh?" She perks up, her eyes shining. "What?"

I make a mental note that she enjoys surprises. Just in case this week goes in my favor.

"I have a trip planned."

Her forehead creases. "A trip?"

I nod. "We leave tomorrow morning."

"We?" She coughs, then gulps some water. "Where?"

"It's a surprise."

Her mouth kicks up in the corner, tugging at a smile. Then her face straightens. "Wait, I can't just pick up and leave. I have clients and appointments."

"I know. Already taken care of."

She shakes her head. "If you mean Misty . . ."

"No, never." I chuckle. Pure fear came over her face at the mention of Misty. "Daisy helped me reschedule people for you this week. She's also going to stop by the salon a few times to check for mail and packages while you're gone."

Adrianne sighs, then takes a bite of her lasagna. Her eyes scan the ceiling as she chews. She's thinking.

"Wait, for how long?"

"We'll be back in town late Wednesday, but you don't have any appointments until Friday."

Her mouth plays with a smile, then finally gives in. "Good. I don't like to be gone too long, but one day isn't enough to relax."

"My thoughts exactly."

She eats another bite, and her thinking face returns. She swallows. "So can you at least tell me how to pack? Like what kind of climate and activities?"

"Definitely warm. Hot as here, if not hotter. I'd pack casual and a swimsuit."

Her face lights up. "Sounds relaxing."

"Good. That was my intention."

We eat a few more minutes, then she stares at Grandpa's empty chair. "What about Grandpa?"

"Daddy and Mama are going to stay with him."

"Okay, good."

My heart kicks into overdrive with her concern for my grandpa.

I have a weird life. I work all day, then come home to an eighty-year-old man. If I'm ever to have a shot at a lasting relationship, the woman will have to accept Grandpa along with me. We're a package deal.

Adrianne gets that. I just hope she's good with it long term. This week should let me know for sure.

Adrianne

I'm now standing in the Atlanta airport, still wearing JoJo's grandma's engagement ring, reading what can only be the result of Jack Jackson's grand gesture that won over his wife.

"No weapons, contraband, or taxidermy."

JoJo looks up from his suitcase and smirks. "I always thought Bradley was making that sign up."

I shake my head. "Apparently it's for real."

We laugh a minute, then continue walking. My chest tightens as I anticipate this trip. For the first time, I'll be totally alone with JoJo.

Sure, we've shared a room for a few weeks and enjoyed one great kiss. Not to mention all the little flirty touches to appease the people of Apple Cart County. I've enjoyed it so much, I haven't questioned him about the state of his grandpa's legal documents in about a week. He hasn't brought it up either.

Does that mean he likes being with me too?

He must to plan a trip with just me for several days. Maybe he's thinking of proposing for real? My heart beats against my chest, and I follow him through the airport in a daze.

We're headed toward the terminals when JoJo stops. He slides my suitcase toward me and hands me a ticket. I glance down at it and smile.

"I love Florida."

He beams. "Great, I thought you would. You're going to have the most relaxing time. The condo I booked has all kinds of amenities and is close to shopping centers. Daisy said you love that area."

"I do." My smile fades slightly.

Something is off. He keeps referring to me and not him. Does he plan on sitting in the room the whole time? If the paleness of his legs are any indication, he's not one to lounge by a pool.

But if he booked a trip to the beach because I like it, then that's even more romantic. We walk a little farther to the terminal on my ticket.

He turns to me and his face twitches. Something is off.

He steps closer to me, cups his hands around my arms, and plants a tender kiss on my forehead. Then he steps back and gives me a look women give right before they add, "Bless her heart."

What is going on?

"I want you to enjoy these next few days of rest. You've earned them."

"Thanks?"

He rubs my arm, then drops his hand again. "You deserve a trophy for putting up with Grandpa and me. The least I can do is send you off to a relaxing place for a few days."

Send me off? Why does this sound so fishy?

"You can call if there's an emergency, but I want you to

take some time for yourself. Clear your head and destress before getting back to normal life. You deserve this."

I ball my hands in fists, then release them. The more he talks, the more confused I become. "What do you mean by call if there's an emergency? Won't you be with me?"

JoJo frowns. "No, I'm going to Texas for a few days."

My mouth dries out like I've swallowed a quilt's worth of cotton. I clear my throat several times before finding my voice.

"Texas?"

"Yeah, there's a lumberyard I've been meaning to visit for over a year now. I thought this would be a great time to give us both a break. You know, from everything."

Wow. I'm literally speechless. He gives me the saddest smile ever and cups his hand around my face.

"Take care of yourself. You deserve a break."

I say nothing because I'm still petrified in shock. Instead, I watch him turn and walk toward another terminal . . . en route to Texas.

Shock, hurt, and humiliation wash over me like a tidal wave as I go through the motions of boarding the plane.

On the drive over, he was so excited about this trip. I'd asked for hints, but he kept selling me on the surprise and saying how I deserved a wonderful, relaxing trip.

I agree, I do deserve a wonderful, relaxing trip after this slap in the face. What a way to break it off with someone. Just when I had hope we might really be eloping or at least getting engaged.

Apparently, our definitions of shipping are totally different.

By the time I make it to my seat, my eyes are so teary that everything is in a fog. One blink is all it takes to open the floodgates. I bat my eyes, swiping beneath my bottom lashes. I grab a tissue from my purse and blow my nose.

The poor man who took a seat next to me turns away and opens a book. I turn away as well, thankful for the window seat. That's the only silver lining in this turn of events.

Did I somehow jinx myself by complaining about guys breaking up with me via text?

I'd always said, "If they would just have done it to my face."

Nope. That doesn't make it any better. In fact, it makes it worse. Instead of staring at harsh words across a screen, I stared into his empathetic face while he gave me the boot.

Did he think sending me packing to the beach would somehow ease the pain of not being with him?

All I've wanted this past month was to be with him.

I don't care if he lives with his grandpa. Taking care of his grandpa is part of why I love him.

Love?

Even though I didn't say it, I slap my hands over my mouth. My lips tingle at the thought of even saying it.

Do I love him?

I use that word a lot to overemphasize things. I love my career. I love my new Marc Jacobs tote. I love tacos.

Perhaps thinking I love JoJo is another extension of this mindset. He's totally cool enough to rank beside designer handbags and Mexican food.

Or . . .

Is he on the level with my family and friends?

Possibly. He's been like my family for the past few weeks, and we're definitely friends now.

Friends with benefits.

I shake my head to try and shake that thought. It's not like we're glued together all the time. Most of our interactions are for show. We've shared one really intimate kiss alone. Even that was in the bathroom, and then he went to sleep on the floor immediately afterward.

Hmmm . . .

Did that kiss mean so little to him that he could brush it off as nothing and fall asleep? Is that even possible?

I've replayed that kiss in my mind at least a dozen times since it happened. It had such an effect on me that I contemplated sleeping on the floor myself after he turned my muscles to mush. He ignited my entire body with electricity, then ripped my power cord out of the wall when he left.

Ever since that kiss, I've longed for more. It's as if I know what I'm missing. I've seen the light and have walked around in a dimly lit fog ever since.

Today I've seen the light in an entirely different way. In the sense that he doesn't care about me the way I do him.

JoJo likes me. Otherwise, he wouldn't smile and joke around me, and he sure wouldn't allow me to stay in his room or pretend to marry me. But he can't love me.

Nobody books separate vacations for himself and the woman he loves.

It might've all started as a relationship of convenience to cleanse me from men and keep his grandpa happy while we figured out a loophole.

But there is no loophole when love is involved. Someone always gets hurt.

I'd naively assumed it would be Grandpa once we tired of the charade and had to come clean. Or maybe JoJo would mourn the loss of taking part ownership on his terms.

Instead, I'm the one hurt. The man I love—and possibly may be *in love* with—is flying to the other side of the country, and I'm stuck wearing his ring.

CHAPTER EIGHTEEN

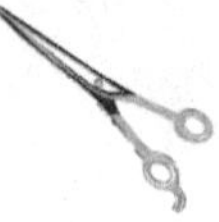

JoJo

Did I make a mistake?

I've asked myself that several times on the flight here and as I tossed in my hotel bed last night.

Adrianne didn't act as excited about the beach as I had hoped. Maybe I should've sent Daisy with her. It wouldn't have cost much more for an extra plane ticket. She's much more social than me. She probably would've preferred a travel buddy.

I sigh and climb out of my Uber ride. If my friend Jimmy hadn't warned me the shooting range was off the beaten path, I'd swear the Uber driver kidnapped me.

A large metal building is the only thing for miles in this desert area. The sun beats on my back as I walk toward it and squint at the cloudless sky. Is that a buzzard overhead? Not a good sign.

The sign I choose to focus on is the one over the door. It

directs me where to go. I'm halfway to the front desk area when Jimmy meets me.

"Hey, JoJo." He extends a hand.

I shake it. "Hey, Jimmy. Good to see you again."

"Same, glad you could make it." He smiles, highlighting the creases in the corners of his eyes.

We met last year at a huge equipment auction. The more I heard him talk about his lumberyard, the more it fed my idea to start one in Wisteria. He'd mentioned several times before the end of the auction how I needed to come to Texas and tour his facilities.

Being the workaholic guy with no hobbies that I am, that's exactly what I decided to do when I took some time off.

"Jimmy Dean, your lanes are ready," a woman calls from the desk area.

Yep, his full name is Jimmy Dean like the sausage. It would be laughable if I didn't admire him so much. He's essentially who I aspire to be in my fifties.

He's worked with timber his entire life in some form and made a comfortable living right where he's always lived. He's also a good family man, always talking up his wife and kids.

Wife and kids.

My mind drifts to that part of the equation. Whether I will find success in that area of life one day is TBA. It all hinges on if Adrianne decides she is better off away from me.

"JoJo, you got your ID?"

"Oh yeah." I reach for my wallet to prove my sanity to the people at the gun range.

Jimmy talks to one of the guys behind the counter about ammo while they google me or whatever. Once I get my ID and pistol permit back, we're good to go.

"I brought some guns you're really going to like." Jimmy pulls several cases from the counter.

"Thanks." I follow him toward a door past the lobby. "I would've brought my own, but I've had some friends get in trouble with trying that at our airport."

He nods. "I get it. One more reason I fly private."

Add private jet to the list of reasons Jimmy Dean is my role model.

He leads me down a hallway to a door with a window. Rows of shooting stations are set up inside. Each one has a target at the end.

We enter and find our two stations on the end. Jimmy opens the cases and describes why each gun is his favorite. I choose a revolver first, then put on ear protection and glasses.

It's hard not to laugh at the man closest to us. He's got to be close to Grandpa's age, though he maneuvers himself better. He's wearing a long round of bullets across his chest and a cowboy hat that is made from some kind of reptile skin. Maybe alligator.

Jimmy notices me staring at him and smiles. "There's all kind of characters here. That's why I'm glad they require background checks and credentials."

I nod. The man could easily fit in Apple Cart County. We have plenty of crazy-looking characters who are harmless once you get to know them. Paul and Woody immediately come to mind.

If I can't have my own guns, Jimmy's make a nice backup. He has some rare guns I've always admired, along with common firearms I've shot plenty.

"When we get to the lumberyard, remind me to take you in my house and show you my gun collection."

"Okay."

In between gun facts, Jimmy mixes in lumber business talk. As much as I enjoy shooting—and can use the stress relief right now—I'd rather talk shop.

"My older son is a missionary now in Europe, but the younger one is set to take over the business one day."

I look up after cocking a gun. "Are you planning on retiring soon?"

"No, I'm just speaking for future planning."

I nod and shoot at the paper bullseye hanging from the end of my lane. My stomach pits as I realize the similarities in Jimmy's situation and Grandpa's.

Grandpa wants me to get married so he can ensure I'll have an offspring to continue the company. Of course, I land more on the practical side that getting married still doesn't ensure I'll have a child or that the child will want the business. But I suppose Grandpa at least wants that possibility.

I shoot a few more rounds, half listening to Jimmy's conversation and half focused on Grandpa. Empathy creeps up as I put myself in Grandpa's shoes.

It's not fair or right for him to demand I get married before playing the role I was groomed to play. The role I want in the company. All my life, I've loved logging and everything I learned from him and Daddy. I know the business inside and out, especially when it comes to our own company. That's why I've had such a beef with Grandpa about that stupid stipulation.

Now I'm viewing it from his side of the coin for the first time. The man came from nothing and built a legacy. It's not so much about the money he's made as the company itself. He isn't keeping it from me to be rude. He's looking past my life and wanting to ensure it has a fighting chance of staying in the family.

Worst of all, I've given him false hope by lying to him about Adrianne and me being together. I've perhaps given myself false hope with that too.

For all I know, she's on the beach flirting with some chair rental guy, living her best life without me and Grandpa.

"I'm going to purchase more ammo," I tell Jimmy.

I need to shoot off some frustration.

Adrianne

"Ma'am."

I grab another handful of cheeseballs and stuff them in my mouth. Half of them fall on my face, and some of those roll toward my belly. I dust them to the side and crunch the cheesy Styrofoam like my life depends on it.

It kind of does considering this is the first thing I've eaten since Sunday morning. Two days of no food and a steady cycle of crying and sleeping. I did at least manage to take one shower in that time.

"Ma'am."

Gosh, I wish whoever the chair dude is talking to would answer already.

"Ma'am!"

I wince at the voice now right above my head and pull my sunglasses down. My eyes were puffy as a panda's when I left the room. No doubt, this heat has made them worse.

"Ma'am, I'm going to have to ask you to move."

I prop up on my elbows and dust cheeseballs from my chest. "You don't have to call me ma'am. We're probably the same age."

Beach-chair bum ignores me and continues. "You're blocking the spot for my clients' chairs. This part is reserved for the chair rentals. You'll have to move closer to the water."

I groan and stand. Cheeseballs bounce off me like ping-pong balls as the wind picks up. I readjust my sunglasses, then grab my bucket of cheeseballs, my beach bag, and blanket.

A stream of sand hits the guy in the face when I lift my blanket. The white particles dot his overly tanned skin like chalk on a blackboard.

I shrug. "Sorry."

He frowns.

Taking that as my cue to leave, I scurry across the burning sand to the area I'm allowed to occupy. It's over-crowded by others like me who chose not to rent an over-priced chair and umbrella.

I settle between a family building a huge shark out of sand and an older couple reading. My blanket fits nicely in the space, and unless there's a sudden change in weather, the tide shouldn't come near me.

Before I can get comfy, my phone rings in my bag. I balance the cheeseball bucket in the sand so I don't lose my remaining mourning food, then answer the phone.

"Hello?"

"Hey, how's your trip?"

My heart sinks at Daisy's voice. I didn't check the ID before answering and had hoped to hear JoJo's voice. When I haven't been crying over him shipping me off to Florida—alone—I've been dreaming of him missing me. I should've known better.

"Ugh," is all I manage to speak. I grab more cheeseballs and crunch, not caring if I hurt Daisy's ears. There have been plenty of times her goats have scared me in the background of her calls.

"Tired? Y'all been having a big time?"

I slap my hand to my forehead and lie back on the blan-ket. "There's no y'all here."

She giggles. "Yeah, I didn't take JoJo for much of a beach

person. It was sweet how interested he was in what all you liked."

My nostrils flare, and I grab another handful of cheeseballs. "Did you think to mention how maybe I don't like taking trips alone?"

"Huh?" The other end of the line goes silent except for a goat bleat in the distance.

"Oh, I don't guess he mentioned to you that he was planning this trip for me alone." I pause, then continue when Daisy doesn't answer. I imagine she's as shocked as I was. "Yeah, he planned this big beach trip for me, then ditched me at the airport to go to Texas!"

The kids beside me stare like I'm the scary shark. I mouth a *"sorry"* to their mom, who gives me her best "bless your heart" face.

I lower my voice. "He booked us two separate trips."

Daisy gasps. "Are you serious?"

"As a heart attack."

"Adrianne, I'm so sorry! Had I any idea, I would've told you."

"I know." I pick up a cheeseball and smash it between my fingertips.

Oddly, it lifts my spirits the slightest bit that I can crush something with my bare hand. I ignore the fact that it's a puny puff of cheese and smash another one.

"Do you want me to come get you?"

I stare at the ocean and slump my shoulders. As much as I want to leave, I want to stay on the beach.

"Nah."

"Are you sure?"

Then I remember riding to the airport with JoJo.

"I think this last day at the beach could do me some good, but I would like a new ride home from the airport."

"Done. Just text me the time and place, and I'll be there."

"Okay, thanks, Daisy."

"Anytime."

We say our goodbyes.

I lie back and toss a shirt over my face. Maybe I can keep my mind off JoJo long enough to get a good tan. Then I'll shower and do a little retail therapy my last night here.

Tomorrow, it's back to the real world. And by real, I mean no more faking it with my fake husband.

My body tenses as I realize this means I may have to move in with Daisy temporarily. I doubt JoJo would rent his basement to me after all this. Not that I would do that to poor Grandpa. We've confused him enough as it is.

Starting tomorrow, no more lies. Who cares what Apple Cart County gossipers have to say? It's time I come clean and regain some power over my own life.

The hard part will be convincing myself to no longer believe the lie that JoJo and I could be together.

One step at a time. First, cheeseballs and tanning.

CHAPTER NINETEEN

JoJo

The scent of fresh sawdust and sound of saws buzzing excites me. Yeah, I'm weird, but I'm also in my element.

Jimmy's face lights up like Christmas as he explains the various operations of the mill. I ask a technical question here and there, but mainly take it all in.

Something like this would be huge for Wisteria, and for the county as a whole. My truck drivers sometimes drive two hours to take our logs to a lumberyard. How convenient would it be to have one on the property?

I suck in one last scent of the wood yard before following Jimmy to his truck. We take off our hard hats and climb inside.

"Some of the guys you met will be at dinner, including my son."

I spent the afternoon touring Jimmy's facilities and

meeting many of his employees. At some point, I agreed to dinner at Jimmy's house.

After leaving the lumberyard entrance, we drive about a mile down a gravel road. It turns into pavement. A large brick house sits at the end of the drive.

Jimmy parks in the garage, and we enter through the side door.

"Hello, you must be JoJo. I'm Eliza," a pretty woman Jimmy's age greets me from the kitchen.

"I am, nice to meet you, Eliza."

Jimmy has mentioned so many random facts and stories about his wife that it's like I already know her.

"Why don't you guys have a seat? Jonathan will be here in a minute." She smiles at Jimmy. "He's bringing the new girl."

"Oh." Jimmy winks at me.

Eliza pulls a pan from the oven and frowns. "Don't let him fool you, JoJo. He's as anxious to meet her as I am. We think this one might be serious."

Jimmy laughs and kisses Eliza on the cheek. I follow him out of the kitchen to the living area. We sit on opposite leather sofas, and he volunteers information on his son's love life.

"Jonathan dated a girl all through high school. They went to different colleges, and she broke it off. Broke my boy's heart." Jimmy shakes his head. "He's tough and never let on like he cared much, but I could tell it bothered him. He hasn't said much about another girl until this one."

I nod, not sure how to respond. I don't know Jonathan, nor do I have any opinion or advice on love. My grand plan was to give my fake wife some space and hope it works out for the best. The whole "free a bird, and if it's yours, it will come back" thing. Maybe it will work.

I swallow, suddenly realizing exactly how inexperienced

at love I am. I've dated and had girlfriends, but I've never been in love before. Unless you count Adrianne.

Wait . . . do I love Adrianne?

"Oh hey, son!" Eliza's enthusiastic voice echoes from the kitchen.

I sigh, thankful for the interruption. Whatever Jimmy was saying ran in one ear and out the other while I drowned my worries in Adrianne afterthoughts.

Jimmy stands, as do I. "Ready for supper?"

"Yes, sir."

We go back to the kitchen, where Eliza is talking with a blonde college-aged girl and a man who looks like someone sent Jimmy back in time. Jonathan is the same size and frame as his father. Their faces look the same minus Jimmy's smile lines and slight eye creases. Jonathan has brown hair, which I assume was the color of Jimmy's before it grayed.

It's odd seeing two men look so similar. But I suppose Daddy and I would, too, if I chose to shave my face rather than my head.

My life flashes before me as I imagine one day turning into my dad, then Grandpa. Half my mind is on fixing my plate, while the other half maps out a possible future for myself.

"Emily and I met in our advanced marketing class."

Eliza smiles at her. "Is marketing your major as well?"

"No, ma'am. It's my minor, so it's really random we had that same class." She smiles at Jonathan as she answers Eliza.

Jonathan's eyes scan Emily's face. I sense he's not only admiring her beauty, but something much deeper. For as little as I know about love, I know this because it's the same way I look at Adrianne.

I take a bite of my pork chop and try not to relate everything back to Adrianne. Which is harder than I'd have imagined. She keeps popping up in my mind at odd times.

A woman working behind the counter at the gun range had the same hair as her. We passed a car like hers on the way to the lumber mill. Even the lotion in my hotel room smells like one of those bottles she keeps in our bathroom.

And it's not just objects I see or smell that bring her to mind. Whenever I'm not totally focused on something, she creeps up in the back of my brain.

"Even stranger is that I grew up not far from here, so it's funny how we never met before that class." Emily grins, and Eliza hangs on her every word.

If the middle-aged women of rural Texas are anything like the middle-aged women of rural Alabama, she's mentally planning a wedding and choosing her grandma name. God help that young couple.

This is the time when I usually wipe my brow and send up thanks for being single. But something's off. I'm not glad not to be them. I'm actually a little jealous.

The only thing that saves me from guilt about Grandpa is what Jimmy says about his business.

"You never know how life is going to turn out. I thought all along my oldest would follow in my footsteps. Then he joined the ministry and met a good gal in the mission field." Jimmy smiles at Jonathan. "Jonathan never showed much interest in running the business at all until college."

Jonathan laughs. "My goal used to be to run the saw. I never cared to be the boss until about a year ago."

We all laugh with him for a minute. Then the conversation shifts back to Emily and Jonathan's relationship. I stare at my plate and soak in what Jimmy and Jonathan said about the lumberyard.

Life doesn't go the way you planned. In Grandpa's perfect world, I'd be married with a couple of kids. At least one would be a boy antsy to follow in my footsteps and carry on the family legacy.

In my own version of a perfect world, Grandpa wouldn't deal with PTSD or memory loss. And Grandma would still be alive to comfort him. I'd carry on the business no matter my relationship status and start my own mill.

That's always been the dream. But . . .

For the first time, that isn't all to my story. I want to explore the personal part of my future as much as the career side. I want to build a life with someone.

And the only woman I want to build a life with is Adrianne.

My stomach churns, and it's not from the bountiful home-cooked meal. It's nervous energy barreling in my gut about tomorrow. I'll take an Uber to the airport. Then I'll fly to Atlanta and wait for Adrianne to arrive.

Once I see her face, I'll know once and for all if she wants to build a life with me.

My palms sweat as I bounce my leg anxiously outside the gate. Any minute now, Adrianne will leave her plane. When my hands are so clammy I can't stand it, I wipe them down my jeans. My knee still jiggles like a nervous tick.

I stand and pace in front of the window to work out some of my nerves. Should I come up with something to say when she gets off the plane?

Hey, Adrianne. How was your trip? Too casual.

I missed you. Too forward?

I've never been in this situation before. Maybe I should say "hi," then let her take the lead. She talks a lot more than me anyway.

I pop my knuckles and pace a few more times. Should I buy her flowers?

I crane my neck for a view of the nearest gift shop. People start coming out of the gate. Shoot. No time for that now.

My boots cement to the floor when I try and move closer. I'm frozen in place, scared stupid about how I'll greet her.

This is ridiculous. I've never been so nervous in my entire life. Not in tight football games, not when I first ran the log crew by myself, not when Grandpa had his first nightmare. Not like ever.

I stuff my hands in my pockets to prevent them from shaking. More people exit the plane. I wait impatiently until brown hair pops up over a kid. More people move, then I see Adrianne's face.

And she does not look happy.

Her entire head is red. With any luck, it's from a relaxing few days in the sun. But her eyes are also puffy. That can't be good.

Did she get sick? Have an allergic reaction to seafood? Some people do.

I manage to pick up my feet as she barrels toward me like a bull out of a shoot. Hmm . . . if she's so excited to see me, why is her face all sulky? She must be sick.

I open my mouth to ask her, then shut it when she pops her hand across my jaw. My cheek throbs like I've had a root canal. I massage my jaw and stare at the floor. Colored circles swirl my vision from disorientation and the shock of her slapping me.

After a solid minute, I straighten, still rubbing my jaw. People stare at us, but I couldn't care less. I don't care what they think. I care what she thinks—and it doesn't look good for me.

"You slapped me."

She narrows her eyes, the clearness of them lighting up

like the center of a bonfire. The blue that's even hotter and more deadly than all the yellow and orange flames we try and avoid.

"You left me!"

I button my lips, calculating what I should say next. A wrong word could earn me another slap. I take a half step back before talking this time to place myself out of her arm's length.

"I sent you on a relaxing trip without Grandpa and me. I thought you'd want a break."

She scoffs. "A break? Don't you mean you wanted a break —from me?"

"No." I shake my head furiously, as if that will help convince her of my case. "I never wanted a break from you. But I had to let you go to see if you came back."

Her forehead wrinkles. "Came back? Of course I was coming back. I live and work in Apple Cart."

I sigh. "I meant to me. You know, the whole 'let a bird loose' thing."

She folds her arms and pops her hip like a sassy teenager. "You're making no sense. All I know is you broke up with me."

I glance at the ceiling and recall why I don't do relationships. I'm horrible at talking to women! When I meet her gaze, it's even more deadly than before . . . if that's possible.

"Adrianne, I can't break up with someone who I'm not in a real relationship with."

Her eyes widen and her lips smoosh into a thin line. I lean back, expecting another slap. Instead, she turns her head and marches in the opposite direction.

"Adrianne, wait!" I follow her toward the exit, pleading my case along the way.

"I didn't mean that I wanted it to be fake, but it was." I continue restating this as many ways as I know how.

Finally, she stops and spins on her heels. I hit her bag with my knee trying to stop in time. She smirks at my blunder, and it's the first smile I've seen from her since I left for Texas.

"Adrianne, I wanted to see if you missed me."

She giggles sadly. "Seriously? That was your grand plan? To ship me off for days by myself?"

I scratch my head. "I thought you'd enjoy time alone to think and decide how you feel about me."

Tears prick the corners of her eyes. "JoJo, I don't need time to think about how I feel. I know how I feel. I thought you might feel the same way." She sucks in a breath, and a few tears fall down her cheek.

I want to wipe the tears away, but I'm sure that would earn me another slap.

"I do feel the same way," I whisper from a safe distance.

She stares at me and slowly shakes her head. "If that one kiss we shared meant to you what it meant to me . . ." She sucks in another breath, and her next words come out shaky. "If you loved me, there's no way you could sleep ten feet away every night and not kiss me again."

"Adrianne, believe me. I was trying to be a gentleman. I didn't want you to think I wanted anything more than a kiss."hear

She sniffles. "All I ever wanted was a kiss."

I lean forward, daring to give her the kiss she so deserves. Before I reach her face, she turns, and her ponytail slaps me this time.

I sigh as she marches toward the main doors. After standing like a fool in a movie, watching the love of my life get away, I race after her.

When I catch up to her, she's in the parking lot with Daisy. Adrianne's death glare is nothing compared to her friend's.

She takes Adrianne's bag and leads her to the passenger side of her car. "I'm taking her home."

When Daisy goes to the driver's side, I attempt to open Adrianne's door. She locks it, so I beat on the widow. She turns her head.

Daisy pulls the car forward and I walk beside it, hugging the window best I can. When the car in front of her moves, she speeds up until I can no longer keep the pace without getting run over.

Fine, I deserve that. I probably deserve to get run over as well. I'm an idiot who assumed she needed space. I know nothing about women except that my mom likes flowers and my sister likes gift cards to the makeup store with the orange sign.

But I know enough about Adrianne to know that I love her with all my heart. And thanks to my stupidity, both of our hearts are now broken.

CHAPTER TWENTY

Adrianne

When Daisy pulls into her drive, I perk up like a puppy at the park. I've never been so relieved to be in Apple Cart.

She opens her door, but I sit for a moment. The past week's emotional drain coupled with the long drive home have exhausted me. Daisy pokes her head back in the car.

"I'm sorry, did you need to stop by your place and get anything?"

I frown. "Everything valuable I own is stored at the salon or JoJo's."

"Oh." Her face drops. "I'll arrange to get your stuff back while you're at work."

"Thanks, that would mean a lot."

She nods and shuts the door. I climb out and grab my suitcase from the back. That's one positive to coming straight from the trip. I have several cute outfits and all my toiletries with me.

My suitcase bounces behind me on the gravel. We step closer to the house and the motion light comes on, saving me from rolling my bag over a chicken.

Mullet stands on the front porch, wagging his tiny tail like a dog. He's way more dog—and human—than goat. At least in my limited knowledge of goats, which comes solely from Daisy's kids.

I laugh to myself at the pun on "kids."

"Hey, good to see you're in better spirits," Daisy quips. She smiles and opens the door.

Another goat stares back at us, and my temporary mood lift deflates.

"Scruffy, move, boy." Daisy grabs the goat by the collar and turns to me. "Excuse me. Make yourself at home."

I watch her march Scruffy toward the back door, while Mullet follows like a lost puppy. I roll my bag inside and shut the front door in case any chickens try and wander in as well.

The familiar scent of essential oils wave toward me. Best get used to it, as I'll be here until my own home is ready.

I sit on the wicker furniture and try to get comfortable. As I'm punching the cushion behind me, Daisy walks back with Mullet.

"Hey, I meant to tell you I bought a futon."

"Really?"

"Yeah, it's in the massage room now. You can sleep on it while you're here."

I go to Daisy and smother her in a hug.

"Whoa." She wraps her small arms around me too.

I pull back and grin. "Thank you, Daisy, for everything. Really. You're my best friend."

"Aww." She gives me a quick squeeze. "You're mine too."

Mullet nuzzles her, and she bends toward him, cupping his head in her hands. "Don't be jealous. You're still my number one," she consoles in a baby voice.

I shake my head and go get my bag. Daisy leads me to the spare bedroom and flips on the light. The futon is bigger than I imagined, and it's got to be more comfortable than the wicker mess in the living room or trying to sleep with my head in the massage-table hole.

"Yeah, this will be good." I plop down on it and sigh.

Daisy props against the doorway and pets Mullet. "Yeah, my clients like it too. Some of my bigger and older ones have mentioned sitting on it while they change clothes."

My cheeks clinch as I try not to think of some overweight older guy sitting in this very spot wearing nothing but tighty-whities. I swallow. She's constantly changing sheets on the massage table and wiping it down. I doubt she does so for this.

"Uh, do you have any sheets I can use on this?"

"Yes, that closet is filled with fresh linens."

I sigh, relieved to have a thin barrier between me and the man in my mind's imprint on the cushions. I'll wash these sheets every day personally if I have to.

"You can keep your clothes in my room since I use this room to work."

"That's fine." Anything is fine as long as I'm not sleeping on a rock surface with chubby-man sweat or goat breath in my face.

Too bad my house was deemed unlivable. I could make it there in twenty minutes walking. Less if I drove.

Crud. My car is still at Grandpa Joe's house.

"Daisy, do you think you could arrange for me to get my car back?"

"Yeah, I can drive you there tonight if you want."

"I was hoping maybe without me, if possible."

"Okay. We'll figure something out."

I nod. "Thanks."

"I'm going to start dinner. Just make yourself at home."

I smile as Daisy pushes herself off the door frame and disappears from view. Mullet trots after her, bleating.

Once Mullet is out of sight, I go to the closet in the corner of the room. Scents of lavender and spices hit my nose when I open the door. I suck in the relaxing smells and grab some sheets.

As I'm converting the futon from a couch to a bed, I glance around the massage room. It's peaceful in here as long as a goat doesn't wander in. Not the full basement apartment with a heavenly bed or JoJo's room with an even comfier bed, but it can do until my house is ready.

Eric said the insurance money should be available any day now, which means I can get a new roof. Maybe this is a blessing in disguise, since my house is old.

I pull the sheets over the sides of the cushiony surface and stare at my makeshift bed. Then I lie down, finally able to relax without fear of someone's germs on my back.

This bed is a far cry from any bed at JoJo's house, but that's not why I can't get comfortable. For the past two weeks, I've gotten used to sleeping with him only a few feet away on the floor.

Silly as it sounds, the fact that he was nearby made me feel safe and comforted. I'm not sure why it mattered so much since I've lived by myself for five years now. I've never felt scared in my own home.

Well, except for when a pine tree crashed beside me.

Still, it's like JoJo is a part of me I didn't realize I was missing. Kind of like when I'm doing someone's makeup and I add a little more bronzer to her cheeks. Then her face glows with a vibrancy it didn't have before.

I had a full life before JoJo and didn't need him. But having him in my life made it vibrant.

Unfortunately, I best get used to a life without bronzer.

JoJo

The sun isn't even up when I start a pot of coffee. After the night—make that week—I've had, I should've started it even sooner.

I took my time driving home from the airport, stopping off at Bass Pro Shop, Buc-ee's, and two gas stations to avoid coming home. On some subconscious level, I associated home with real life. As long as I wasn't back in Wisteria, life without Adrianne wasn't reality.

But I have a business and a grandpa at home to tend to. I can't live at Buc-ee's, even if the brisket sandwiches are a nice incentive to try.

By the time I got home, Grandpa was in the bed. Daddy was nodding off in the recliner and ready for bed himself. It was so late that we basically told one another "hi" and "bye" before he went home to sleep.

I may have dodged a conversation there, but eventually he will ask about Adrianne. That talk has been due for a while now, since neither he nor Mama has addressed the marriage.

I suspect one of two things. Either they somehow know it's fake or they don't care because they like Adrianne. Neither knows her on the level Grandpa does, but all their interactions with her have been positive. Of course, they're also used to me doing my own thing and living a very private life. So it wouldn't be totally out of character for me to get married at a courthouse without telling anyone.

The coffee fills the pot, and the kitchen fills with the

scent of morning. I inhale the roast as I pour a mug. It's barely cooled down enough for me to sip when I hear shuffling behind me.

I turn to Grandpa in his slippers, easing toward the kitchen. "Do I smell coffee?"

I glance at the time on the microwave. "You're up early."

"I smelled coffee."

I chuckle and pour an extra mug for him. He eases around the corner and takes it.

We walk to the living room and sit in our respective recliners. I make sure Grandpa is settled with his coffee so it doesn't spill before I let him release his cane.

"Did y'all have a good trip?"

And here it is. The conversation I've avoided for a while. I should've known it would come from Grandpa. Daddy is more reserved like me, and he also treats me like the adult I am with my own life. Grandpa would ask anyone about anything and not blink an eye—especially me.

"I did." I down a gulp of coffee to clear the lump in my throat.

"What about your bride?"

I cough, sending the coffee down the wrong pipe. I drink more to try and correct it. After one more coughing fit, I catch my breath and notice Grandpa staring at me for an answer.

I set my cup on the coffee table and sigh. "Grandpa, there's something I need to tell you."

"What's that?" He sips his coffee and raises his bushy eyebrows in anticipation.

I lean forward and pinch the bridge of my nose. "How do I put this?" I clasp my hands together and face Grandpa. "Adrianne and I never really got married."

"I know."

If I weren't already sitting, I'd fall. "You knew?"

"Yeah." He sips more coffee as casually as if he'd just commented on today's weather.

"Then why go along with the lie? And why force us in the same room?"

He smirks deviously. "I thought y'all could use the extra time away from me to talk things out, and maybe you'd realize you were right for one another. That's why I was happy to see you two kids go on a trip."

I slap my forehead and run a hand down my face. "*We* didn't go on a trip."

"What's that supposed to mean?"

I waver my head. "We both went on a trip, but not together. I went to Texas to see Jimmy Dean's sawmill, and I booked her a stay in Florida."

Grandpa scowls and bats his cane at me. I lean back, and it barely misses my nose.

"Boy, that's the dumbest thing I've ever heard. Why would you take two separate trips?"

I rest my back against the chair. "Yeah, I'm beginning to understand I'm the only one who thought that was a good idea." I sigh. "Somehow I assumed if she were away from me . . ." I hesitate. "And you . . ."

Grandpa nods for me to continue.

"Maybe she could get some clarity on how she really feels about me and our situation. Would she miss me? Would she want us to be in a real relationship?"

"And what happened?"

I wince. "She slapped me when she got back to the airport. Apparently, she took the whole splitting our separate ways thing the wrong way."

Grandpa shakes his head. "Or you did. That's the dumbest idea I've ever heard. You have a good-looking, kind-hearted woman here with you, and you send her away."

I nod. "Yes, we've established I'm an idiot."

Grandpa continues, having more to say on my idiot status. "You were never going to meet a woman in the woods or eating at hole-in-the-wall diners with me. This was your one opportunity, and you blew it."

"You act like she's the last woman on the planet."

"She may be the last one who gets you. You're not that easy to live with."

I glare at Grandpa. "Well, excuse me. You're not exactly a breath of fresh air yourself."

"Boy, you love her. Whether you know it or not, I do. I can tell. Why do you think I told everyone y'all were married when I knew you weren't?"

"To harass me?"

"No." He wields the cane again.

I grab it and set it on the other side of my recliner. "You don't need this to sit in your chair. You can have it back when you stop swatting at me."

"I'm trying to knock some sense into you. I all but served a woman up to you on a silver platter, and you dumped her out in Florida."

"Grandpa, I know, and I have to live with this mistake. If I could undo it, I would. Have you ever done something you regret so badly that it eats you alive?"

His face goes soft. "Hand me my cane."

"So you can beat me? Nope."

He makes a grabbing motion with his hand. "No, I need to go to the office for something."

I narrow my eyes, testing him. I hold out the cane, but lean back in case he's bluffing.

He uses it to stand and starts down the hallway. I relax momentarily, then watch my back in case he changes his mind. Between him and Adrianne, the last twenty-four hours have been brutal.

I finish my coffee and rock in the recliner. It's so early,

I can take a nap before work. Too bad my mind won't shut off. I should probably go out to the site soon anyway.

While I pined over Adrianne yesterday, I came up with another one of my grand plans. This time, I'm ninety-nine percent sure Adrianne will like it.

We finish logging behind her house soon. While we're still there, I have roofers coming in to reroof her house. I made calls in between gas station stops yesterday. She'd mentioned what kind of roof she'd get if the entire thing needs replaced, so I found the materials.

Sometime today, a roofer is coming out to start the work. I've wanted to do this for her ever since the tree incident, but mainly out of guilt. Now I want to do it for her to give her a place to live since she doesn't want to live with me. I'm paying enough to have them repair it as soon as possible and hope to surprise her soon.

She may hate me now, but I want to do one last gesture to prove I'm not a total goob.

A mental checklist of everything I need to discuss with the roof contractor is running through my mind when Grandpa interrupts.

"Boy, this is for you."

He's behind me holding out a folded piece of paper. I take it and wrinkle my forehead as I turn it in my hand.

"Unfold it and read it," he demands as he sits in his recliner.

I do as I'm told and spot Angela's logo at the top. It's a letter drafted by her in legalese that basically states Grandpa is reversing his previous letter and signing his shares of the company over to me.

My hand goes numb. I slowly turn to him. "Is this a joke?"

He shakes his head. "Nope. You inherit your idiot ideas

from me. I've finally realized that you run things well and deserve the power to make decisions."

"But what about the marriage thing? You don't care anymore?"

Grandpa clasps his hands together. "I wanted you to get married for selfish reasons. I wanted more offspring to see my company stay in the family. What I should want is for you to be happy with someone like I was my Silvia."

I nod. "Thank you. That's what I want too."

He shrugs. "I thought you'd finally found it with Adrianne. That's why I kept pushing you two together."

"I thought so too." I rub my beard and sigh.

"If I can give some words of wisdom."

I smirk. "You always speak freely, please don't hold back now."

Grandpa chuckles, then his face goes serious. "Don't give up on her. You're a hard worker, and you fight for what matters. You fought for the company, and you fight to help me every day. Fight for her, boy."

I fold the paper and rest it on my knee. Then I rock slowly and let Grandpa's words of wisdom sink in. I want to fight for her so badly, but right now it's a losing battle.

Instead of fighting to win her back, I'll fight to make it up to her.

I stand. "I'm going to fix you some breakfast, then head to work."

Grandpa laughs. "This early? I know we're loggers, but aren't you just logging in Apple Cart right now?"

"Yeah, but I've got some more things to do today."

Like fight for Adrianne's happiness.

CHAPTER TWENTY-ONE

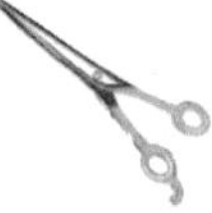

Adrianne

The last time I dreaded going to work this badly was when I agreed to come in on a Saturday and do pageant hair for ten girls under eight. I haven't opened on a Saturday since.

This time, I dread work for an entirely different reason.

I'm coming off a trip most of Apple Cart assumes was my honeymoon. Heck, I assumed it could be for a hot minute too.

Instead, I have to either lie more and dig a deeper hole or fess up to the fact that we went on separate trips and are no longer together. Which, by the way, means a divorce to all the folks currently believing we're married.

There aren't enough "bless her hearts" in the county to cover that dysfunction.

I unlock the door to the salon and step inside. It's quiet and warm from nobody entering in a few days. I crank up the AC before plugging in all the appliances that will add even more heat.

Today will be busy to make up for being gone. That can be great or horrible. Great in the sense that busyness will keep my mind off things. Horrible if the clients decide to ask about my trip, not only activating my thoughts, but making me speak on them.

I huff and go to the counter to check my book. Carolina is first. Relief washes over me when I see her name. Most Fridays are filled with older ladies getting their hair "set" for Sunday. Some of them moved to other salons when I moved to no Saturday appointments, but several are still on my books.

The front door opens, and Carolina sticks her head inside. "Morning."

"Hey, girl. Come on in." I grab a smock from a drawer at my station and hand it to her.

She buttons it around her and sits down.

I stand behind her and smooth my apron. "What were you thinking?"

She holds her shoulder-length hair behind her head. "Maybe like an updo, but not so formal."

I nod. "What does your dress look like?"

Carolina beams as she pulls out her phone. She scrolls to a photo and hands it to me.

I put a hand over my beating heart. "Oh, Carolina. That is breathtaking on you."

"Thanks." She blushes. "Now I've got to delete it before Jonah sees it."

I frown. "Text it to me first in case I want to refer back."

"Okay, but I'm cropping my head off first."

I laugh. "Whatever you need to do."

My phone pings, and I save the photo. I zoom in to get a better view of the neckline.

"Do you know what kind of jewelry you'll be wearing?"

"Not a necklace since it has a bit of a collar. Earrings—probably pearls."

"Studs or dangly?"

"Studs."

"Okay, that helps." I take her hair in my hands and play with positioning it behind her head.

A high ponytail-like updo with curls cascading down would look beautiful. Yep, that's what I'll do.

"Great. I'll start curling you before we do your makeup."

"Sounds good." She claps her hands. "I'm excited."

"You should be. After all these weddings, you get your own fairy tale."

She laughs. "I guess. It's getting stressful. You're smart for eloping."

I pause from combing a section of her hair. I'm not good at hiding guilt, and I'm sure my face says it all.

"What's wrong?" Carolina's teeth clinch as she looks at me from the mirror.

I sigh and resume sectioning off hair to roll. "Well, it will get out soon enough, so you may as well hear it straight from the horse's mouth." I take a deep breath before describing how one thing led to another, eventually leading to the separate trips.

Carolina's face morphs into a dozen different expressions as she listens intently to my story. When I finally finish, she's wide-eyed, with her whole hair in curlers.

"Adrianne, I never would've—I mean y'all seemed so real." She puts her hands on the sides of her head, then snatches them away when they touch the hot curlers. "This is like déjà vu from Hannah and Tanner."

"Not really. They actually did elope." I click my tongue. "They did for real, right?"

Carolina laughs. "Totally. I was the witness for that."

I nod. "Glad it worked out for somebody."

I start dismantling my makeup case on the countertop of my station. Carolina squirms in the chair to get comfortable.

"Now wait a minute. I called bull on Tanner fake liking Hannah, and I call bull on JoJo too."

I roll my eyes and beat a bottle of makeup primer against my palm before I squeeze it out. "You can't compare the two. Tanner is your brother. You barely know JoJo."

"True." Carolina winks. "But I know love when I see it."

A crash comes from the front of the salon, and I almost smear foundation across Carolina's neck as we both turn. Misty stands near the counter staring at us, with a potted plant broken at her feet.

"I'll clean that up," she mutters.

She passes by us for the broom. I glance at the plant, then back at her.

"Wait, when did you come in?"

She shrugs. "About twenty minutes ago."

"Why didn't you say something?"

Misty props against the broom and sighs. "Your story was so impactful, I wanted to hear it all without interrupting."

I want to correct her by saying she means eavesdropping. Instead, what comes out of my mouth is, "What's with the plant?"

"Oh." Misty perks up. "A gift from Woody. I was going to bring it here and let it sit in the sun. Then my arms got tired, and I dropped it."

I half smile. "Why don't you get a large color-mixing bowl from the back? You can sweep the plant and dirt into it until you get a new pot."

"Thanks."

Misty cleans up her mess while humming a Dolly Parton tune. When I recognize it as "Here You Come Again," it makes me think of JoJo. I want to throw a makeup brush, but that would do nothing except smear bronzer across my mirror.

"You okay?" Carolina asks when she stares up at me so I can apply her mascara.

"Yeah." I shake my head. "I don't know." I puff out my cheeks and finish the eye I'm on, then take a step back.

"If I may?" Misty returns with the flower in a color bowl, holding it by the handle.

I want to throw the mascara wand at her. It would be worth the mess. Maybe it's jet lag from my trip to hell—I mean Florida—or lack of sleep from last night's futon, but I don't say a word of rebuttal. I actually listen to Misty.

"I'm the only one in here who's been married. And I've been married several times." She drawls out the word "several" and laughs.

Carolina laughs with her.

"My point is I may not be the best for advice, but I've had enough husbands to tell when I've got a good one. Woody is a good man." She points a red nail at Carolina. "Jonah is a good man."

Carolina grins.

"And JoJo is a good man," Misty adds.

I open my mouth to say she doesn't know him, but she holds up a hand to shush me.

"Before you say I don't know him, I know him through you. You're a cheerful person, Adrianne, but there's been something extra peppy since you've been with JoJo. Real or fake, I can tell he's good for you."

I sigh. What kind of twilight zone are we in that I'm taking relationship advice from Misty?

However, she does make a valid point. I lick my lips, then continue applying makeup to Carolina's eyes. When I look up, Misty is frowning at me.

"What?"

"You need to talk to him."

I screw the lid back on the mascara and take a deep breath. "I can't."

Both Misty and Carolina give me sad stares.

"I'm sorry. This whole fiasco proves that I was right to go on a man fast. I need a break from all these emotions. I need to just work and focus on getting my house back in order."

Misty and Carolina exchange a sad smile. Then Misty walks away to put the flower in the sunlight. Carolina changes the subject to the house she and Jonah are renovating for someone.

Everything goes back to normal for a few minutes, and I let out a sigh of relief. Work, small talk, and Misty wasting time. This I can handle.

Pining over JoJo, not so much.

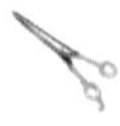

JoJo

The front door opens, and I turn to my older sister walking in. She smiles at me and raises her eyebrows.

"You ate and ran."

"No, I just had some stuff to do here at the house."

She frowns at the TV. "You're watching NASCAR."

"Yeah, well, maybe that was my thing I needed to do."

She walks up to my recliner and knees me in the leg. Then she sits on the couch and stares at me. I observe her from the corner of my eye, waiting on her to leave me alone. She doesn't.

"What?"

"You're avoiding me."

"No, I'm not."

"Then why did you eat and run?"

I roll my eyes. "I'm tired, okay?"

I'm also annoyed that she's on to me. Mama rarely cooks big family meals anymore. We're all busy and on different schedules. Whenever Dana comes home from Tennessee, Mama makes a spread. The only thing better than Dana coming in is when she brings her husband and daughters too. Then we get a full-on feast.

"JoJo, talk to me."

I sigh and feign a yawn. "I'm tired."

"So am I. We're all getting old and tired. More reason not to neglect precious time with your favorite sister."

"Only sister," I remind her.

She rubs my head like I'm a puppy. "There's my smart-butt little brother."

I roll my eyes and pop the legs on my recliner. Grandpa moseys in and takes a seat beside me in his. "Why are we watching this? It's stupid."

"It's a big race."

Grandpa huffs and grabs for the remote. "All they do is drive in circles. What kind of racing is that?"

Dana laughs. I release the remote without much of a fight, and Grandpa finds a game show.

"Yes, because this is so much more interesting," I say.

"It's educational," Grandpa argues.

Dana shrugs. "Fair argument."

"Speaking of arguments, what were you kids fussing about a minute ago?"

Dana grins, and I shoot her a look that warns her not to poke the bear. Unfortunately, she jumps at the chance to pit Grandpa against me.

"JoJo's being a sourpuss, Grandpa Joe. He hasn't seen me in two months, and he won't even talk to me."

"Oh, don't mind him. He's been in a mood ever since he lost his woman."

Holy cornbread. He just had to bring up the word "woman." That's music to Dana's ears. She perks up like a squirrel under a pecan tree. "A woman?"

"Yeah. What's her name again? The hair cutting girl in Apple Cart," Grandpa says.

"Adrianne," I remind him through clinched teeth. Saying her name aloud is like a shot to the heart all over again.

"Adrianne?" Dana taps her finger to her mouth.

"You don't know her. She's younger than me, and *much* younger than you," I tell her.

Dana slaps my side and I lean away. I've taken quite the beating these past few days.

"She's a good girl. Pretty and can cook. She even went to church with us until JoJo screwed it up."

Dana hangs on every word from Grandpa's mouth, then turns to me. "You've got to tell me what happened."

I shake my head. "None of your business."

"Then how does Grandpa get to know?"

I stare at the TV and cross my arms. "This whole thing started because of him being stubborn."

"And it ended because JoJo's stubborn." Grandpa frowns at me.

I pout at him, then face the TV. An Asian man is spinning a large colorful wheel. I've never seen this game show before, and it doesn't make much sense. I assume it didn't last long since everyone is dressed like the 1970s.

"It didn't end because of me. It ended because she wanted it to."

"You drove her away," Grandpa counters.

I stand and stretch. "I'm going outside."

They both stare at me as I walk out the door. Sunday is my one off day when I watch TV, or clean my shop, or lately, hang out with Adrianne.

Dana and Grandpa are hogging the room with the big TV and my recliner, and the shop is clean. As for the last option . . . Well, that's not exactly an option anymore.

I sigh and open my truck. When I reach across the seat for my cap, a tube of lipstick rolls out from under it. I pick it up and open the lid.

No question whose it is or where it came from. I stare at the reddish-pink color for a second. Memories of Adrianne running it over her lips whenever we would go somewhere race through my mind. I put the lid back on it and toss it in my glove box.

How many more items like this will I find? How long will her memory plague me and make me regret everything?

Yesterday, two of her friends came by to pick up her car. I hid in the shop when they drove up just so I wouldn't have to watch her car drive away for the last time. How pathetic is that?

I sigh and kick a rock in the driveway. Now I'm standing in the yard, hiding from an old man and my sister.

Enough.

I walk back to the house and swing open the door. Dana and Grandpa are sharing a pack of Oreos, and apparently still discussing my love life.

"Care to join us?" Dana lifts an Oreo.

I buckle my lips but go and sit on the couch, since she's now migrated to my recliner.

"What all did Grandpa tell you?"

She wiggles her eyebrows. "Everything."

"Oh Lord." Of course he would remember the details of my screwup.

Dana smirks. "I'm just happy to know you're in love."

I open my mouth to call bull, but I can't. Because it's not bull. Not even a little. I do love Adrianne.

"She doesn't love me back."

Grandpa frowns. "She did until you screwed it up."

I hold up a hand. "Grandpa, we all know your opinion. I'd love to have Dana's."

Dana arches a brow as she chews a cookie. "Wow, that's a first."

I narrow my eyes at her.

"Okay, I'll be serious. You're stubborn. You need to be honest with her and tell her you love her."

"I tried."

"When?" Dana scratches her head as if thinking. "Let's see, would that be after you lied about y'all eloping, or before you sent her to Florida without you?"

I lean back and grunt. "When she got back to the airport. But she slapped me."

Dana tries to hide a giggle and fails. "Sorry, but I can only imagine what you might've said to her." She clears her throat. "Sarcasm aside, I'm speaking as someone who's been married a while. It's never easy, and avoiding someone after you've messed up isn't going to help."

"And it's not like you can hide from her forever," Grandpa adds.

"I've stayed away from her up until hitting her house with a tree. I don't see why I can't now."

Grandpa shakes his head. "So you're going to go back to hiding in the woods and eating catfish with me like someone on one of those survival shows?"

"It's worked so far."

Dana shakes her head too. "And what happens when Grandpa's gone?"

My ears burn and my throat closes. "Don't talk like that, Dana."

Grandpa stares at me. "She's right, boy. I won't be around forever. You can't just work, eat, and sleep. That's no life."

I stare at my boots. They're right, and I know it. The hard part is admitting that. After a long awkward pause, I look up.

"I love her, and I have no problem admitting that, but she's got to love me back. I can't beg her to love me. It's got to be her decision."

I take the remote from the coffee table and change it back to NASCAR. Then I drop it on the couch beside me like a proverbial mic drop.

This conversation is over.

CHAPTER TWENTY-TWO

Adrianne

I blow a stray strand of hair out of my face and slump my shoulders. Mondays always exhaust me. Why I schedule most of my late appointments then is beyond me.

Oh wait, it's because I think I'll have more energy after taking off Saturday and Sunday. For most of the day, I do. Then somewhere around that six or seven mark, I hit a wall.

Today, my wall was built with about a thousand highlighting foils, which my wrist is currently paying for. I cross the room to lock the front door before I sweep the last piles of hair and call it a night.

When I reach for the lock, the door opens. I flinch and dart my eyes around for the nearest weapon I can grab. A can of hair spray? I could spray it in the thief's eyes.

The door opens wider to a woman about forty with a cute brown bob. Her eyes are kind, and I doubt she plans to harm me or my property.

"Sorry, I'm closed."

"I was hoping you'd say that." She steps across the threshold before I can stop her. "I'm JoJo's sister."

JoJo's sister? I couldn't stop her now if I wanted to. I'm frozen in place like a 1980s prom hairstyle.

She slides past me and closes the door. I'm a little above average height, and she has a few inches on me. Her eyes lower, and she scans me up and down.

A smirk crosses her face. "You're very pretty. I'd love to have been there when my brother walked up on you at the pool." She laughs.

My mouth opens, and I tilt my head. *How did she?*

"I'm sorry, you're Dana, right?"

She nods her head. "Yes, so sorry. Where are my manners?" She extends her hand, and I shake it.

"Adrianne."

"I know." She smiles mischievously. "The one my stupid brother let get away."

I scratch my head at my ponytail and widen my eyes. "More like he pushed me away."

"I know. He's an idiot."

I laugh a little. I like her.

"Could I give you a little background on JoJo that might help you understand?"

I lift then lower one shoulder. She seems to be on my side, so what could it hurt? I swing my arm toward the couch.

"Have a seat."

Dana sits while I lock the door. Then I join her on the other end of the couch. I sigh and raise my eyebrows, signaling her to go ahead.

"JoJo is terrible with women."

I laugh. What a way to start the conversation.

"No, seriously. He's not good with people at all, really."

Dana bites her bottom lip, then continues. "He's rough and introverted and doesn't relate to people well."

I sit back and fold my arms. Dana continues to paint a picture of JoJo that proves maybe he is different around me.

"He started working with Daddy and Grandpa Joe in the summers when he was like ten. Being in the woods with a bunch of old men kind of aged him too early. He's always been a great boss or leader, in football and in work. The problem is he doesn't know how and when to turn off the take-charge, old-man boss tone. That is, until you."

I squirm, unsure of whether to walk away from this conversation or settle in with a bowl of popcorn.

"It doesn't help that he lives with Grandpa Joe. That man is still holding a grudge over losing land in a poker match to Ed Mayberry way before we were born."

So that's why Grandpa doesn't like the Mayberrys.

"As soon as I got here, I could tell something was off with JoJo. He acted almost depressed. Grandpa ratted him out and told me about you. Then JoJo finally fessed up and told me the whole story."

"Including the separate trips," I add.

She nods. "Yes, which I agree was a bonehead move. As he was mainly raised in the woods by old men, it makes a little sense to me." She holds up her thumb and index finger, making the tiniest of spaces between them to indicate just how little sense it makes. "Still, not acceptable."

I sigh and slump back into the couch, wishing I had that popcorn about now.

"I'm not trying to make excuses for my brother. I'm just saying that there's no way he sent you to Florida to get rid of you. He sincerely thought he was giving you time to decide if you really missed him and wanted your relationship to be real." Dana winces. "Honestly, he's that dumb when it comes to women."

I laugh. "I'll say." I stare at my shoes and shift a little before looking back at her. "Does he know you're here?"

She shakes her head. "He's at home sulking."

I roll my eyes. "Of course he is."

"I tried to convince him to tell you everything he told me."

"Thanks, but I already lived it. There's nothing new I need to know."

Dana leans toward me. "Has he told you he loves you?"

My nerves flare. *No, he hasn't.* My silence gives me away.

"That's what I thought. I suspect he was afraid to, and he's afraid to now. As tough as he is, JoJo is a real wuss when it comes to love."

I hear her, but it's muffled. My pulse beats in my ears and my body flares like I'm in an illegal-grade tanning bed. After a minute of staring dazed and confused, I find my voice.

"He literally said he loves me?"

She nods. "Even in front of Grandpa."

I blink. "Wait, what does Grandpa think about all of this?"

She shakes her head. "Apparently, he knew about your ruse the whole time and played along?"

"You're kidding."

"Nope. He was trying to play Cupid."

I twist my mouth and recall the times he told us to kiss or reminded me to wear the ring. Then my anger swells when I remember him throwing us under the bus—or pew—in church by announcing our fake elopement.

"That little—"

Dana laughs. "He's a sneaky one. I have to say that the church announcement was a nice touch."

I shake my head. "What do your parents think about all this?"

I've only met JoJo's mom a time or two and would see his

dad in passing when he worked in the shop. Both were super kind, but had no comments on JoJo's personal life.

"I'm sure they're still convinced the marriage was real."

"I never understood how they were so cool with it."

"They've wanted him to find a good girl for a while. Take it as a compliment that they like you. And for what it's worth, they could see he really loved you too."

I sigh and run my hands over my hair before dropping them in my lap. "So you're saying everyone who knows JoJo best saw a change in him when we started . . . whatever you call what we had."

She nods. "Exactly."

"And he's really in love with me."

"Yep."

"Then why isn't he here telling me?" I throw up my hands, then slap them on my knees.

Dana groans. "That's the hard part. He's dead set on all this being your decision. He doesn't want to sway you in any way." She shrugs. "And I suppose he's a little scared that you won't have a reason to be with him, since your house will be fixed soon, and he's got half the company."

Half the company? My mind backtracks as I try and recall if Angela found something. I stare at the wall and come up blank. "Hold up, he has half the company, even though Grandpa knew our marriage wasn't real?"

Dana nods. "Yep. Grandpa signed it over a week ago. Said he felt bad about hanging marriage over JoJo's head."

I wrinkle my forehead, trying to make sense of it all. "Then why would Grandpa push the stipulation and pretend we're married?"

"Grandpa may be stubborn and have a few marbles loose, rolling around in his memory section, but he's still wise. He fessed up to seeing how JoJo was in love with you. He was trying to play matchmaker long as he could until y'all figured out what he already knew."

"Huh." I take a long breath and let that sink in. "I'm not sure whether I should thank him or get mad."

Dana laughs. "JoJo said the same."

I half smile. Either JoJo and I are more alike than I thought, or sharing a room has made us think similar. Kind of like how college roommates find their periods syncing after a semester together.

Dana stands. "I'm going to get out of your hair." She shakes her foot to dislodge a stray ball of hair caught on the sole of her shoe. "Literally." She smiles.

I stand and walk her to the door. She stops before stepping onto the sidewalk and turns back.

"Will you promise you'll talk to JoJo?"

I suck in a breath and exhale slowly. "I promise I'll think about it."

She frowns, then shakes her head. "He deserves that."

The corners of my mouth kick up. "Good night, Dana, it was nice to meet you."

"You as well." She turns and leaves.

I shut the door once more and lean against it. Closing my eyes, I slide down until I'm sitting on the cool concrete floor.

JoJo deserves love. But I'm not quite sure if he deserves me.

JoJo

The roofers hammer away under the hot sun while I clean up some of their scraps around the side of the house. From what I gathered through Daisy—before my trip blunder—Adrianne thinks the insurance people are starting on it next week.

By the time they get started, I'll have her an entirely new metal roof installed. Every day I've hidden any clue that we might be working on it before I go home. Cleaning the worksite and re-covering the entire roof with the tarp have become my nightly ritual.

It will all be worth it, though, when she sees the new roof.

I wish I could see the look on her face when she discovers it. That's doubtful, considering she probably never wants to see me again.

I sigh and bend down to pick up a piece of tin. A hoof is on top of the sheet of metal. My eyes follow it to a tiny goat that bleats in my face. I blink, then stand to see Daisy holding it on a leash.

"JoJo?"

"Daisy?"

"I came by to check on the tarp for Adrianne. She's stuck at the salon and worried about last night's wind." She nods at the goat. "We were already out walking."

I rub my beard and watch the goat lick the ground. This woman needs a dog.

Daisy folds her arms and gazes at the roof. "I thought they were just supposed to replace the shingles in the middle. Her homeowners' insurance must be better than mine."

I straighten my hard hat. "Insurance didn't pay for this. I did."

She raises an eyebrow. "Why?"

"I'm responsible for the roof damage, I screwed up her staying at my place . . ." I pause before confessing what I've confessed a lot the last two days—mainly to myself. "I want to do something nice for the woman I love."

Daisy's jaw drops. She stares at me without moving until the goat nudges her. Then she drops a hand to its head and shakes her own head.

"What?" I ask.

"I'll admit, I thought you were a butthole with the whole trip thing, but you really were just that stupid."

I scowl. "Why does everyone keep saying that?"

Daisy pets the goat and watches the roofers for a minute. A smile creeps across her face, and she snaps her head to me. Her eyes are wild and mischievous.

"Do you really want to win her back?"

I take a step closer to her, then step back when the goat bleats. Daisy laughs.

"I just want her for real."

Daisy's smile widens. "I think I can help with that. You got time to talk?"

I stare at the roof and then my truck. "Tell you what. Let me check on my men in the woods real quick, and you get that goat to leave me alone."

Daisy cups her hand around the goat's head and pulls it close to her. "Don't talk about my baby, JoJo Culp, if you want my help."

On that note, I head to my truck. I'm even worse than I thought for forcing Adrianne to stay with a crazy goat lady.

I drive down the logging trail until I get to the work site. Homer is in charge, which should tell you my desperation. I roll down the window and motion for him to come closer.

He sets down his chain saw and hurries to the truck.

I swat my hand out the window. "Go cut that chain saw off before you set it down. What's wrong with you?"

He grunts, then takes his time walking to the saw and back to me. "What's up, boss man?"

"I'm going to be at the house site a few more minutes. Why don't y'all go ahead and break for lunch."

"Yes, sir." He perks up like a dog at the word "treat."

I nod, then back up the truck. I really don't want them to eat this soon. That will lead to complaining about wanting more breaks later in the day. But it's the best option when they're unsupervised. I can at least trust them to feed themselves.

By the time I turn around, they're already opening coolers. That figures. I shake my head and drive back to Adrianne's house.

One of the roofers is petting the goat. He stops and acts busy when he sees me pull up. Daisy stands from the porch steps. I meet her on the porch and nod toward my truck.

"It's quieter over here."

She takes the goat by the leash and follows me to the truck. I pull down the tailgate for us to sit. She jumps to get on it, and her short legs dangle.

I reach into the cooler behind us and pull out two bottles. "Water?"

"Thanks." She takes one.

The goat literally paws her leg like a dog. She holds the bottle out and pours a stream of water into its mouth like he's a linebacker on a water break.

I shake my head and drink my own water. "What were you gonna tell me?"

"You two should have a real wedding."

I laugh so hard, I spit water across the dirt. "Very funny."

"No, I'm serious. You could surprise her with a real wedding."

"Yeah. Since she loves my surprises so much?" I harden my expression. "Is this your way of getting back at me about the trips?"

She shakes her head. "Not at all. I think she needs a big act of love to show how serious you are about her."

"And your first idea was to give her a wedding?"

"No, my first idea was for y'all to both go to the beach. But you ran off to Texas."

I cross my arms, and she presses her lips shut.

"So it's not enough that I get left at the airport—you want me to get left at the altar too?"

"No." She sighs. "Please take me seriously, I know Adrianne better than anyone."

I narrow my eyes. "I know her pretty well now."

She laughs. "Yeah, *so* well."

I growl.

"Sorry, I'll stop with the trip jokes."

"I'd appreciate it."

"Look, Carolina could throw her dream wedding together in no time. You could surprise her, and y'all could really get married." Daisy holds up her hands as if this makes more sense than anything in the world. "And I could be maid of honor, and offer a ring bearer goat—"

"No!" I yell in her face. So loudly that the roofers stop working and turn to us. I lift an arm and wave at them. "Not y'all. Carry on. Good work."

They give me a puzzled look before starting back to work. Daisy has hurt written all over her face. I've gotten a little better at reading women thanks to my time with Adrianne.

"What I mean is I won't have a goat in my wedding."

A smile slowly forms across her face. "So you're not saying no to the wedding?" She raises a brow. "Or to me being the maid of honor? I mean, it's cool if you don't want me to, but—"

"Yes, we can do the wedding." I remove my hard hat and rub a hand over my head. "I can't believe I'm agreeing to this."

She laughs. "But you want to marry Adrianne for real."

"Yeah." I waver my head. "But the courthouse was more of my dream wedding."

Daisy rolls her eyes. "Just promise you consult me before planning a real honeymoon."

I grin. "Promise."

She stands and pours the rest of her water for the goat to drink. Then she sets the empty bottle on the tailgate. "Recycle this, please."

I stare at the bottle, knowing good and well I'm going to chuck it in the trash soon as she leaves.

"I'm going to talk with Carolina."

I start to tell her no, but she's already speed walking toward the driveway with her goat. Before they get out of sight, she turns and smiles.

"I'll call you with the details."

I raise my hands as she turns and jogs away.

What have I gotten myself into?

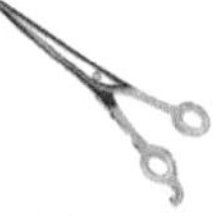

JoJo

Daisy grins up at me after checking her phone. "Adrianne will be here in a few minutes."

I take a deep breath meant to calm my nerves. Instead, it gives wind to the butterflies in my belly and sends them swirling.

The hairs on my forearm prick when Daisy rests her tiny hand on it. "It's going to be good. Trust me."

I gaze down at her smiling. After one more deep breath, I nod.

This is it. No turning back.

"Is everything else good?" I ask once my throat opens a bit.

"Yes. Everyone's at the lodge putting the finishing touches on everything. Both families are there, and Carolina's in charge."

I nod. "Maybe this will go the right way."

"It will." Daisy pats my arm before releasing it. "She loves you too. I know this will work."

I close my eyes and try to relax. For a moment, I dream Adrianne is talking to me.

"JoJo?"

My eyes blink open to Adrianne standing in front of me. Okay, this really is real. It's all or nothing.

"Adrianne."

"What are you doing here?"

Daisy offers me an encouraging smile from behind her. "I wanted to check on your house," I say.

"Why?"

I clear my throat. This is not how I planned on this going, but whatever. "I know the guy who's going to fix it."

"You do?" She wrinkles her nose. It's adorable and I want to kiss it, but I'm still a little afraid of getting slapped.

"Yeah." I step back and touch the edge of the tarp, which isn't tied down.

"I was worried about this," Adrianne says, running her hand over the tarp. "It's not even secure."

Our fingers brush lightly, and my arm tickles. I want to grab her hand, but restrain myself a little longer. Instead, I fist the end of the tarp and tug it.

"JoJo!" Her mouth flies open.

Now I'm really anticipating a slap, but it will all be worth it soon. I whistle, and the guys appear from the other side of the roof, then roll the tarp so it can fall. I pull Adrianne to the side of the house, and together we watch the new roof glisten.

Her mouth remains open, and her eyes widen.

"Like it?"

"A whole new roof? Why? How? When?" She blinks at the metal beaming in the sunshine.

"I fixed it."

She jerks her head my way. "You fixed it?"

"Well, I had a roofing company do it, but yeah, I handled it all."

"What about the insurance?"

"You'll still get it, but now you can pocket that money and put it into your business or use it to buy a new pool or something."

Her mouth closes slowly, and tears start to fill her eyes. "I told you that you didn't owe me anything. It was a mistake."

"No, it was an accident. The mistake I made was assuming you'd like going on a trip without me."

She laughs through her tears. "I'm still having a hard time believing you thought that was a good idea."

I fumble around with the pocket of my shirt until my hand stops shaking enough to grab Grandma's ring. Daisy had returned it to our house when she came for Adrianne's car. Of course, to me that indicated maybe she did want rid of me.

Time to see if that theory holds true. Maybe not.

"I have one more good idea. At least, I hope it's a good one." I pull the ring out and get down on one knee.

Adrianne

Everything goes blurry. I'm sweating and shaky and staring at the diamond ring I wore so many times over the past month. The one JoJo presented to me almost as a joke.

Is this a sick joke?

His eyes study me like he's committing this moment to

memory. There's no sneakiness in his gaze. Just sincerity—and love. However, I have a good bit of trust issues, and for good reason.

"Is this like really real?"

"If you want it to be." He stands and holds the ring between us. "I love you so much. The only thing I regret about our fake marriage is that it was fake. I miss having you in my life."

A few tears prick the corners of my eyes. That's all I ever wanted to hear, but before I can say something in response, he continues.

"No pressure. I no longer need a wife for the business, so the only string attached is that you'll have to live with Grandpa until I make other arrangements."

I sniffle, then smile. "Well, my house is fixed now."

He scratches his head. "Well, there's one more thing."

"What's that?" I'm not sure if I can take any more surprises.

"I kinda planned a wedding in case you might want to marry me today."

My eyes bug. "You what?"

Daisy comes from around the house. "Don't be mad. I helped him. It was my idea. He prefers the courthouse."

I glance at Daisy, then back at JoJo. "So like we could get married today?"

He starts tucking the ring back into his shirt pocket. "I knew this was a bad idea. I'm sorry."

I grab his hand and pull it out of his pocket. "No, it's perfect." My heart rate kicks up as he loosens his grip and allows me to take the ring from his hand.

"It is?"

Daisy winks. "I told you."

"Yes." I giggle and wipe a stray tear from my face. "I can't believe you went through all this trouble." I point toward the roof. "Giving me a new roof, and now a wedding." I shrug. "Are there any more surprises? Because I don't think I could handle them."

He takes my hand and slides the ring up my finger. "You have a choice."

"Yes, I choose you." I jump and wrap my arms around him.

JoJo laughs and hugs me back. "I'm glad, but the option I mean is to get married at the big wedding at Jack's place or right here, just us, and let Jack's be the reception."

I pull back and study him for a moment. All my life, I've dreamed of walking down an aisle in an elaborate white gown with my hair just right. Flowers would flank all the rows of chairs, and everyone I knew would admire my style and elegance.

Now that I'm grown, and I have my Prince Charming, all I want is to share this moment with him.

I stare into JoJo's eyes. "I actually like the idea of just us."

"Really?" His grin stretches ear to ear.

I nod. "I do. It's more special." I shrug. "Besides, everyone thinks we got married already anyway."

Daisy steps closer. "Yeah, but the new rumor is y'all split on your honeymoon."

I thump her nose.

"Ouch. Don't abuse the witness."

"Witness of what?"

Daisy whistles like she does for her goats. I expect Mullet to trot around the side of the house. Instead, Brother Billy steps out the back door with a Bible in hand. "Ah-ha. The signal. So you chose door number two."

I wrinkle my forehead at JoJo. He laughs and takes my hands in his.

Brother Billy stands in front of us, opens the Bible, and turns to Daisy. "Does the maid of honor have the rings?"

"Yes."

I tilt my head as Daisy pulls two gold bands out of the pocket on her yoga pants. "Where did you get those?"

"Etsy."

I roll my eyes. "Of course you did."

She holds them in her palm. "Do you want them or not?"

"Yes." I smile at her, then JoJo.

Brother Billy clears his throat and goes through the usual wedding vows. We repeat them, hand in hand, eyes locked. JoJo's face is a mixture of seriousness and playfulness, which is perfect. With his words, he promises to protect and cherish me. With his expression, he promises to mean everything he just said, but also make life fun.

I vow the same, then we exchange rings.

"You may now kiss your bride."

For the first time since that random night on the bathroom floor, our mouths meet. He kisses me as passionately as he did then, but with deeper meaning. In this kiss, he translates that it will be my last first kiss, but the first of many more to come just like it.

Daisy squeals as we pull back, then hugs us. I laugh as Brother Billy congratulates us and pulls out a marriage certificate for everyone to sign.

Daisy signs the witness line, complete with her signature flower to dot the "i."

JoJo wraps his arms around me and pulls me close. I relax against his chest. This is finally really real. If only my parents were here.

"Wait, my family. I've got to call my mom. She's already mad about me supposedly eloping." I cover my face with my hands.

Daisy laughs. "She's at Bianca's waiting on you."

"What?"

JoJo nods. "All our family and friends are there. We can do a ceremony again for them, if you want."

I smile. "Two weddings?"

"Three if you count the mythical one we had at the courthouse." He smirks.

"Two will be fine." I giggle as JoJo leads me to his truck.

Daisy rushes to her car. "I'll meet y'all there. Adrianne, you're going to love your bridesmaids' dresses!"

I climb in the truck and shut the door. "Please tell me she didn't pick them out." Nightmares of hemp and earthy tones flood my mind.

"She said Carolina picked everything out." JoJo glances at his worn jeans. "Which means I've got to change too."

"Oh, thank God."

He frowns at me.

"I didn't mean that toward you, just everything in general."

He halfway grins.

I poke his arm and add, "I just married you wearing that."

He smiles. "Yeah, you did just marry me."

Indeed, I did.

CHAPTER TWENTY-FOUR

Adrianne

At the entrance to Gamer's Paradise is a sign that reads, "Congratulations, Adrianne and JoJo."

I turn to JoJo. "Pretty sure of yourself with that sign, huh?"

He rubs his beard. "Let's see. We supposedly got married at the courthouse, which some speculate is a shotgun wedding, by the way."

"Oh, I haven't heard that one."

"Yeah, well. Then we supposedly split on the honeymoon, and now we're actually married going into our official wedding. Why not chance a sign?"

I laugh. "I'm glad it worked out for you."

He smiles and takes my hand. We continue down the driveway and pass a parking lot full of vehicles on our way to Jack and Bianca's house.

"Wow, we've got a lot of guests. That must've cost you a fortune to plan this."

"Actually, your dad wanted to pay for most." He raises his eyebrows. "The insurance money should cover Mary's catering."

I laugh. "Oh, what about me getting a new pool?"

"I thought maybe we could put an in-ground pool in at Grandpa's house. He could use some good water aerobics anyway."

I laugh harder, imagining Grandpa in swimming trunks. "Good luck with that."

JoJo parks in front of Jack and Bianca's house. I perk up when I notice my parents' and sister's vehicles.

"Your people are here to help you get ready. I'm going on to the big house to put on a tux or something. Whatever Carolina got me."

I kiss him gently on the lips. "I'm sure you'll be very handsome."

He sighs. "Well, I've already had my dream wedding in the backyard in jeans. It's your turn."

I smile and hop out of the truck. I watch him drive toward the lodge, then practically skip onto Bianca's porch. After I knock one time, the door flies open.

My mom engulfs me in a huge hug and starts rocking me back and forth. We talk on the phone every week and have an ongoing text thread with my sister. They didn't know everything was fake until after my trip in Florida.

Once the rumors started flooding through their friends left in Apple Cart, I had to fess up.

"Mama, I'm so sorry. I know this is crazy."

She holds me at arm's length and shakes her head. "No. It's crazy that you thought you couldn't just tell me the truth to begin with. And y'all are both crazy for lying to everyone so long, including yourselves." She pouts.

"I'm sorry."

She hugs me again. "It will all work out, baby girl. In less than an hour, you'll be married."

I should probably tell her I'm already really married, but I don't. That can be a funny story for the future. For now, I'll let her enjoy thinking she saw her daughter get married for the first time—and hopefully the last!

Mama lets go of me, then takes my hand and leads me toward Bianca's bedroom, where she and Carolina are waiting with the most beautiful couture wedding dress I've ever seen.

My jaw drops. "Where did you get this?"

Carolina bounces on her toes. "Daisy showed me a picture of a dress you liked in a magazine. She told me the few parts you said you'd change, and ta-da." She opens her hands toward the dress.

Bianca twists the hanger in her hands. "What do you think?"

"It's breathtaking!"

"And it should fit like a glove. Luckily, you have enough clothes that I could sneak away and go by. I took it to my favorite gal in Atlanta."

I smile. "I can't believe it."

"Just wait, she did the bridesmaids' dresses too," Bianca adds.

"I have bridesmaids?" I smile wider. They've thought of everything.

"Just Daisy and your sister, who are already at the lodge. We didn't want to crowd the space since there's a ton of flowers already."

I love wedding flowers! I leap forward and hug them both. "Y'all are the best!"

Bianca holds the dress to the side so I don't wrinkle it. "Okay, let's get you ready, then."

I breathe in, then out, and follow Carolina to Bianca's

bathroom. All my makeup for events is laid out on the counter.

"We would do your hair and makeup, but . . ." Carolina shrugs. "You do better."

I laugh. "Y'all have done enough." I sit in front of the vanity and start curling my hair.

My entire body jitters with excitement as I finally get myself ready for my own wedding. I swear, the getting ready part is almost as exciting as the wedding itself. Maybe even more so, since I'm technically married already.

I keep that tidbit to myself for now as we talk about the proposal and JoJo fixing my roof. My mom thinks the roof repair is the most romantic part. Must be her age.

In half an hour, I'm transformed from everyday cute to wedding day glam. Carolina picks up my train and helps me to my mom's car. She stuffs it in the back seat and climbs in beside me to keep it from wrinkling.

"Where's Daddy?"

Mama turns back and smiles. "Waiting on you at the lodge."

"Perfect." I smile back. My hands shake, as I can hardly stand the few minutes it takes us to pull up to the lodge.

We park, and Carolina opens the back door. An older man who looks vaguely familiar is standing there, waiting for us to get out. Mama hands him the keys.

"Thanks, Ronald," Carolina says to him. "I'll let you know when we need the getaway vehicle."

I stare at Carolina, who grins. Best not to ask right now. Instead, I focus on the front doors to the lodge, which are flanked with a spray of summery flowers. When we reach them, Carolina knocks, and they open.

Bradley smiles at us and offers his arm to Mama. She takes it, and he leads her to a seat up front. My pulse races as Daddy meets me.

"Daddy," I whisper.

He kisses my cheek and takes my arm. "You look angelic," he whispers back to me.

I smile and try to regulate my breathing. I shouldn't be nervous. We've already said our vows. This is just a formality.

We step toward the foyer and the wedding march begins. Everyone stands and stares at me. My heart beats in overdrive as I put one foot in front of the other and walk toward JoJo.

His dad and Grandpa Joe are by his side. Daisy and my sister are standing there for me in gorgeous bright pink gowns.

It's almost like I'm floating as Daddy leads me down the aisle. He hands me to JoJo and kisses me on the cheek one more time.

We go through the formalities we did about two hours earlier in my backyard. Except this time, JoJo and Brother Billy are in formal wear rather than denim, and I'm wearing the most magnificent dress I could imagine.

We stare in one another's eyes and repeat our vows for all of Apple Cart County to hear. And I do mean *all*, as everyone and their brother are literally packed into the lodge.

When we're wearing our wedding bands—again—Brother Billy directs us to a small table with three vases. We are to pour sand from two of them together into the largest vase as a form of unity candle.

I pick up my vase, and almost drop it when Misty's voice comes over a microphone. She's singing "I Will Always Love You" by Dolly Parton. I cut my eyes at JoJo, who is trying not to laugh.

"Did you know about this?" I whisper through clinched teeth.

He shakes his head. We finish combining our sand and rejoin the preacher. I glance at Daisy beside me.

She frowns, then whispers, "She bribed me. She said she'd tell you our plans if she couldn't sing."

I press my lips together to keep from giggling, but it doesn't work. My shoulders shake as I try and hold it in, and I end up snorting. That makes Daisy and JoJo laugh, then my sister joins them. We continue until even some of the guests laugh.

Brother Billy starts to speak to try and sum it all up. JoJo beats him to the punch by pulling me close and kissing me.

The crowd roars with applause as JoJo releases me and leads me down the aisle. If I was floating before, I'm flying now.

We sail out the front door, laughing and smiling as we circle the property to the reception area. I guess the third time is a charm, because this is one wedding to remember.

JoJo and I enter the patio area after being pronounced husband and wife—for the second time today. I'd say that should seal the deal that nothing about our relationship is fake.

Mary spots us from the kitchen and waves frantically. She barrels out the door and engulfs us in a hug.

"My babies got married." She pulls back after squeezing me lifeless for a second. "I knew it." She wags her finger in my face.

JoJo half smiles at me. Mary swears she has a sixth sense in which she can spot love connections, often before the couples can. Whether that holds true is a mystery, but she's been pretty spot on with a lot of couples in Apple Cart County.

"Thanks again for catering on short notice," JoJo says.

"Well, of course. I'd be offended if you'd asked anyone else." Mary gives both our arms a gentle squeeze. "I've got to head back inside. Enjoy your reception."

"Yes, ma'am." I smile as she hurries inside.

Carolina squeezes through the back door before Mary can close it. She's wearing a headset like a football coach on the sidelines.

"What's that?"

She taps the headband part. "It's connecting me to Jonah and Bianca. Saves a lot of time and stress in managing the various parts of a wedding."

"Nice."

"Yeah, that's been my best investment this year." She snarls her nose. "Unless you count making Jonah take a few refresher courses in piano in case we need him again."

I laugh. Jonah had to fill in last minute to play piano at his cousin's wedding to Bianca. He ran out of songs to play and started "Great Balls of Fire."

"Thanks again for all you've done."

"My pleasure." Carolina sighs, then laughs. "I mean, you're welcome. Something about this earpiece makes me channel a Chick-fil-A drive-through worker."

We laugh as she answers a message from Bianca and hurries off to check on the cake.

"So there's cake?" I raise an eyebrow to JoJo.

"Yeah, and you didn't even have to make it."

I smile. "I'm afraid my cakes will be a letdown after you've had Mary's."

"You could never be a letdown." He wraps an arm around me and winks.

My body relaxes as I melt against him. For the first time, I'm confident that he's really mine and I'm really his.

The guests start arriving around back and everyone stops by to congratulate us. Several people comment that they knew we would work things out. I thank them and try not to laugh.

If they only knew what we've gone through to get to where we are today. All the confusion and pretending. Even worse than pretending I was married to JoJo when I wasn't, was pretending to him like I didn't want to be.

All that's over now.

"Excuse me, everybody." Bradley's voice in the microphone catches everyone's attention. "We'd like for the bride and groom to have their first dance, then everyone else can join on the next song."

He bends the microphone in front of his guitar and strums a few chords.

JoJo holds out his hand, and I take it. "I'm not much of a dancer."

"That's fine. Just don't step on my dress."

He glances down at his feet. "Oh shoot. Did I step on it?"

"No," I giggle. "Hang on." I reach behind, gather the train, and pin it to the hook on the back of my gown. "Now."

I place my hand on his chest, and we start to sway. We lock eyes, and everyone else fades into the background. The music dulls, and all I see or hear clearly is my husband.

My husband. How cool is that?

"We haven't talked about this yet, but if it's okay, I think we need to stay with Grandpa until I can make other arrangements for him."

"Of course." My heart sinks. I can't imagine Grandpa not living with JoJo. "There's no way we're leaving him. He's like my grandpa now too."

JoJo's face lights up. "Are you sure? I could arrange for him to move in with my parents or get some hired help."

I shake my head. "No way. It shouldn't be any different than before. Except we're actually married this time."

He sighs. "You don't know how much it means to me for you to say that. I didn't want him to leave his house, and I don't think he'd like someone not in the family coming in."

I wrap both my arms around JoJo's shoulders and pull him closer. "We're a family now, and I love him. I can rent my house out. It's much smaller, and it has a brand-new roof."

"Yes it does." He winks. "But I did arrange for Dana's family to stay with Grandpa a few days."

"Oh?" I'm intrigued to hear his plans for a *real* honeymoon.

"I know we can't take off work again spur of the moment, but I thought we could spend our first few nights at your place, alone." He pulls me even closer as a mischievous smile crosses his face.

"That's a great idea. My bedroom has carpet, so you'll be much more comfortable on my floor."

JoJo's face contorts as he tries to pull off a mean look, but his laughter seeps through. I burst out laughing too.

"I am NOT sleeping on the floor tonight, Mrs. Culp."

My breath catches when I hear him refer to me as Mrs. Culp for the first time. I open my mouth to say how much I love the sound of that.

But he kisses me before I have a chance to speak. Good thing a kiss is worth a thousand words.

EPILOGUE

A Few Months Later

JoJo

I never know what I'm going to come home to. But as long as I know who I'm coming home to, I don't much mind.

Adrianne's laughter carries through the house, warming my insides. I follow her and Grandpa's voices to the back porch.

They're playing poker around a table with Grandpa's buddies and Adrianne's dad.

Her parents came into town to help put her house on the market. They're staying in it and helping us paint and stage it before the Realtor takes photos. Mr. Rick and Grandpa have become fast friends over the past few days.

I prop against the doorway as they lay down cards. Wendall growls when Adrianne's dad beats him.

"Shoot, Rick. When do you go back to where you came from?"

Everyone else laughs as Rick pulls an armload of chips his way. And by chips, I mean actual snack-sized bags of chips, not poker chips. That's today's booty. Apparently, they're running low on soft peppermints, so Grandpa raided the pantry.

I know this because it's happened before with peanuts. I make a mental note to put chips on the grocery list.

Adrianne smiles at me, and then Grandpa notices me for the first time.

"Hey, boy. Want to play?"

I shake my head. "No, can I borrow Adrianne for a bit?"

Wendall frowns at her, then at me. "Take her! Less competition."

Everyone laughs and pokes fun at him. Adrianne stands, patting Wendall on the back as she leaves the back porch.

"Bye. Y'all have fun." She waves, and everyone but Wendall tells her bye. He pouts at his cards as Grandpa deals them out.

We go inside the house and sit in the living room. "Interesting day?"

She sighs. "Always with that crowd. Did you get the truck fixed?"

"Almost. Daddy's on the phone now ordering a part."

She nods. "What's up?"

I pull my phone from my side and open it to a web page, then hand it to her.

She twists her mouth as she scrolls down the page. "What's this?"

"A travel site. You get to pick our honeymoon."

She raises her eyes to me and opens her mouth to speak.

"Before you say anything, I know we're all busy with

businesses and selling your house, and Grandpa. Everything, really. That's why I'm giving you complete control."

She smiles. "So I get to plan where we go?"

I nod. "That, and when we go, how long we stay, whatever. You can even send me on a separate trip if you like."

She pops my arm. "Stop it."

I rub my arm and laugh. If I can't use my own mistake to aggravate her, what kind of marriage do we have?

"Seriously, you choose. I have a budget in mind, because most of my savings are tied up in starting the lumberyard, but other than that, you have complete say."

She grins widely and stares at my phone for a minute before looking back at me.

"Are you sure? I don't want to cause any stress while we're doing the new business."

I pulled the trigger on starting a mill a month ago. We both agreed it's a good venture, and even Grandpa was on board with the idea. Personally, I think he liked it being close to the house. He's mentioned several times that he would be available to go "supervise" everyone while I'm in the woods. Even though we all know that will be Daddy's job.

"Yes. We deserve a good, fun, relaxing trip, alone."

Adrianne narrows her eyes. "Alone, together."

"That's what I meant."

"Just checking," she quips.

I snatch my phone from her and cover her face in kisses. She giggles, then kisses me back.

In all honesty, the trip is for her. We could stay on this couch for eternity as far as I'm concerned. As long as we're together. But I intend to spend my life spoiling her with trips and whatever else she wants.

Who knows? We may even take Grandpa with us on the next adventure.

INSPIRATION FOR THIS NOVEL

Often when writing, I throw in new, fun side characters to add some comedy to a scene. This was the case with JoJo in *Hammered by Love*.

I wanted a grumpy, super-manly guy who might rub the other Bama Boys the wrong way. I had no intention at the time of giving him a love story, but immediately thought of making him a logger.

This image is my maternal grandpa, who we affectionately referred to as "Papa." He started a logging business at age nineteen that is still running strong in my family today.

The oldest of five brothers, he involved all of his younger siblings in the business. At different times, they branched off on their own, to the point that the Clark family was known for logging and timber in my hometown.

Ettie and Denver Clark, 2005

He and my "Grannie," Ettie, were married almost sixty-one years before he passed away from cancer, nine days before he turned eighty.

Before getting cancer, he suffered from early dementia and would often forget little details like what he was looking for or the day of the week. However, he could recall in detail stories from the past, which I always found fascinating. Like JoJo, I helped my granny care for him a lot.

He died two months before my wedding, in which he was supposed to walk me down the aisle. My cousin walked with me instead. Ironically, he is also named Denver after our grandpa. I consider this a "God wink" as I had already designed and printed the programs. "Denny" now carries on the family logging business with my uncle Jim.

Papa and Grannie were my biggest influences growing up. I lived within walking distance from them and would spend most afternoons and summer days at their house. Both worked—a lot, but when they were home, they were always doing something outside. Grannie did tax and accounting work until a year before she passed away at ninety. She also started a local Christian TV station that ran on cable back before everyone streamed TV service.

Together, they had the biggest impact on my life. They had a strong Christian faith, wonderful marriage, welcoming home, and entrepreneurial spirit. They started from nothing and always lent a hand and/or dollar to anyone in need.

If I am half the person either of them were on this earth, I will consider my life well lived.

ACKNOWLEDGMENTS

First, I'd like to thank God for giving me creative ideas and placing the right people in my path to help see them to fruition.

My husband, Blake, gets credit next for always supporting my writing endeavors, even if he finds my stories a little too "girly."

Thanks to one of my cousins for allowing me to use his tattoo for JoJo. (Yes, someone in the world really has a bulldog skidding logs on their skin!)

I also want to thank my readers and ARC team for their support. You. Are. Awesome! I could not do what I do without my readers and support team. I love y'all!

Of course, I'd like to thank my editor, Joanne. She's always a pleasure to work with and polishes my books to help them shine.

ABOUT THE AUTHOR

Kaci Lane is a journalist turned fiction writer who believes all stories should have a happy ending. While unsuccessfully trying to learn Spanish for a decade, she has become fluent in sarcasm, Southern belle and movie quotes. She is married to a Southern Gentleman and has two young children who help keep her humility in check. Connect with her on kacilane.com or Facebook.

BOOKS BY KACI LANE

Bama Boys Series*

Hunting for Love

Chicken about Love

Hammered by Love

Cutting out Love

Apple Cart County Christmas

Christmas in Dixie

Crazy Rich Rednecks

Schooled on Love Series

Taco Truck Takedown

Side Hustle

Buggy List

Off-Season

Books in Shared Series with Other Authors

No Time for Traditions

A Perfect Match in Silver Leaf Falls

*If you enjoyed the Bama Boys books, revisit Apple Cart County with the Christmas in Applecart series, starting with *Christmas in Dixie*. Set in Apple Cart, Alabama, it includes secondary characters from the Bama Boys series.